Chocolate Kisses

"In *Chocolate Kisses*, three hot treats are served up that are sure to satisfy the appetite."
—Eric Pete, author of *Gets No Love* and *Don't Get It Twisted*

Acclaim for the Title Story

"The best love story I've read."
—Mary B. Morrison, national bestselling author of *Nothing Has Ever Felt Like This*

Chocolate Kisses

FRANCIS RAY
MARYANN REID
RENEE LUKE

A SIGNET ECLIPSE BOOK

SIGNET ECLIPSE
Published by New American Library, a division of
Penguin Group (USA) Inc., 375 Hudson Street, New York, New York 10014, USA
Penguin Group (Canada), 90 Eglinton Avenue East, Suite 700, Toronto, Ontario,
Canada M4P 2Y3 (a division of Pearson Penguin Canada Inc.)
Penguin Books Ltd., 80 Strand, London WC2R 0RL, England
Penguin Ireland, 25 St. Stephen's Green, Dublin 2,
Ireland (a division of Penguin Books Ltd.)
Penguin Group (Australia), 250 Camberwell Road, Camberwell, Victoria 3124,
Australia (a division of Pearson Australia Group Pty. Ltd.)
Penguin Books India Pvt. Ltd., 11 Community Centre, Panchsheel Park,
New Delhi - 110 017, India
Penguin Group (NZ), cnr Airborne and Rosedale Roads, Albany,
Auckland 1310, New Zealand (a division of Pearson New Zealand Ltd.)
Penguin Books (South Africa) (Pty.) Ltd., 24 Sturdee Avenue,
Rosebank, Johannesburg 2196, South Africa

Penguin Books Ltd., Registered Offices: 80 Strand, London WC2R 0RL, England

First published by Signet Eclipse, an imprint of New American Library,
a division of Penguin Group (USA) Inc.

First Printing, January 2006
10 9 8 7 6 5 4 3 2 1

SIGNET ECLIPSE and logo are trademarks of Penguin Group (USA) Inc.

LIBRARY OF CONGRESS CATALOGING-IN-PUBLICATION DATA:

Chocolate kisses / by Francis Ray, Maryann Reid, Renee Luke.
    p.   cm.
    ISBN 0-451-21749-7
    1. Love stories, American. I. Luke, Renee. Chocolate kisses. II. Ray, Francis.
Chocolate affair. III. Reid, Maryann. Good man is hard to count.

PS648.L6C494 2006
813'.54—dc22   2005018106

Set in Century Old Style

Printed in the United States of America

PUBLISHER'S NOTE
These are works of fiction. Names, characters, places, and incidents either are the product of the author's imagination or are used fictitiously, and any resemblance to actual persons, living or dead, business establishments, events, or locales is entirely coincidental.
    The publisher does not have any control over and does not assume any responsibility for author or third-party Web sites or their content.

Contents

A Chocolate Affair

by FRANCIS RAY

This anthology, my thirty-first title, is dedicated to my loyal readers.
I couldn't have done this without your prayers and support.
Wishing each and every one of you love and happiness.

Prologue

LOVING MIRANDA COLLINS was Lucian Faulkner's greatest pleasure. There was nothing about her that didn't please and entice him. From the exotic beauty of her face to the lush softness of her body, she was exquisite and all his.

He'd been fighting his arousal since he'd picked her up for dinner at her dormitory at Columbia University, where she was a sophomore fashion design major and he was a senior marketing major. Finally they were back at his apartment. He drew her into his arms the moment he closed the door, his mouth closing hungrily over hers. She was with him all the way. Her slim arms slid around his neck; her fingers held his head close as she kissed him back with just as much hunger and need.

His impatient hand slipped beneath the heavy sweater she'd worn in deference to New York's sharp November wind and closed around the fullness of her breast. She shivered, then whimpered as his thumb and forefinger closed around the turgid peak of her nipple.

In one deft motion he pulled her sweater and T-shirt over her head. Her bra quickly followed. Before the clothes had hit the floor he'd picked her up and carried her to his bedroom. Her feet had barely touched the carpet before his mouth and teeth closed around her nipple.

His name was a ragged whisper of sound. Her knees buckled.

Gathering her in his arms again, he laid her on the bed. He released her only long enough to undress them both; then he covered her body with his. This time he was the one who shivered, as he always did with the initial impact of bare flesh against bare flesh, hard against soft, fitting so perfectly together. No woman had ever pleased him more, nor had he ever wanted to please one more.

His hands couldn't seem to get enough of touching her, his lips of kissing her. There was no place that was forbidden to either of them as they teased and pleased each other. Trailing kisses down her body, he found her hot, silken core and drew cries of ecstasy from her.

When both were pushed almost to their limits, he quickly sheathed himself and brought them together. Her legs and arms wrapped around him as if she'd never let go.

Feeling her response beneath him as he drove them both toward completion always made him feel as if he were on top of the world. They shattered together. Their breathing labored, he rolled to his side, pulling her with him, unwilling to release her. She was his sweetest addiction.

When Lucian woke up Saturday morning he knew Miranda was gone. The couple of times he'd enticed her into spending the night with him, she'd awakened him to tell him she was leaving and they always ended up making love, causing her to be late for class or work at a restaurant near their university. She was working today. He wished she were still with him, but they had a date for tonight. He'd see her then. Or so he thought.

That night Lucian was heading out the door to get Miranda when she called to cancel, saying something had come up. Before he could question her, the line went dead.

A moment of unease swept though him. She'd never canceled before. On top of that, she'd sounded strange. He started to go to her dormitory to check on her, then decided he was worried about nothing. He'd see her tomorrow.

Lucian saw Miranda the next day, but it wasn't the same. She didn't smile and barely looked him in the eye. She refused to make a definite date to see him again, claiming she had class projects to work on, tests to study for. She didn't know when she'd be free, she told him. He didn't take her rejection well and became angry. A couple of days later he cooled down and called her, but it was the same story—she was busy with school.

He offered to help her study or work on her projects, but she always played it off, saying she did better by herself. After weeks of being turned down it finally sank in to Lucian's head that she didn't want to see him.

It was difficult for him to accept that she could turn her back on what he'd thought was a perfect relationship. He'd wake up at night wanting her, needing her, missing her. Once the bewilderment ebbed, anger set in. Miranda might not want him, but there were plenty of other women who did.

When he graduated in May, Lucian promised himself that when he left New York he was leaving Miranda and her memory behind. But if their paths ever crossed, he'd treat her the same heartless way she'd treated him.

Chapter One

Since graduation from college, Lucian Faulkner III had become a very wealthy man by satisfying women. He enjoyed every gratifying moment, and took pride in his accomplishments. In his opinion, few things could compare to the exquisite expression on a woman's face at that exact moment she reached the peak of satisfaction. Eyes closed, head tilted slightly back, she'd emit a long, low moan of pleasure, then slowly glide her tongue over her lower lip, searching for that last, lingering taste of chocolate.

To Lucian's delight, there was a great deal of moaning going on in the rose-covered terrace of the two-story mansion that beautiful summer afternoon in Dallas. Like a proud father, Lucian looked on as the happy group of women munched their way through an assortment of rich, decadent chocolates. Branching into catering had been his idea and a natural progression in the family-owned business, A Chocolate Affair, that his paternal grandmother had started thirty-five years ago.

With one hand in the pocket of his tailored beige slacks, Lucian watched the thirty-odd women stuff themselves with an assortment of irresistible chocolate goodies ranging from fudge-covered popcorn to a chocolate mousse cake—all of which his superior staff had freshly prepared for the bridal shower.

More than one survey stated that 50 percent of women enjoyed chocolate more than sex. Lucian wasn't going to argue the point.

Few people probably realized that orgasms and chocolates both released endorphins into the body for the ultimate high.

Lucian caught the eye of the hostess, who had an orange-filled chocolate cream in one hand and a flute of champagne in the other. She raised the glass in acknowledgment of a job well done. He bowed from the waist, a courtly gesture women seemed to love. Lucian always aimed to please. Women, either as buyer or as recipient, made up 90 percent of his customer base. Whatever pleased them invariably pleased him.

What began as Grandmother Faulkner's way of helping put her son through college at Morehouse had grown to a thriving business with over two hundred employees. A Chocolate Affair had grossed well into seven figures the year before and shipped all over the world.

The busy Dallas plant sat on three picturesque acres with a small lake inhabited by several black swans. The logo of a black swan surrounded by gold was immediately recognizable, and guaranteed customers the ultimate chocolate experience when they sank their teeth into one of A Chocolate Affair's delectable chocolate products—or their money back.

Lucian's paternal grandmother had retired two years ago; his parents had followed the next year, leaving him and his younger brother, Devin, in charge of the operations. He was president and chief operating officer, and Devin was vice president and chief financial officer.

Neither of them had any intention of letting down their family, their loyal customers, or the new ones they intended to acquire. It had been Lucian's idea to add a variety of unique chocolate bakery goods and other chocolate products, but their staple was, and always would be, candy.

In honor of the bride-to-be, a chocolate lover, Lucian had created individually wrapped chocolate cakes tied with the guest of honor's colors of pink and burgundy. There was also a brownie hot-fudge sundae, a rich fudge brownie layered with brownie chunks and chocolate ganache. The chocolate-covered strawberries coated with crunchy gourmet toffee and elegant chocolate twirls were admired, then quickly devoured.

The bubbling laughter and risqué conversation were soon sprinkled with a few giggles. Lucian had suspected the combination of the endorphins in the chocolate with the liqueur in the dessert cakes and the champagne might prove too much for a few of the ladies.

He had just turned toward a waiter to tell him to make sure the coffee was ready to serve when a strikingly beautiful woman, arms open, rushed onto the terrace from inside the house. Lucian froze and then tumbled back in time. The hostess, bride-to-be, and several other women squealed and surged toward the woman. At five-foot-seven in her stocking feet, wearing stilettos, the elegant newcomer towered over the others, allowing Lucian an unimpeded view of the woman who had devastated him when she walked out on him almost ten years ago.

He looked for flaws and clenched his fists when he found none. She hadn't grown fat, as he had hoped. If anything, the years had defined her exquisite features. She was the most tempting woman he had ever seen, then or now. She possessed high cheekbones, naturally arched black satin brows over deep chocolate eyes, and a mouth that he was well aware could drive a man crazy. Her body had remained lush, with long, shapely legs that could wrap around a man's waist and draw him deeper into her satin heat.

Desire hit before he drew his next breath. His hand in his pocket clenched. He'd promised himself long ago that if he ever saw Miranda Collins again, he'd treat her the same way she had treated him, blithely dismissing her as if they had never shared intense emotions and an even more intense passion.

"Please forgive me for being late," Miranda said, her sultry voice as sexy as ever. Her jet-set life hadn't changed the cadence that made a man think of long, moon-draped nights, silken sheets, and naked flesh against flesh. "Bad weather at LaGuardia kept the plane on the runway for almost an hour."

"You're forgiven," Emma, the bride-to-be, said, a smile on her pretty face. "I could never be angry with my favorite designer and good friend. I'm just glad you're here. We're about to open the gifts."

"*If* we can get everyone away from the chocolates." The hostess chuckled, and everyone laughed with her. "Ladies, let's go inside. I promise there are more chocolates to come." She turned to Miranda as the women filed inside, some taking one last serving of chocolate. "Help yourself. We'll be inside."

Miranda watched them leave, then turned to the array of chocolate on the twelve-foot table before her. Picking up a twenty-four-carat-gold-rimmed dessert plate and sterling flatware, she studied the offerings. Her gaze stopped at the hot-fudge-sundae silk pie. The drizzle of dark chocolate over the white-chocolate mousse caused an old, forbidden memory to surface: a stream of warm chocolate poured over her breasts and licked leisurely away by a man she'd sworn to forget, but never had.

"Having trouble deciding?"

Miranda started, her eyes going wide with recognition, her heart pounding as she stared in stunned surprise at the man she had just been thinking about. "Lucian."

Hearing her say his name in that breathless tone caused his body to harden even more. With an effort he kept the pleasant smile on his face and withdrew his hand from his pocket. "Hello, Miranda." He waved his hand toward the laden table. "Not to your liking?"

She moistened her lips and swallowed, finally dragging her gaze away from him and back to the table. She'd always wondered what she'd feel if they met again, wondered if she'd experience the same wild exhilaration, feel her pulse race, her body tighten with need. She didn't have to wonder any longer. Lucian still affected her as no man ever had.

She'd always hoped his perfect white teeth had decayed, or he'd gained weight from eating his products—or perhaps at the very least lost that thick head of hair so she could stop thinking about how soft it had felt beneath her fingertips or how arousing against her bare skin. None of it had happened. He remained devastatingly handsome, with a well-conditioned body that a god would envy.

"I'm trying to talk myself out of eating anything. I have a weakness for chocolate, and I'm afraid one wouldn't be enough," she finally said.

His nostrils flared. She realized she had said the wrong thing. Once, she'd dared let herself dream of a future with him. Back then he had often told her that after making love to her, once could never be enough. She was his sweetest addiction, and he had been hers.

Lucian picked up a bourbon bonbon and held it close to her slightly parted mauve-painted lips. "Everyone should have one guilty pleasure."

And you were mine, Miranda almost said. Instead she stepped back, trying to find her equilibrium, to smile and act as if pushing the man standing before her out of her life at nineteen hadn't been the most difficult decision she'd ever had to make. "My seamstress would throw a tantrum if I'm not able to fit into the designs I'm wearing for the trunk show in two weeks."

Lucian's dark eyes slowly swept her incredible body, from her four-inch heels, along the fishnet stockings, past the black-and-white couture suit with feather details on the sleeves and hem, to the open vee of the black silk blouse that showed the rounded curve of her full breasts, to the caramel-colored face that would stop any man in his tracks, to the breezy layers of straight black hair. "One won't hurt. I'll help you work it off."

Miranda's heart thudded. Her mouth dried. There was no mistaking the type of work he was referring to, or her body's eager reaction. She wanted him, but nothing had changed. There was no place for Lucian or any other man in her life. She took another step backward, and placed the plate and fork back on the table. "Thank you, but I've learned it's best not to give in to temptation. Good-bye, Lucian."

Lucian watched Miranda walk away, and wasn't surprised to feel the same anger and hurt he'd felt after she'd done the same thing when they were in college. They'd met when she'd dropped her books in the library and he'd picked them up. One look and he had been a goner. It had taken him two very long weeks to wear down her resistance to go out with him. A month later they had become lovers.

He hadn't planned on it happening. Fact was, he'd been scared of doing anything that might push her away. He could tell she hadn't much experience with dating and even suspected she was a virgin. They'd been at his off-campus apartment testing the chocolate syrup his grandmother was thinking of carrying. She had wanted him to try it out. He had—just not in the way she had ever imagined: on a woman's skin.

One moment they had been laughing as they made chocolate sundaes; the next moment he was licking the syrup off her fingers, the corner of her mouth. Things had rapidly progressed to his wondering how the chocolate syrup would taste on other parts of her body. He'd found out, and the experience had blown his mind. The taste of her had been incredible, an experience he would never forget.

They'd seen each other every chance they got for the next three weeks. . . . Then Miranda broke a movie date and afterward never went out with him again. He moved on to other women.

But no woman since then had even come close to making him feel a fraction of the emotions or the connection he'd felt with Miranda. Suddenly he realized just how much he'd missed that connection and how he had looked for it with every woman he'd dated since college.

Before Lucian knew it, he had followed the women into the house. At the door to the great room, he immediately found Miranda in the crowd of women. He hadn't had to look for her; it was as if they were connected in some way.

Suddenly she looked toward him. Desire lanced between them

like a current of electricity. Her eyes rounded; her parted lips trembled. It wasn't over between them. The question was, what, if anything, did either of them plan to do about it?

Desire coursed through Miranda, and there was nothing she could do about it. Lucian had always had that effect on her. That was why back in college she had so long resisted going out with him. He drew her like metal shavings to a magnet. She had looked at him holding out her books to her the night they had met and forgot her own name. She'd been lost in the midnight black of his eyes, his sexy dimpled grin.

Instinctively she had known that caring too deeply for him could derail her plans of becoming a top fashion designer. But Lucian had been a hard man to resist. They'd had three fantastic weeks before reality had set in. She could have him, or a successful career. She'd made her choice and tried not to look back.

Since then she'd accomplished what she had set out to do, but a designer was only as good as his or her last collection. The upcoming fall/winter collection, in which she planned to preview her newest designs of scarves and belts with her day- and evening-wear collection, was four months away.

All of the designs were complete except for one magnificent gown that would be the crowning touch to the night and mark her as a designer who remained fresh and innovative. She had to keep her mind clear and focused. She couldn't do that with Lucian around.

She turned and gave her attention to Emma, who was opening another gift, this one from Miranda. White paper and thick gold ribbon were cast aside in greedy and acceptable haste to reveal a set of handcrafted sterling toasting goblets. There was a collective indrawn breath as Emma held the goblets up for inspection.

"They're exquisite, Miranda. Thank you," Emma said.

"I hope you'll use them to toast each other on your wedding night and every anniversary thereafter," Miranda said. "Your initials and the marriage date are inscribed on the inside of the handle, so each time you pick up the goblet it will remind you of your special day and your love."

There was a mixture of sighs and oohs. Emma crossed the lavishly decorated room to hug Miranda, then went back to her seat on the sofa and picked up another gift. Miranda was glad the attention was no longer on her. She didn't want anyone to see the sadness in her eyes. She was happy for her friend and client. If, at times, Miranda felt sad that she would never experience such happiness or be married, it was her own secret.

Lucian had listened intently to Miranda and wondered if he was the only one in the room who heard the ache in her voice, the loneliness—if he was the only one who saw it in her face when she embraced the bride-to-be with her eyes closed. Or did they think the sheen of moisture in Miranda's eyes afterward was due to happiness?

Why had she turned her back on love? At almost thirty-one, he found the words didn't scare him as much as they might have at twenty-one. Good sex could make some men do anything and be as possessive as hell. He and Miranda had had great, mind-blowing sex, and he hadn't known how to handle her not being as caught up in the relationship as he had been. He was stunned to realize that Miranda didn't plan on letting herself care about him or any man.

While that fact might soothe a wounded ego that still smarted after all these years, it did nothing to take the edge off his wanting to make her his again. He didn't think it would be any easier this time than the last to persuade her to go out with him.

Miranda could feel Lucian's eyes on her. Clasping her hands in her lap, she kept her gaze straight ahead, refusing to succumb to his will. Giving him even a hint that her body still craved his would not only be foolish—it would be disastrous.

Emma pulled a frothy ivory bit of nothing negligee from a box, and the women broke into bawdy comments and suggestions. Miranda laughed, but didn't comment. The first time she'd actually planned on spending the night with Lucian she hadn't wanted him to see the cheap cotton gowns she slept in, so she had said she'd forgotten hers. He'd told her she didn't need one, and he had been right. They'd made love most of the night. She'd awakened content and naked in his arms to make love again. With the right man, what you wore or didn't wear was immaterial.

"Thank you, everyone," Emma said, a tremulous smile on her lips. "I can't believe I'll be married in four weeks to the most wonderful man in the world. I wish all of you could feel the happiness I feel."

Amid applause, the hostess stood. "Let's go back on the terrace and finish decimating the desserts. I've also asked the caterer to set out a couple of trays of goodies to nibble on."

"I wouldn't mind nibbling on Lucian Faulkner," a woman near Miranda whispered.

"Get in line," replied another woman beside her. "I bet he's as yummy as any of his chocolates."

Miranda didn't expect the spike of jealousy as she watched the two women making their way outside. But their comments reinforced her decision to stay as far away from Lucian as possible. Just like her father, Lucian was too handsome and too charming for a woman ever to be able to completely him call her own. Her mother had taught her that depending on a man for anything was asking for disaster. She'd known that since she was seven years old.

Chapter Two

MIRANDA PROMISED HERSELF that she was not going to be tempted. She lost her resolve less than an hour later as the bridal shower finally broke up. She'd hung back on the terrace. As the last woman filed inside, Miranda glanced around to make sure she was alone, then picked up one of the bonbons Lucian had offered her earlier. The women had raved about how scrumptious they tasted. Since she couldn't have the man, she'd settle for one of his exquisite chocolates.

The rich flavor of the imported chocolate burst on her palate. Closing her eyes, she savored the taste. A moan slipped past her lips.

"Just as I remembered. Only your moan wasn't caused by chocolate."

Caught, Miranda snapped her eyes open. She spun around to see Lucian walking toward her in what could only be called a predatory swagger. Damn, he was gorgeous and dangerous, which made him all the more tempting. He made a woman want to throw caution and common sense to the wind.

But she'd done that once before, with almost disastrous consequences. She popped the last bit of chocolate into her mouth to give herself time to think. "We've both moved on since then," she finally said.

He kept coming until she could see her own reflection in his eyes. She looked just the way she felt, panic-stricken and aroused. "Have we?" He ran a blunt-tipped finger down her jaw, causing her to tense, then shiver with awareness.

She thought he'd grin with triumph. Instead his gaze centered on her trembling mouth. "I still want you just as much as you want me."

With her body almost melting at his feet, lying would be a waste of time. She'd resisted once; she could do so again. "Wanting isn't enough." She stepped back and held out her steady hand to show him she controlled her emotions. "Good-bye, Lucian. Please give Devin my regards."

His large hand closed over hers, his thumb raking across her open palm, causing her to jerk. "This isn't over."

Pulling her hand free, she resisted the urge to rub her palm against her skirt in an attempt to stop the tingling sensation. But that wouldn't help, because the disturbing spark had spread rapidly, centering in the middle of her body. Turning, she went inside to call a cab. With each step, the ache deepened. Her mother had been right: She had been a fool to have come to Dallas . . . even if she'd believed the chances of seeing Lucian again were a million to one.

Once Lucian made up his mind about something, he seldom veered from his decision. Almost ten years ago he'd vowed he wouldn't take Miranda back on a silver platter. Now, parked across the street from where the bridal shower had been held, he admitted he'd take her any way he could get her.

It hadn't taken a rocket scientist to figure out that Miranda had come from the airport in a cab and, being her independent self and after living in New York, she was used to getting herself where she needed to go. Only this time, he was taking her.

He glanced at his watch: 6:32 P.M. He didn't know if she planned to fly back out or stay overnight, but he was going to find out. A cab pulled up across the street in front of the house and the recessed front door opened. Miranda hugged the hostess, then started toward the cab, pulling a rolling suitcase behind her. She was at least staying overnight.

Lucian had a wide grin on his face as he emerged from the SUV. The grin evaporated when Miranda saw him and stopped, then started forward again. This time her lips were pressed tightly together in annoyance.

"I'll take you where you need to go," he said, reaching for the handle of the Gucci suitcase.

She deftly stepped around him. "That won't be necessary. And if you don't mind, I'd like not to be the topic of gossip for the next month."

Lucian looked over his shoulder and saw Callie, the hostess, and her best friend, Sydney, closely watching them. Both were wonderful women, but, like a lot of women, they probably enjoyed nothing better than to be able to be the first one with new gossip. He waved to the women, who dutifully waved back. "Thanks again, Callie. Take care, Sydney."

By the time Lucian turned, the cabbie was loading Miranda's luggage into the trunk of his cab. Hands in his pockets, whistling as if he didn't have a care in the world, Lucian strolled to his Navigator and pulled off, thankful that Callie lived on a cul-de-sac and the cab would have to turn around. When it did, Lucian planned to follow.

Miranda breathed easier on seeing Lucian pull off. She hadn't thought he'd give in so easily. She tried to tell herself she wasn't disappointed and almost convinced herself. Digging into her oversize bag, she pulled out her cell phone, then hesitated before placing a call to her mother. Miranda loved her mother; she just didn't always agree with her.

Jessica Johnson Collins, pampered only child of lower-middle-class parents, had married a rich man who had promised to love and take care of her forever. Instead, after eight years of marriage he had left her for a younger woman. Miranda and her mother had been forced to move from the big house with a swimming pool and servants on Long Island to her grandparents' two-bedroom apartment in Brooklyn.

While Miranda missed her father, she had gradually adjusted. Her mother refused to. She had loved living the life of luxury her marriage afforded her and was bitter that it had been snatched from her, that another woman was living the life that should have been hers. Her anger increased on learning that alimony and child support wouldn't even pay for the weekly trips to the upscale salon that she had grown accustomed to, or the two-seater red convertible Mercedes she loved, or her numerous shopping trips.

Miranda's father's death in an automobile accident two years later hadn't appeased her mother's anger or sense of betrayal. He'd been deep in debt at the time, and once his creditors were paid there was nothing left. In her mother's opinion, her husband had failed her twice.

After the funeral, her mother had been even more relentless in teaching Miranda never to be dependent on a man to take care of her, as she had been. Consequently, Miranda dated very little. Her entire focus had been to sharpen the skills and talent her instructors had seen in her designs, to make enough money to give her mother the things she desperately seemed to need to be happy. Nothing had come close to disturbing her focus on doing just that . . . until Lucian.

Miranda's hand tightened on the cell phone. She pressed the code to dial her mother's number. She didn't want to think about Lucian.

"Hello."

"Hi, Mother." Miranda settled back into the cushioned seat. "How are you?"

"Better if my back didn't bother me so much. My inept doctor wouldn't know how to treat a bunion," her mother grumbled.

Miranda wondered why she'd asked. Her mother seemed to

take pleasure in being miserable. Miranda rubbed her forehead at the unfairness of her thought. The divorce had not only humiliated her mother—it had thrust her into a world she was unable to cope with. They might have ended up homeless if not for her grandparents. As it was, with only a few hours of college credit, her mother had never seemed able to hold a job longer than a few months.

"I want another doctor," her mother continued.

Miranda refrained from reminding her mother that she had been through five doctors in the past two years and not one of them could find anything wrong with her. "We'll see. How is the decorating coming?"

"Wonderful." Her voice perked up. "My friends are green with envy that I have a top interior designer working for me."

"I'm glad you're happy," Miranda said as the driver turned onto a long driveway. With her success, her mother had once again been able to move in the social circles she had enjoyed when she was married.

"You don't sound happy," her mother said. "You saw him, didn't you?"

There was no reason to elaborate on who her mother was talking about, but Miranda wanted to lie. A twenty-nine-year-old woman should be able to stand up to her mother.

"Miranda, answer me this instant."

"Yes. He happened to be one of the caterers at the bridal shower," she explained.

"Bet it knocked him for a loop seeing you again and knowing how far you had come on your own," her mother said gleefully.

Miranda doubted Lucian thought about her success. He was too much his own man to worry about or envy anyone else.

"You don't need him or any other man," her mother reminded her. "You listened to me, and see where it's taken you? Straight to the top. It's lucky for you that I came up that weekend to check on you and put a stop to that nonsense."

Miranda had been embarrassed to find her mother waiting for

her when she'd come back to the dorm after spending the night with Lucian. Jessica had arrived the night before. Two of Miranda's professors had contacted her mother because Miranda hadn't done well on a major exam and had been late with two design projects. If her grades fell, she'd lose her academic scholarship.

When her mother hadn't been able to contact Miranda by phone all day Saturday, she'd gone to her dormitory. Miranda's roommate told her mother that Miranda had signed out for the night and gone on a date.

Her mother had met Miranda at the door of her dorm room. She had never seen Jessica so upset and angry. She accused Miranda of throwing away her life for a man who probably had forgotten about her as soon as she left. She'd end up just like her, alone and with nothing.

Miranda might have tried to reason with her mother if Jessica hadn't told her that two of her professors were worried about her. If she lost her scholarship, there was no way she could afford to remain in college. Scared, she finally agreed with her mother that she shouldn't see Lucian again. She broke their date for that night to the movies, and never went out with him again. She'd graduated at the top of her class and tried never to look back.

The cab stopped in front of a single-story ranch house with late-blooming pink azaleas bordering the house and ringing the two giant oak trees in front. "I'm at Simone's place. I'll call you later."

"You do that. I want to tell you the idea I had for the vaulted ceiling in the bathroom. I saw it on *Oprah*. My friends' eyes will pop."

Her mother was happiest when she was impressing people. "All right. Bye, Mother."

"Bye."

Miranda disconnected the phone and climbed out of the cab while the driver retrieved her luggage from the back. Including a generous tip with the fare, she took the suitcase and went up the winding walkway, feeling more relaxed already. Maybe coming to Dallas for a few weeks to finish up her design wasn't such a bad idea after all.

She unlocked the door and pushed it open. Hearing a vehicle motor behind her she turned and blinked, then blinked again on seeing Lucian's SUV pull up. Seconds later he hopped out, closed the Navigator's door, and started toward her with a pleased smile on his face.

"You followed me," she accused.

"Guilty, but you left me with no choice."

"What part of 'no' didn't you understand?" she asked. She should have known he wouldn't give up that easily.

"I understood the 'no' coming out of your mouth, but your eyes and body language were saying something entirely different," he told her, inching closer. "It's not over between us."

Her heart thumped. "Yes, it is."

"Seems I'll have to prove it."

Guessing his intention to try to kiss her, she took a hasty step backward. "Touch me and I'll scream."

His black eyes blazed with barely banked desire. "I remember your screams of release when I was buried deep inside you. I remember the way your body would clench around me. I remember thinking I was the luckiest man alive."

Her eyes closed in helpless frustration. She remembered as well. "Please."

"If you're asking me to leave you alone, I can't. I want to know why you suddenly cut me out of your life," he demanded.

Her eyes opened and she stared into the face of the man she had once thought she loved, would love forever. "Because it was the only way to save myself." Stepping inside the house, she closed the door.

Stunned, Lucian stood in front of the closed door. What did she mean? The thought that she could have been in some type of trouble or danger sent cold chills down his spine, quickly followed by a ruthless fury that anyone would harm Miranda.

Why hadn't she come to him? Anger that she hadn't asked him for help overtook his fury. Hadn't she known he would have done anything for her? He needed answers. He lifted his hand to ring the doorbell, but let it fall on recalling the sadness in her eyes, the same sadness he'd seen in her face when she was at the bridal shower.

Somehow he knew the two were connected. If she hadn't told him when they were in college, he didn't hold out much hope that she'd tell him now. At least for the moment he knew where to find her.

Hands in his pockets, Lucian walked back to his SUV and got in. For a long moment he simply stared at the house. With everything within him he wished he were there with her, holding her, comforting her.

He frowned. In the past he'd wanted to do a lot of things to Miranda, but comforting her had never been one of them. He had offered her mind-blowing sex, but nothing else.

It didn't sit well that he might have failed her. He rubbed the back of his neck. No woman had ever confused, and, yes, pleased him as much as Miranda had. He didn't have to think long to recall him telling her in the past he'd thought he was the luckiest man alive when he was buried deep in her satin heat. He hadn't realized until now that just being with her made him feel like he was on top of the world.

Blowing out a breath, Lucian rubbed his hand over his face. For a man who hadn't made up his mind about going after Miranda, he was doing a lot of mental gymnastics.

"Miranda, why is it that only you can move me and make me as angry as hell?" Starting the motor, he turned around in the driveway, determined that she hadn't seen the last of him. This time he'd find the answer to his question: What was bothering her?

Chapter Three

"YOU LOOK LIKE A MAN with a lot on his mind, bro."

Lucian glanced up from his seat in the backyard to see his brother coming down the stone steps from the terrace, then past the end of the rectangular-shaped swimming pool. They usually got together every Sunday afternoon at Lucian's place. Although they worked in the same building, they might not see each other for days at a time.

Two years younger, Devin had good looks and an easygoing smile that drew people to him. He was also a mathematical genius, which was probably for the best, since he had to juggle so many women. Lucian frowned as Devin took the chair across from him at the glass-topped table under the spreading branches of a maple tree.

"What?"

"You never seem to have problems with women," Lucian said, still frowning.

Devin chuckled, then picked up the pitcher and poured himself a glass of iced tea. "So a woman put that look on your face." He sipped and slouched in the chair. "Since we're obviously not going to watch the baseball game now, do I know her?"

"Miranda."

Devin's eyes narrowed. Slowly he put the glass down. He'd been there ten years ago to hear his brother talk nonstop about a girl he'd met, a first for Lucian. Devin had finally met her and understood why. She had the kind of sultry, sexy beauty that would always turn heads. He'd also been there to see what her leaving had done to his brother. "When did you see her?"

Lucian told him everything, then waited for his brother's response, but there was none. "Nothing to say?"

Devin placed both arms on the tabletop, his gaze level. "Depends."

Lucian pushed his sunshades up on top of his head. "On what?"

"If you've still got a thing for her." Devin plucked a few green grapes from the bowl of fruit on the table, but his sharp gaze remained on his brother.

Lucian might have expected as much. Devin was fiercely loyal, but he was also cautious. Lucian couldn't ever remember Devin doing anything rash in his life. Lucian sighed. "I haven't made up my mind yet."

"It's not like you to be indecisive."

"Yeah." Frustrated, Lucian leaned back against the chair. "Tell me something I don't know. By the way, she said to tell you hello."

Devin nodded. "If you're doing this much thinking, I take it she's still off the chart and still saying no."

Lucian shot his brother a look. Another quality about his younger brother: He called them the way he saw them, no matter the consequences. "Right on both counts." He chugged his tea.

"You gonna let her call the shots this time?"

Lucian's eyes narrowed. There was no mistaking the challenge in his brother's voice. A slow grin spread across Lucian's face. Everything clicked into place. He made his decision: He was going after Miranda and this time she wasn't getting away from him. "No. I'm not," he finally answered.

Devin grinned, stood, and picked up his glass. "Now that that's settled, let's go in and watch the game. Sandy said she left a spiral ham, potato salad, and a peach cobbler for us."

Lucian shook his head and followed his brother inside the ultramodern home filled with sleek furniture in tones of black, beige, and slate. "How is it you know more about what my cook and housekeeper prepared than I do?"

"Maybe because I asked," Devin said easily on his way to the kitchen.

Lucian stopped dead in his tracks. Could it be that easy? He rushed after his brother to find him pulling the spiral ham and potato salad out of the built-in stainless-steel refrigerator. He placed both on the elongated slate-covered island. "You asked?"

Devin pulled two plates from the frosted-glass cabinets, then picked up two trays on the granite counter already prepared with napkins and flatware. "Women want to be needed; they want to feel they have value. I have never understood why men can't see that simple fact."

Lucian eased down onto a backless barstool. He couldn't remember any of his and Miranda's conversations except when she had started brushing him off. Even now all he had talked about was their hitting the sheets again. He winced.

Devin saw his brother's expression. "I thought you were smarter."

"I thought I was too," Lucian mumbled.

Devin handed Lucian his tray, then pulled two beers from the Sub-Zero wine chiller. "Don't worry. Nothing a woman likes better than to see a man groveling after he's made a mistake and worked up the courage to admit it."

Lucian took his beer and studied his brother. He thought he knew the answer, but he asked anyway. "I take it you never had to grovel?"

Devin looked offended. "That will be the day." He headed for the den and the fifty-one-inch plasma TV.

Lucian didn't know whether to laugh or give his brother a swift kick for being so arrogant, but considering he might have helped him with Miranda, he decided to let it slide. If there was any justice, there was a woman out there somewhere who would give Devin a run for his money. It didn't seem fair that Lucian was having all the problems with a woman.

As for himself, Lucian knew he had better start thinking about ways to get Miranda to talk to him. He followed his brother, but he paid little attention to the unfolding baseball game. He'd done a lot of thinking since leaving Miranda last evening. One thing that kept running through his mind was her saying she didn't want to be the subject of gossip for the next month.

He couldn't imagine that word of his taking her to the house would reach New York, or interest anyone, for that matter. On the other hand, if she were here in Dallas, it would be of interest. He didn't like to think about it, but he was considered, along with Devin, to be among the most eligible bachelors in the state. There had even been an article in a national magazine. Her concern could mean only one thing.

"She's staying here," he murmured to himself.

"Are you blind?" Devin was on his feet, yelling at the TV and the umpire who'd called the Red Sox player out on third base. "He was safe by a country mile."

"I have to make a run. Lock up if I'm not back by the time the game is over." Lucian stood with his untouched plate.

Devin's dark brow lifted. He grinned. "Going to grovel?"

Lucian didn't like the sound of that. "Talk."

"So you say. Get out of here, and tell Miranda I said hi."

"I will." The crack of a bat against a fastball had already drawn Devin's attention back to the game. Lucian was about to put the food back in the refrigerator when a thought struck. Placing the stoneware on the granite counter, he went in search of a picnic basket.

Miranda hadn't slept well. She'd wakened Sunday morning as restless and uncertain as she had when she'd fallen asleep. She didn't take long to think of the reason: Lucian.

Arms folded, she stared out at the huge backyard bursting with flowers. She loved flowers. They filled her terrace at her Manhattan apartment during the summers. She had a standing order for a fresh bouquet to be delivered every Monday to her office. They were one of the few extravagances she allowed herself. The lean years growing up had taught her to save as much as possible.

She'd learned that lesson, so why couldn't she learn to forget Lucian? Shoving her hand through her hair, she picked up her sketch pad from the chair beside the open French door, this time determined to make progress in creating a design for the finale of her fall/winter collection. Her pen remained motionless, just as it had for the past two weeks.

In her New York office her drafting table faced the Hudson River. Looking south, she enjoyed a magnificent view of the Empire State Building and downtown Manhattan, yet it didn't inspire her as it once had. Fear momentarily seized her before she determinedly shook it away. She just had to concentrate. Everything was in place for the fall/winter runway show. If she didn't create that last gown no one would know . . . except her.

The ringing of the doorbell spun her around. She wasn't expecting anyone. Very few people in Dallas knew she was staying in Simone's house while her friend was on a modeling assignment in Paris. Miranda had thought the change of scene might break her mental block, thought that getting away from the demands of her business and friends might help. So far it hadn't.

The doorbell sounded again. Tossing the pad back into the chair, she went to the front door and opened it.

"Hi, Miranda."

Somehow she'd known it would be Lucian. He was as sexy as ever in a white shirt with the sleeves rolled back to reveal his strong wrists. His long-fingered hands were beautifully shaped and could be gentle or demanding on her skin, but always, always arousing. She shivered in remembrance, then frowned on seeing the picnic basket in his hand.

"Lunch—or dinner, as the case may be," he said with a dimpled smile as he held up the wicker basket. "It occurred to me that you didn't have a car to go out to eat. I wasn't sure what the food situation was here," he explained.

It was a roundabout way of asking about her living arrangements, but it was also sweet and unexpected. "I'm house-sitting for a friend who exists on cottage cheese, fruit, and yogurt."

"Then this should come in handy." He held the basket out to her. "Ham, potato salad, and a special treat."

"Lucian—"

"I don't have to share." He gestured with the basket, and this time she took it. "No strings."

"Thank you," she said, still trying to find the catch. Lucian had never been the spontaneous type while they were dating.

"Well, I'll let you get back to whatever it was you were doing."

Thinking of you and being scared.

He frowned. "Is everything all right?" He glanced behind her as if expecting to see someone.

He'd also never been able to read her so easily. "Fine. I'm just having trouble with a design," she admitted, tired of holding her fear in.

"That can drive you crazy," he acknowledged. "I'm having a bit of a problem myself. I want to bring out a new confection with a new look for the box, but nothing sticks." He tilted his dark head to one side. "Maybe we could toss some ideas around . . . if you have time?"

"I'm not sure." Spending time with Lucian wasn't a good idea.

"Well, think about it. I put my card inside. Enjoy." Lucian took a couple of steps, then turned. "Almost forgot—Devin said to tell you hi."

He was halfway back to his SUV before she realized he was really leaving. "You don't want to stay?"

Stopping, he turned. Even from a distance of fifteen feet she felt the heat of his gaze. "More than anything, but it's what you want that's more important." He opened the door to the SUV.

She was no longer sure what she wanted. She wasn't supposed to feel this strange yearning or this aching loneliness that had begun when she saw his picture in a magazine over a month ago. She'd been shocked that he had remained single. "Thank you."

She looked as confused as he'd once felt. "You're welcome. Take care."

Miranda watched him drive away, then went to the kitchen and began removing the items from the basket. The special treat was thick slices of fudge bursting with almonds. There was a note in Lucian's neat handwriting. *One temptation deserves another. Lucian.*

"Oh, Lucian." Her eyes closed, her throat clogged. "Don't do this to me. I'm not strong enough to resist or get over you again."

By 8:15 Monday morning Lucian was in the massive commercial kitchen of A Chocolate Affair. Once he'd stopped fighting the irrefutable truth that he'd never gotten over Miranda, he'd decided to go all out to get her back. This time she wasn't walking away from him.

Heads and questions followed him, his executive secretary, the production manager, and the pastry chef. Everyone knew that Lucian detested wearing the disposable paper cap required of everybody in that area and that he came only for his routine monthly inspection, as he did for every part of the plant operations.

Since he had been there just the week before, the employees were understandably concerned. The intense look on his usually smiling face wasn't comforting as he went from one handmade chocolate confection to the next. Suddenly Lucian stopped and smiled.

"A miniature of that goes out today," he said. "I want it wrapped in chocolate-colored foil and tied with a huge white organza-and-satin ribbon."

There was a collective sigh of relief from the production manager, the pastry chef, the kitchen staff, and the woman putting the final touches on a chocolate espresso cake—drizzling chocolate syrup over the whole pecans an inch high.

"Certainly, Mr. Faulkner," chorused the production manager and the pastry chef.

LaWanna Johnson, Lucian's longtime executive secretary, studied the pleased smile on her boss's handsome face over the gold rims of her glasses, then noted the requirements. He was a man on a mission, and if her guess was right, he was about to launch an all-out campaign to dazzle some lucky woman.

"Now, let's see about tomorrow and the rest of the week," Lucian said, setting off again.

The two men traded confused glances, then quickly hurried after Lucian. LaWanna simply smiled. It was always so satisfying when she was right.

Miranda held the beautifully wrapped box with hands that refused to stop trembling. Her legs weren't much better. She'd known it was from Lucian even before the messenger handed her the heavy vellum envelope embossed with a black swan and Lucian's name and title. She didn't stop until she was outside at the small wrought-iron table where she liked to sit and think.

Placing the box on the table, she moved aside the terra-cotta garden bowl overflowing with pink geraniums and English ivy, then moved the box to the center. Why her heart was beating so fast she didn't know.

Yes, she did. She'd always been a sucker for gifts. They'd been few and far between after her parents divorced. Picking up the envelope, she removed the notecard.

Studies have shown that a deep love of chocolate may lead to a happier life. I agree, but there is one other thing that I require; the pleasure of your company for dinner.

Lucian

Miranda sighed. He'd put a telephone number at the bottom. If only it were possible to throw caution to the wind and to accept.

Laying the note aside, she took a deep breath and slowly lifted the top of the box, glad she didn't have to dismantle the lush white bow that had at least two yards of ribbon.

Her breath caught. Reaching in she withdrew the miniature cake, inhaling the rich aromas of cocoa and coffee. Unable to resist, she popped one of the pecans in her mouth and sighed with pleasure. But as delicious as it was, there was another taste that she remembered, craved . . . Lucian's.

Her eyes popped open. Quickly she placed the cake back into the box, put the top back on, and took it to the kitchen as if she could put away the erotic memories of Lucian as easily. He was *not* disrupting her life again.

On Tuesday, Miranda received a chocolate-raspberry tart wrapped in chocolate-colored foil and tied with another beautiful bow, this one raspberry-colored. She'd eaten the tart in one sitting, just as she had eventually eaten the cake last night.

By Wednesday morning at 8:45 she was waiting for the messenger, who had arrived promptly at nine both days. If she didn't stop eating all that chocolate she wouldn't be able to fit into the clothes for the trunk show.

Since she had no willpower, there was only one way: She had to refuse the delivery. She was torn by her decision because she wouldn't know the chocolate treat he'd sent, or read the sweet note. Tuesday it had read:

Chocolate was once thought to be a sacred source of power and strength. You possess those same qualities. Your design will be stunning. Dinner?

Lucian

She had to give it to Lucian: He was as persistent now as when they were in college together. And since she now knew the intense pleasure found in his arms, resistance was much more difficult. For too long there had been no time for a social life. She'd sometimes worked eighteen-hour days to get where she was.

But his note had inadvertently reminded her of why she couldn't take him up on his offer. She was no closer to coming up with the design than she was a month ago.

She glanced at her watch: 9:05 A.M. Brushing the sheer drapery aside, she looked out the bay window in the living room. There was no white delivery van in sight. Nor was there one at nine thirty or ten.

Miranda didn't know what to think. Had Lucian stopped sending the treats because when she'd called both days to thank him she had left the message with his secretary, refusing to wait until she was connected to him? Or was the messenger running late?

She peered out the window again. She certainly couldn't call and ask. Nor could she stand there for the rest of the day. She headed to her room for her sketch pad. Today was going to be different.

"Everything is ready for your inspection, Mr. Faulkner."

Lucian glanced up from the monthly report he had been going over. Closing the folder, he stood. "Thank you, LaWanna." He glanced at his watch: 6:15. "Is the limo here?"

"Waiting with a chilled bottle of Dom Pérignon and a single red rose."

"Excellent." He came around the desk. "Thanks for staying late."

"I wouldn't have missed it," she said, following him out of her office on the fifth floor of the office building to the elevator, her notebook in her arm.

He chuckled. "I bet the employees are wondering what's going on."

"I think they have a pretty good idea," she said.

The elevator door opened. Devin, his expression thoughtful, stepped back. "Just on my way to see you."

"The office grapevine is working well, I see," Lucian said without heat. Stepping inside he punched G.

Folding his arms, Devin leaned against the oak-paneled wall. "You're a fast learner."

"You sound disturbed," Lucian answered.

"You're making it very difficult for the rest of us to top you."

"You haven't seen anything yet," Lucian said, stepping off the elevator.

"That's what I was afraid of," Devin said, and followed.

Chapter Four

Miranda OPENED THE REFRIGERATOR Wednesday night and groaned. It was as bare as it had been the other times she'd looked. She didn't know how Simone subsisted on yogurt, fruit, and cottage cheese, but she had warned Miranda. She'd planned on taking a cab to the grocery store today, but hadn't gone for fear of missing the deliveryman. The door closed with a thud.

She had waited all day for nothing. Served her right. She shouldn't have been so sure Lucian would keep sending her chocolates.

Putting your faith in any man is the first step to heartache.

Miranda heard her mother's words as clearly as if she had been standing in the room. She threaded her fingers through her hair. Her mother was right again, and Miranda's stomach was paying the price.

So she'd order takeout again. She opened the drawer for the phone book just as the doorbell rang. *The deliveryman.* Shoving the drawer closed, she hurried to the front door.

Whatever he had, she was accepting. Maybe that was Lucian's plan; to throw her off guard and catch her at a weak moment. She was too hungry to worry about his strategy or the pounds.

Unlocking the door, she swung the door open. Her eyes widened in surprise. "Lucian."

The smile on his face disappeared. "You didn't check to see who it was first?"

"I—I thought it was the deliveryman," she confessed, darting a quick glance at the stretch limo in the driveway.

His dimpled smile returned. "In a way you're right." He handed her a long-stemmed red rose. "The rest was too big to deliver. You'll have to go to it."

"Lucian, I'm not sure about this."

"I am." He knuckles tenderly grazed her cheek. "Come with me. If you don't like the surprise or want to stay, I'll bring you back."

Was it sensible to go with a man who with just one touch could make her knees weak? What would happen if he did more . . . if he touched her in all the secret places she still craved to have him touch, no matter how hard she tried not to?

"Please. I promise to be on my best behavior."

Having a man as handsome as Lucian practically begging her to go with him was difficult to resist. Besides, if nothing else, she could ask him to stop for takeout on the way back. It was partly his fault that all she'd had to eat that day was an apple.

"I have to change."

"No, you don't," he told her, taking in her slim-fitting black slacks and white blouse. "You look perfect."

Since he wore a houndstooth sports jacket with a white shirt and no tie, she decided not to argue. "I'll get my purse."

In her bedroom she gasped on seeing her hair standing up on her head and her face devoid of makeup. She quickly took care of both. It wasn't primping. She didn't know where Lucian was taking her. People expected a fashion designer always to be flawless.

"Ready."

He closed the front door, then took her by the arm and led her to the limo. As soon as they were seated the driver took off. "Champagne?"

She shook her head. "Not on an empty stomach."

"Haven't been grocery shopping yet," he correctly guessed.

"I plan to do it tomorrow," she said. She wasn't about to tell him why the pantry was still bare.

"How did the design go today?" he asked.

She sighed. She'd rather not talk about that either. "Not very well."

"What are you aiming for?" he asked, giving her his full attention and appearing genuinely interested. It was all the encouragement she needed.

"Romantic, glamorous, alluring." She lifted her slim hand, only to let it fall again. "A fabulous creation that will make a woman feel seductive yet elegant." A thought struck. "When you look at a woman, what draws your attention?"

He shifted uncomfortably in his seat. "I don't know."

She smiled and folded one long leg underneath her. "Come on, Lucian. You said we'd toss ideas."

"Yes, but I didn't know they might get me in trouble." He frowned. "Why don't you talk with Devin? He's the ladies' man."

"You were listed in *People* as an eligible bachelor as well." Her gaze narrowed. "In fact, a couple of women at the bridal shower were practically drooling over you."

"I was too busy drooling over you to notice," he said softly.

Her pulse raced. She had been doing the same thing over him. "Th-that will not get you out of answering the question."

"All right. Let's see." His gaze slid over her like silent fingers, lingering on her parted lips, her full breasts. "I assume you mean clothes?"

She drew in a shaky breath. "Do you notice her or the clothes first?"

"Depends on the woman. It could be the seductive innocence of a young woman on the verge of learning the power of her sexuality, or the lure of a woman who knows her power."

Miranda's breath snagged. He was talking about her when they had first met and now.

Lucian fingered the silky material of the collar of her blouse, then lowered his hand until his knuckles rested lightly on her breast. "If she's wearing soft, feminine clothes that shape to her body, it makes a man wonder if her skin is as soft underneath. If he already knows the answer he anxiously waits for the time they'll be alone so he can explore all the hidden places that only he is allowed to see, to taste, to savor."

She couldn't have spoken if her life depended on it. All she could do was wait for his mouth to slowly descend toward hers. The first, tender brush of his warm lips caused her eyes to close, her body to shiver, the ache to sharpen.

"Miranda. Sweet Miranda."

As if she were a piece of his delectable chocolate, he nibbled on her mouth, slowly driving her senseless with need. By the time he finally covered her mouth with his to deepen the kiss, she was whimpering and clinging to him. His large hand gently cupped her breast; his thumb raked across the nipple, wringing another cry from her.

His head lifted and he crushed her to him. "I should have waited to kiss you, but you're too tempting." Taking a deep breath, he set her away from him, rebuttoned her blouse, and ran a shaky hand though her hair. "I hope you'll forgive my bad manners when you see your surprise."

Miranda realized they had reached their destination and blushed. She'd been too lost in Lucian to notice.

"We've only just stopped," Lucian reassured her as if reading her mind. Getting out, he reached back to help her.

Fighting embarrassment, she took his hand and stepped out. She straightened and gasped. On the bank of a small lake was a beautiful harem-style tent in bold colors of red, blue, and gold. The opening was tied back with gold rope and tassels to reveal two high-backed red-cushioned seats and a table with a lamp on top. Several waiters stood nearby.

"I take it you approve," he said.

"Lucian, it's breathtaking."

"If it makes you happy, it must be." Circling her waist, he escorted her to her seat.

Almost immediately they were served the first of six courses that consisted of lobsters, sablefish, and lamb laced with Valrhona chocolate from France. Soft music played in the background. From their seats they could see the full moon suspended over the placid water of the lake.

When the waiter started to serve the white-chocolate cheese-cake with a brownie crust, Miranda shook her head. "I couldn't eat another bite."

"Please box it," Lucian requested. "Coffee?"

"No, thank you. I can't eat or drink another thing," she said, smiling across the table at him. "I've never eaten a more scrump-tious meal."

"I'll convey your comments to my chef. Few people realize that chocolate has the ideal flavor profile to coax out the subtler quali-ties in food." He stood. "I'd like to show you something."

She didn't hesitate to give him her hand. "Lead on."

Smiling, he circled her waist, pulling her close. "We should be able to get a glimpse of them in the moonlight."

"Them?"

"Yes. We'll have to be quiet. Just a few yards farther."

Willing to follow instructions, Miranda walked beside Lucian, en-joying the beautiful night, the tender way he held her, the heat and hardness of his body against hers, the spicy scent of his cologne.

"There."

It took Miranda a few moments to stop thinking about Lucian and follow the direction he was pointing. At first she didn't see any-thing, but as her eyes adjusted to the night and with the help of the full moon she finally saw what he was pointing at—several black swans.

"Lucian, they're beautiful," she whispered.

Stepping behind her, he curved his arms around her waist, drawing her back against him. "This end of the lake is more of a wetland for them, and far enough away from the main plant that they're undisturbed." He kissed the top of her head. "They're very territorial and mate for life."

"Too bad people aren't the same way," she said, unable to keep the regret out of her voice.

Slowly he turned her to him, staring down into her face. "You never talked much about your parents except to say they divorced when you were young and that your father died two years later."

She shrugged. "What else was there to say? On the other hand, you always talked about your close-knit family and the crazy things you and Devin did while growing up."

He studied her closely. "It wasn't that easy for you, was it?"

"I made it, and that's all that matters." She turned toward the swans. "How did they get here?"

For a long moment he was silent, then: "It was my parents' idea to acquire the first pair after seeing them in Australia when they were on their second honeymoon. By the time the swans were settled it was decided that they would be the perfect symbol of love and devotion for our chocolates." His hands rested on her shoulders. "They're nesting now. If you plan to be here for the next few weeks, you can come back to see their chicks."

"I'd like that." She glanced over her shoulder at him. "Can we go back now?"

Once again he hesitated. "Certainly." Taking her hand, he led her back.

They were twenty feet from the tent when a gust of wind caught the end of the flap loosened by the workman taking it down and sent the silk brocade material flapping in the night breeze. With the night backdrop and the lanterns around the tent, the sight was a beautiful dazzle of color.

"Looks like I'd better give them a hand," Lucian said.

"Wait!" Miranda caught his arm, her eyes glued to the unrestrained cloth.

"What is it?"

"The way the light catches the material gave me an idea for my design."

"Leave it alone," he shouted, causing the two men unsuccessfully trying to catch the material to stop and stare at him. The chef and the servers had already left.

Eagerly Miranda started forward. "I need pen and paper."

Lucian handed her a pen and a small notepad from the breast pocket of his jacket. She shook her head. "Bigger."

"I have a notebook in my briefcase in the limo."

Lucian was back in no time, giving her a tablet.

"Thanks." Her hand flew across the page, noting color as she sketched a voluptuous, floor-length black cape lined in red satin over a long-sleeved clinging red gown that plunged to a waist, cinched with a sparkling jeweled buckle.

Lucian watched Miranda's hand dance across the page, her brow knitted in concentration as she stared at the tent, her mouth softening when the idea hit, then after ten minutes, a pleased expression taking over her face when she finally turned to him.

"Can I see?"

She didn't hesitate. "It's not finished, but it's a good beginning. Thanks to you."

"I can see you in this," he said. "The cape will make people wonder what is underneath, and when they see, they'll be spellbound."

"You understand," she said, amazed.

He stared down at her. "It's what I feel when I look at you."

Emotions clogged her throat. "Lucian, don't do this to me."

"Do what?"

"Make me want you." She hugged the sketch closer to her. "I can't go though that again."

"Miranda . . ." he began, but she had already turned and started toward the limo.

Lucian's troubled gaze followed; then he turned to the two men. "You can continue now. Thank you." He wasn't sure how the wonderful night had gone so terribly wrong, but he intended to find out. Miranda was not walking out on him again.

Miranda was miserable. Arms folded, she stared out the window of the limo, too aware of Lucian's silent presence beside her to pay attention to the passing scenery. She only hoped he thought the sniffling sounds she kept making were from a cold and not her attempt to keep tears from falling.

She'd badly miscalculated her ability to resist Lucian and his effect on her. Not even the final breakthrough of designing the gown helped eased the emptiness she felt. Without him she would still be stuck, and each time she thought of or saw the gown she'd remember him and his words that had gone straight to her heart.

It's what I feel when I look at you.

"We're here."

Startled by his voice, she looked at him sitting at the other end of the seat. "What?"

"Grocery store," he said simply. "You'll probably be too busy tomorrow to think about grocery shopping. I don't want you hungry." Opening his door, he came around and opened hers. "Since you don't have much, this should be pretty easy."

Miranda got out of the car and stared at Lucian. She had rejected him and he still thought of her welfare. "Why aren't you angry with me?"

His hand tenderly cupped her face. "My anger helped drive you away before. I learned my lesson."

She shook her head, misery in her face and voice. "It wasn't your fault. I couldn't stay."

He stepped closer, staring down into her troubled face. "Why, Miranda? Was it something I did or didn't do? Why did you leave?"

"My dream," she whispered softly, then stepped back on legs that wobbled. It was time. "My work has to take precedence over everything. It did then and it always will."

Chapter Five

Lucian NEEDED ANSWERS, and he planned to get them tonight. It was all he could do not to pressure Miranda while they were in the grocery store. Back in the limo she was just as quiet as she'd been on the drive from the lake. When the limo pulled up in front of her house, he helped her out, then picked up the two bags of groceries.

"Thank you, Lucian. I'll take them."

"It's no trouble. Besides, you can't carry these, the boxed cheesecake, the notepad, *and* your purse." Turning away, he went to the front door and waited.

Left with little choice, she followed him to the front door and glared up at him. He stared right back. Her shoulders slumping in defeat, she opened the door. He stepped past her into the entryway. "Where should I put these?"

She bit her lower lip. "I'll show you."

Lucian followed her through the great room and into a small but well-equipped kitchen. He placed the bags on the counter and pulled out a carton of milk and a package of cheese.

"I can do that," she said, placing the boxed cheesecake and pad on the counter and extending her hands.

"There's no reason why I can't help." He deftly stepped around her and opened the refrigerator. He frowned on seeing the meager contents. "You should have gone to the grocery store days ago."

"It's unimportant," she said. "Thank you again."

He turned. Fear and uncertainty were etched on her face. He never wanted her to look at him that way again. "Miranda, what is it? Talk to me."

Swallowing, she shook her head and reached toward the paper sack. Lucian moved faster.

With his only though to comfort her, he pulled her into his arms. She might have opened her mouth to rebuke him. Lucian didn't care. He took advantage of the opportunity to shamelessly remind her of a time when they hadn't been able to get enough of each other.

They both needed this. He needed to know that he hadn't lost her. She needed to know that she could never lose him.

The kiss was hot and wildly erotic. While his tongue mated with hers, his hand slid down her slim back to her buttocks, pressing her closer to his straining erection. She moaned against his mouth, her arms going around his neck, pulling him closer.

Teetering on the edge of sanity, he lifted his head and crushed her to him. His breathing labored, he rubbed his cheek against hers, unwilling to relinquish touching her completely.

"Why . . . why did you stop?"

He lifted his head and stared down into her passion-dazed eyes, her lips soft and pouty from his mouth. Her pulse still beat wildly in her throat. "Because when we make love again—and we will—I have to know it's a beginning and not the end."

Closing her eyes, she placed her head on his chest. "I'm not sure I can give you that."

Tenderly he lifted her chin and stared down at her, then wiped the tear cresting her lashes with his thumb. He refused to let the fear he felt be heard in his voice. "All right, then let's take this one step at a time, beginning with the conversation we should have had years ago."

Taking a seat in one of the straight-back chairs at the kitchen table, he pulled her onto his lap. "Why did you have to shut me out to have your dream?"

Miranda felt the hardness beneath her hips and wanted to move against it. "Why can't we just have sex?"

"Because I want more than just sex from you, and I think you feel the same way about me." His thumb grazed across her lower lip, causing her to shudder. "We haven't forgotten each other any more than our bodies, our hearts, our minds have."

Miranda clasped her hands together and looked away.

"Have we?"

"No," she answered quietly. "I thought I had. No, that's not the truth." She drew a deep breath and continued, "I tried to forget you, but I never was able to, not completely. Then I saw the *People* spread. I was surprised you were single and wondered if the pictures had been airbrushed."

Lucian lifted an eyebrow. "I didn't even want to do it," he confessed, "but Devin thought it would be good for business."

"That wasn't all it was good for," she said, unable to keep the jealousy from her voice.

"Nope, it brought you back to me."

She started to reprimand him for intentionally misinterpreting what she'd said; then she realized he'd meant what he'd said. "Lucian, this can't work."

"Tell me why. I'm listening."

"The driver is waiting on you," she reminded him. There was no need to discuss what couldn't be changed.

"He left as soon as we were inside," he told her calmly. "And before you jump to conclusions, I called Devin while you were shopping. He's picking me up."

"Oh," she said.

He grinned. "Disappointed?"

"What if I were?" she confessed, surprised at her boldness.

His arm around her clenched, his breathing quickening. "Why is it that you'd rather tempt me than tell me what's going on inside that head of yours?"

She was no longer surprised that he read her so well. "When did you become so perceptive?"

"When did you become so evasive?"

She started to get up, but his arm tightened. Glaring did no good.

"Talk, Miranda."

If he wanted the truth, so be it. "You can't depend on a man."

"I beg your pardon?"

She sighed in exasperation. "You heard me. Men are undependable. A woman has to take care of herself. Becoming a top fashion designer was my dream and my life. It had to be my only focus."

"Other women have career and relationships," he told her.

"Perhaps on the surface, but who knows what goes on behind closed doors?" she told him, her voice becoming tight. "The divorce rate goes up yearly, and the children are left with the fallout."

"Like you were," he said softly.

This time she made good her escape. Standing, she wrapped her arms around her waist. "Yes, like me, but it was tougher on my mother, who believed a man when he said he'd love and cherish her forever. He left us with nothing. We had to move back with my grandparents. She taught me never to be dependent on a man."

"She taught you," he repeated incredulously, coming to his feet.

"Yes." Miranda paced the length of the small kitchen. "If it hadn't been for her I might have lost my academic scholarship and everything I dreamed of becoming to help both of us." She stopped pacing and turned to him. "The morning after spending that last night with you she was waiting for me. We were spending so much time together my grades were suffering. I realized that I couldn't go on seeing you."

"You realized that, or was it your mother?"

She shoved her hand through her hair. "It was my decision. I know it may be difficult for you to hear, but I chose my career over you then, and I'd do so again. My career will always come first."

He'd asked for it, and she'd given it to him. He'd come in second, maybe third, and always would. "You couldn't make it any clearer." He thought he saw her wince, or was that what he wanted, hoped to see . . . some sign that she wasn't as cold and unfeeling as she had sounded?

Or had Miranda made the best decision for herself at that time? He'd never had to worry about his tuition or his grades. He'd been blessed with wealthy, loving parents and a sharp intelligence that let him finish summa cum laude. Miranda, on the other hand, had worked as a waitress to earn extra money, and made many of her clothes. He might not have liked her decision, but it had been hers to make. Now he was the one with a decision to make.

"So you don't expect me to be around very long, and you think I'll bail if things get complicated." It wasn't a question.

"Both of us have busy careers," she said. "It's just the way things are."

He grunted and turned away. Miranda almost reached out for him, but clenched her fist instead. It was best. "What are you doing?"

"Finishing putting up the groceries." He opened the refrigerator and placed the butter and orange juice inside. "You want the meat in the freezer or refrigerator?"

She stared at him. "Didn't you understand what I said?"

"Every word." He left the groceries and went to her. "Now hear me. Maybe I wasn't mature enough to handle your decision while we were in college, but know now that in any relationship there has to be some give and take. I understand how important your career is to you. You have a right to be proud." His arms circled her waist. "All I ask is that you try to find time to fit me into your schedule."

Her eyes narrowed. "You aren't the humble type."

He nuzzled her neck. "I can learn to be a lot of things."

She sank more heavily into him, turning her head to give him greater access. "I'm leaving in a little over three and a half weeks."

"Then we'll just have to make every moment count." He picked her up and started out of the kitchen.

She bit him on the earlobe. "What about the groceries?"

"They'll keep. I won't," he practically growled.

Laughing, feeling freer than she had in months, she pointed to the bedroom she was using. She'd take this time with Lucian and deal with the consequences later.

He eased the partially closed door open with his shoulder, then strode inside. Miranda had just time enough to reach the dimmer, throwing a soft light into the room and revealing the king-size bed in the middle.

Lucian flicked back the ecru duvet cover. "I don't think I could have gone much farther."

She palmed his face. "I've dreamed about you being here with me."

His sharp intake of breath cut through the air. "You won't regret letting me into your life again."

Miranda didn't want any promises. They could have only this time. "Love me."

They tumbled into bed together. Once their clothes were shed, he worshiped each part of her body, relearning her taste and craving her softness. Her panties and bra were black and lacy bits of expensive nothing, unlike the plain white ones she'd worn while they were in college.

He rolled over her and made her his in one powerful lunge. Her silken walls closed around him. It was all he could do not to release. Her long legs wrapped around him, drawing him deeper, more snugly within her. He closed his eyes as a feeling so intense it shook him rolled though him.

Looking down into Miranda's face, her lips slightly parted, her eyes dazed with desire, he felt himself falling in love. "Miranda," he whispered her name, emotions clogging his throat. "Sweet Miranda."

"I've waited so long for this, for you."

His mouth and body fused with hers. Spinning out of control, he felt her release and his at the same time. Together they tumbled over the precipice.

He'd never felt so content. Miranda was curved against him, her arm around his neck. He never wanted there to be a time when they couldn't be this way. "Loving you is like nothing I've ever experienced."

He felt her tense beside him and struggled not to press the issue. Deep down she might want permanence in their relationship, but he knew she didn't believe it was possible. She cared for him, but didn't believe in him enough to let go of the past and trust him.

He kissed her bare shoulder. "I'd better go put up the rest of the groceries." She started to get up, but he stayed her with his hand. "I can do it."

Miranda smiled up at him. "Thought you said they could keep."

"I might have stretched it a bit, since you bought ice cream." Kissing her again, he bounded out of bed and reached for his pants. Unlike when they were in college, she didn't tuck her head in embarrassment. When and how had she become so blasé about a man's nudity?

"You have a beautiful body," she said, staring at him with open admiration.

He tried unsuccessfully to keep the jealousy out of his voice. "Glad you approve."

Sitting up in bed, she dragged the sheet up with her over her breasts. "My first job was an assistant designer for menswear. After a while you become a bit jaded and it's just a body you need to clothe. You, on the other hand, make me very glad to be a woman."

"Keep talking like that and the ice cream is on its own."

"We can always buy more," she teased.

She didn't know how much he wanted them to be a *we*. "Stop tempting me." He started from the room, then stopped and turned. "I'm going to call Devin and tell him I'll get a cab home."

"Then I guess you'd better go put the rest of the groceries up if you want bacon for breakfast," she said, and this time she did blush.

"You want anything?"

"Just for you to hurry back."

"You got it."

After Lucian put the groceries away, he looked around the kitchen to make sure he hadn't overlooked anything. He saw the white bakery box and lifted the lid. Tucked to one side of the white chocolate cheesecake was a small jar of chocolate-raspberry syrup. The warm syrup was to be drizzled over the cheesecake just before eating.

Sensual memories flooded him. Memories of the first time he had tasted the syrup . . . on Miranda's finger, then her mouth, before moving on to other delicious areas of her body. He had intended Miranda to see the chocolate syrup tonight and be reminded of the first time they'd made love, a night like no other. The pleasure had been intense and left him feeling awed and powerful and incredibly fortunate to have found a woman like Miranda.

His brows bunched as he recalled the pain her leaving caused. He'd do whatever it took to help her realize they belonged together.

Picking up the jar, he headed back to Miranda. The morning after they'd first made love he'd called his grandmother and given her a rave review on the chocolate-raspberry syrup. It had become one of their best sellers. Lucian often thought he wasn't the only one who had found another use for the syrup.

A few feet inside the bedroom he heard the shower running, and he smiled in anticipation. Opening the jar, he sat on the side of the bed nearest the bathroom and waited.

Moments later Miranda came out of the bathroom, a fluffy white towel wrapped around her sleek body, an alluring smile on her glowing face. The heady scent of jasmine followed in her wake. "I thought I'd take a quick shower."

"The next time we'll take one together, just like before." He held up the chocolate syrup.

Miranda's eyes widened and her breath hitched. "I was so scared, but you made the night beautiful for me."

"You remember?"

"How could I forget heaven?" she asked.

Lucian felt a catch in his throat. "I was nearly crazy with wanting you. I wanted to please you so much."

"You did. In every way." She sat beside him and placed her head on his broad shoulder.

His arm curved around her waist. "Making love to you hasn't lessened the need, the hunger."

"For me either," she admitted softly.

"I've relived that night a dozen, a hundred times." He reached for her hand, feeling the slight tremble.

She tucked her head for a moment, then lifted it and met his bold gaze. "So have I."

Desire raced hot and heavy through him. "Let's see if our memories did that night justice." He dipped one of her fingers into the syrup. "We won't need the ice cream this time."

With his eyes locked with hers, he smeared the right corner of her mouth, the exact spot where she'd gotten the syrup when they were making sundaes years ago in his apartment. As then, he licked the chocolate from her finger before moving to her mouth. Both of them were breathing erratically by the time the chocolate was gone.

Releasing the towel, he dipped his finger into the chocolate syrup, then rubbed it over her nipples, the insides of her thighs, the dip of her navel. He stretched her out on the bed and proceeded to drive her wild with desire as he tasted her, savored her. By the time he reached her navel she was moaning his name. He kept going downward until he reached the very essence of her. She gasped in sweet agony, then came undone.

While she was still quivering he entered her, his mouth fusing with hers, his tongue in tandem with the pumping motion of his hips as he drew cries of ecstasy from her lips. The pleasure was pure and explosive. They climaxed in an incredible flood of sensations.

"Lucian," Miranda murmured. Drained and satisfied, she drifted off to sleep.

Tucking her snugly against him, Lucian kissed her damp forehead. Each time they made love it was more miraculous than the last. Winning Miranda's complete trust wasn't going to be easy, but he had no intention of failing. He loved her, and this time she was not getting away from him.

Chapter Six

Mɪʀᴀɴᴅᴀ ᴡᴏᴋᴇ with a smile on her face and the warmth of Lucian's lips on hers. Opening her eyes, she wound her arms around his neck. "Good morning."

"Good morning." He bent from sitting on the side of the bed and lifted a breakfast tray. "Scoot up."

Her eyes rounded in surprise, going from the perfectly scrambled eggs and crisp bacon to Lucian's pleased face. "You burned water in college."

"Still do, except for breakfast." He settled the tray over her lap. "I usually jog every morning and enjoy a good meal afterward. I finally got tired of eating out on the days Sandy doesn't come."

Miranda's hand paused in midair over the toast. "Sandy?"

Lucian's grin broadened. "Cook and housekeeper. She's happily married with grandchildren."

She munched on her toast. "I like her already."

He kissed her on her lips, then stood. "I'm taking a cab home. It's almost seven thirty, and I have a meeting at nine or I'd stay. How about dinner tonight at Papas?"

She opened her mouth to accept, then remembered the design. "I'll be busy today going over details with my seamstress and staff. I need to find the right fabric." She placed her toast back on the plate. "I might need to fly to New York this afternoon."

He sat back down on the side of the bed and took her hand. "I'm available after eleven to take you to the airport, or I can put a driver at your service."

She hugged him, almost upsetting the tray. He couldn't have said anything more right. "I can manage."

"Your fall/winter show is going to make heads turn in the fashion industry." He set her away. "Eat every bite before you start on what promises to be a hectic day. Let me know if you have to leave."

"I will." Her hand gently touched his cheek. "Have a good day."

He kissed her palm, then her lips. "You too." Standing, he was gone.

Miranda had never felt less like eating, but she picked up the fork to please Lucian. She'd give him all she could, but there was one thing she couldn't, and that was forever.

Lucian gave the cabdriver his address and sat back to stare out the window. So it had begun already. He didn't mind the fact that Miranda's work took her away from him. He was truly proud of her accomplishments. What bothered him was not knowing whether she'd come back.

Sighing, he leaned back heavily against the seat. The odds weren't exactly in his favor, but he had no intention of being anything but supportive. Somehow he'd show her that she could have a successful career and a man who loved her.

Thank goodness Simone had a fax machine, Miranda thought. Moments after her design had reached her office in New York, the phone rang. Every one of her staff loved the gown and couldn't wait to start. There were several companies where they could look for the right material, but the consensus was that the best place to start was Italy.

Miranda hesitated, knowing the only reason she did was Lucian. "Make the arrangements. I'll go by the Dallas Market Center in Dallas today and, if nothing catches my eye, I'll fly back to New

York tonight. You search our usual sources there. We'll compare notes, and if nothing flies I'll be on the earliest flight to Italy."

"I'll call you back with your itinerary," Melody, her assistant, told her.

"Thank you. See you all tomorrow at nine." Miranda hung up the phone, unable to keep the misery at bay. It didn't seem fair that the moment she and Lucian became lovers again, she'd have to leave. But the world wasn't fair. Another hard truth she'd learned growing up.

"Mr. Faulkner, Ms. Collins to see you."

"Please send her in." Lucian replaced the phone in the receiver, then came around the desk. He'd been waiting for a phone call all day. Her coming didn't bode well. He was halfway across his office when Miranda opened the door. She didn't have to say a word. Her expression told him what he'd feared.

"What time is your flight?"

"Nine," she said warily, watching him.

He stopped inches from her, wanting so badly to take her in his arms. "When will you be back?"

She bit her lower lip. "I'm not sure. My assistant may have located the fabric, but I'll have to see it first. If it's not what I want, I plan to go to Italy as soon as I can get a flight out."

"Italy!"

"Imported silks are often the best. Then I've been thinking of a special weave for the hem and cuffs," she finally said.

His hands circled her upper arms. "If we didn't import ingredients from all over the world I'd think you were out of your mind." His forehead touched hers. "I know you have to go, but I don't like it."

"Neither do I." Placing her hands on his chest, she lifted her head. "Any idea what we can do in the four and a half hours we have left?" she asked, letting her body sink seductively against his.

"Plenty," he rasped, his breath hot against her ear. Straightening, he caught her hand and left his office. "LaWanna, I'm taking the rest of the day off and going home. Unless there's an extreme emergency that Devin can't handle, I don't wish to be disturbed."

"Since Devin would say there is no such thing, please enjoy your day," LaWanna said with a smile.

"I plan to." His arm circling Miranda's waist, they were out the door.

The second they entered the house he'd picked her up and carried her to his bedroom. They raced to get undressed. Lucian finished first. Kneeling in front of Miranda he peeled off her thong, his hot mouth following its downward descent. He kissed the arch of each delicate foot, behind her knees, her quivering stomach, and then came up on the bed on top of her.

"There is no place on you that isn't sweet and addictive."

"The same goes." She pushed against his chest until he lay on his back. She straddled him. His breath hissed between his teeth as her woman's softness grazed his groin. Smiling like a siren, she darted her tongue across his turgid nipples, his broad chest, his quaking stomach.

With a fierce growl Lucian came off the bed and brought them together. Miranda cried out in pleasure and wrapped her legs around him. She met and matched the fast tempo he set. Their mind-blowing release came together. It was a long time before either of them was able to speak.

"I love your house, what little I saw of it," Miranda said, facing Lucian as she lay against him in his king-size bed, the gray silk sheets draped over her breasts. From the floor-to-ceiling windows she'd briefly been able to see teak furniture on the extensive terrace, the edge of the pool, and huge pots overflowing with flowers.

His hand lazily stroked her bare back, then over her hips before moving up again. "I was in a bit of a hurry. When you come back you can explore to your heart's content."

Smiling impishly up at him, she circled his neck. "Why can't I do it now?"

"Because you're going to be much too busy." His mouth and body covered her.

Her cell phone rang with a familiar ring tone. She tensed.

"Leave it." He nuzzled her neck.

"I can't." She pushed lightly against him to sit up. "It's my mother."

Frowning, he straightened, looked around the room for her purse, then retrieved it for her.

"Thank you." She dug inside for her ringing phone.

"I hope I can say 'you're welcome' when you're finished."

So did she. "Hello, Mother."

"What took you so long? Where have you been? I've been calling the house all day," her mother complained.

Miranda threw a glance at Lucian. "I was out searching for fabric for my new design. It's going to be sensational."

"That's good, Miranda. The architect says the vaulted ceiling I want will cost an extra ten thousand dollars. I told him to go ahead. That was all right, wasn't it?"

It shouldn't have hurt that her mother was more interested in her renovations than her daughter's career. "That's fine, Mother. I'll put the check in the mail tomorrow. I may have to go out of the country for a few days."

"Where? Perhaps you could look for something for the house."

Miranda fingertips rubbed her suddenly throbbing temple, then almost jumped when she felt Lucian's hand massaging her tense neck and shoulders. "I-Italy?"

"Excellent. You could pick up a statue for the gardens."

"I'll try. Mother, I have to go."

"All right. Don't forget my statue."

"You know I will if I can. Good-bye." She deactivated the phone and kept her back to Lucian. As close as he was he'd heard most of the conversation. His parents were nothing like hers. She'd gone to his graduation and seen his family. There were at least fifty of them, and all of them had been smiling and congratulating Lucian. At her own graduation there had been only her mother. "I have to go."

Lucian continued massaging her shoulders as if he hadn't heard her. "I've been thinking about the new chocolates, and I wanted to run an idea by you, if you have time."

It would be rude and selfish not to listen. "All right."

"We are known for having premier chocolates, so trying to improve on perfection will be tough. But I finally figured out a way, and I have you to thank."

Forgetting her embarrassment, she twisted toward him. "Me?"

His expression was so tender it brought tears to her eyes. "You. You're a rare woman. A woman who takes the hard knocks life has dealt her and doesn't complain; she just works harder to make her dream come true." His mouth quirked.

"Then there's your exquisite taste that, like chocolates, I can't get enough of. The handmade haute-couture collection of twenty-nine pieces, your age, of chocolate truffles in unique flavors will be called M, and come in a limited-edition wooden box with a swan charm hanging from the gold closure. Like you, they'll be rare, dazzling, and luscious."

She was stunned and deeply touched. Nothing could have pleased or scared her more. Tears crested her eyes.

His eyes widened in alarm. "Please tell me you aren't getting ready to brush me off again."

She sniffed. "You make me feel . . . I'm just happy."

Trembling arms drew her to him. "Do you think that from now on you can be happy without the tears?"

She brushed the moisture away from her eyes and smiled up at him. "I'll try."

"Good." His mouth took hers and they tumbled back on the bed.

Lucian had kept an eye on the clock to ensure that there was time for a quick dinner before taking Miranda to the airport. He walked with her in the security line. "Why do I get the feeling that I may be losing you again?" he asked when he was standing with her several feet from the baggage check.

"I'm coming back."

And then what? he wanted to ask, but was afraid of the answer. "I don't like you getting in so late."

She smiled. "A car will be waiting. I'm a Brooklyn girl. I can take care of myself."

"Call me just the same when you land, when you meet your driver, and when you reach your place," he instructed.

She grinned. "My mother doesn't worry this much."

He saw the smile disappear the moment she realized what she'd said. Her mother had a great deal to answer for. "Because she knows she taught you to be self-sufficient. On the other hand, I'm a Texan, and we're overprotective of the women we care about. Call."

This time the smile wasn't as bright, but it was there. "I will. I think you're running out of rope."

Her line was about to curve. "Come back to me," he said, and kissed her, unmindful of the people watching. "Travel safely."

"Good-bye, Lucian."

Lucian watched her until she went through the security checkpoint; then he could have kicked himself when he realized he didn't have her cell number. He berated himself as he made his way out of the airport. Just as he was getting in his SUV, his cell phone rang.

He grinned on seeing OUT OF AREA. "Hello, beautiful."

"Those words had better be for me," Miranda said.

"Out-of-area gave you away. Please give me your cell number," he said, opening the glove compartment for a pen.

She gave him the number, as well as that of her office and home in Manhattan. "They're boarding. Lucian, I . . ."

His grip on the phone tightened. "Yes?"

"Nothing. I'll see you when I get back. Good-bye."

"Good-bye, honey." He placed the phone back in his jacket. It was going to be a long, lonely night.

*   *   *

Miranda's hand glided across the black velvet, the black ranch mink, the red silk, and in her mind she saw the design truly come to life. "The fur will edge the cape's hood and sleeves. I've decided against the red lining."

There were murmurs of agreement from around the table, where her staff sat. She'd had the idea after dreaming about Lucian and thinking how soft and touchable his hair was.

"Looks like you won't have to go to Italy," her assistant said, then smiled. "Although I'm not sure that's a good thing."

"It is for me." Miranda picked up the large sketch. "I want the material here in two hours, even if someone has to go pick it up. We start on this today."

Everyone stood. It was her pattern maker who asked, "Are you staying until it's completed?"

If they made the gown top priority it would still take at least three days. "Yes," she answered, although she wished it could be different. That knowledge scared her as everyone filed out of the room. Wanting, needing Lucian was asking to be hurt. She knew that. She was just having difficulty convincing her heart.

"I have good news and bad news, Lucian," Miranda said a short while later when she telephoned from her office. "The fabric is perfect, but I've decided to stay until the design is finished."

A long sigh drifted though the phone. "It's tough being the boss."

"Is there a problem there?"

"Just had a meeting with my pastry chef. He can't get the exotic flavors I wanted for the M collection until next week. I'd hoped we'd be able to sample some of the chocolates this weekend."

"That would have been nice." She propped her arms on the desk. "I'll be here through the weekend."

"Any objection to having a houseguest?" he asked.

Her heart raced. She was tempted, but it was too dicey with her mother living so close to her. "Luc—" There was an abrupt knock on her door. "Hold on. There's someone at the door," she said, knowing she was intentionally putting off telling Lucian no. Her rejection would hurt him just as it was already hurting her. "Come in."

The door opened and her assistant came in. "I just got off the phone with Elizabeth Bass. She insists on having a private showing at her home tomorrow night. She has dignitaries from London visiting her. They wanted to see your designs, but have to fly out Saturday morning. She promised she could get you to preview a few pieces from your upcoming trunk show next weekend."

Miranda's eyes widened in alarm. Elizabeth Bass was one of the most powerful socialites in New York. It was her patronage that had plucked Miranda from obscurity. Her displeasure could also send her plummeting back.

"There's no way," Miranda cried, telling her assistant what she already knew. "I'm modeling two of the designs, but the other models are booked. I promised LaMier's an exclusive showing."

"She wants you to call her. Sorry." The door closed softly behind the assistant.

Miranda lifted her hand to massage her temple, then realized Lucian was still holding. "Lucian, I have to go."

"I heard everything, and I think I know a way to help."

"Lucian, I appreciate your interest, but you know nothing about fashion. I can handle this."

"I wanted to help you in college, and you told me the same thing. This time don't turn your back on me. Let me help."

"This could ruin me," she said softly.

"I won't let it," he said fiercely. "Let me help."

Standing, she went to the window and stared out at the Hudson River. Peering south she could see downtown Manhattan. She'd worked too hard, sacrificed too much to give up without a fight. "I appreciate your help, but I can take care of this myself. Good-bye." Hoping she was right, she hung up the phone.

Chapter Seven

LUCIAN DIDN'T LIKE DECEPTION, but in this case he'd had no choice. Sitting at his desk, he waited for the phone to ring. Miranda's future and possibly his with her hinged on the outcome of the call to the CEO of LaMier's. Miranda probably wouldn't have gone for the plan he had in mind if he'd told her, but it still smarted that she wouldn't even listen. He'd help her with or without her consent.

His fingers drummed impatiently on the polished cherry surface. He'd had a lot of experience dealing with men and women who could give the devil pointers on being vicious if crossed. He wasn't personally acquainted with Elizabeth Bass, but, from the fear he'd heard in Miranda's voice, he suspected she was in that group.

After Elizabeth boasted to her friends, she wasn't about to admit she couldn't deliver. Miranda would be the scapegoat. There was no way he intended to let that happen.

The phone rang. Lucian pounced on it before the sounded ended. "Yes?"

"Lucian, I have Mr. Carter, the CEO of LaMier's, on line one," LaWanna told him.

"Thank you." Lucian pressed the blinking button. "Good evening, Mr. Carter. Thank you for taking my call while on vacation."

"I was told it was urgent," he said, his voice as clear as if he were in the next room instead of in Geneva.

"It is to both of us. For the past ten years you've allowed A Chocolate Affair to be the exclusive chocolate you've carried. For that, we are deeply grateful."

"So grateful that you tracked me down on vacation to tell me?"

So he was smart, but Lucian hadn't expected otherwise. "In a way. I'd like to talk to you about a way to keep one of your best customers happy, help a talented and dedicated designer, and make the trunk show next weekend at your store the talk of the fashion industry."

"I'm listening."

It took Lucian an hour to iron out all the details with Carter. The man was crafty and had pushed hard for every possible advantage. Lucian had balked, as any good trader might, but he would have given much more to help Miranda.

He picked up the phone as it rang again. "Yes, LaWanna?"

"The cab is waiting to take you to the airport, and Sandy is here with your bag."

"Thank you. I'll be right out." He strode out of the office to find not only his housekeeper, but his brother. "Thanks, Sandy." He reached for the overnight bag and the handled A Chocolate Affair shopping bag beside it. "Devin, I need to fly to New York. I'll be back sometime tomorrow. I'll call when I'm in the air. We have to prepare a chocolate party for a trunk show at LaMier's in New York next Friday afternoon."

"Is that all?" Devin asked drolly when Lucian reached the door.

"No. You're coming with me with as many of the other bachelors in the *People* spread as you can talk into coming." He smiled. "We're going to be escorting models."

Devin blinked, then grinned like a fox in front of the open door of a henhouse.

Miranda hung up the phone in a state of shock. First the CEO of LaMier's had called to assure her that he understood her dilemma with Elizabeth Bass, who was one of his good customers. Modeling a couple of pieces for her visiting friends would be acceptable. He planned to call Elizabeth personally to invite her to the trunk show.

He'd gone on to say that it was going to be an event to remember, with several of the bachelors from the *People* magazine spread escorting the models. Lucian Faulkner had promised a chocolate feast that would be talked about for weeks. The CEO had practically been giddy when he'd hung up.

The phone rang again. This time it was Elizabeth Bass, apologizing for the position she had unknowingly placed Miranda in, and gushing with joy that the CEO had called her from Geneva to personally invite her to the trunk show. Her visiting friends had a single daughter and were thinking of returning with her. They'd all eaten and enjoyed chocolates from A Chocolate Affair, and were anxious to meet the two men in charge. Elizabeth was going to hunt up her issue of *People* and show her friends.

That last sentence hadn't sat well with Miranda. The daughter could have Devin, but Lucian was hers.

Miranda groaned. No matter how much she wished otherwise, he couldn't be hers, but he was making it difficult to keep remembering that. She owed him more than she could ever repay. He'd come through for her. Picking up the phone, she dialed.

"Lucian Faulkner's office. May I help you?"

Miranda recognized his secretary's voice. "Hello, LaWanna, this is Miranda Collins. May I speak to Lucian, please?"

There was a slight pause. "He's not here. Is there a message?"

Disappointment swept through her. "When do you expect him?"

"Tomorrow."

"If he's not in an important meeting, perhaps I can get him on his cell phone?"

"His cell phone has been turned off," she said. "But I'm sure he plans to contact you before the night is over."

Miranda brightened. "You think so?"

"I'd bet my next paycheck on it," she said with a laugh.

Miranda found herself smiling. "Thanks, LaWanna. Good-bye."

"Good-bye, Ms. Collins."

Miranda stood, clipped her cell phone to her belt, and headed for the workroom. If Lucian tried to call her she wanted to make sure she didn't miss him. The least she could do was thank him.

Lucian's grandmother was fond of saying that man planned and God unplanned. She'd never been more right. His three-hour flight to New York had turned into a nightmarish six after their plane had engine trouble and was diverted to Atlanta, where they had to wait for another plane. By the time a cab dropped him off in front of Miranda's apartment, it was close to ten.

Nodding to the concierge, Lucian entered the posh interior and headed for the elevator. He was tired, hungry, and irritated at the inefficiency of the airline. He wasn't looking forward to getting back on a plane from the same airline tomorrow morning.

Stepping off on the thirty-second floor, he quickly found Miranda's apartment and rang the doorbell, then rang again. No answer. It was the perfect ending to a horrendous day.

What else could go wrong? His head fell, then snapped up as he heard the lock disengage.

"Lucian!"

Miranda launched herself into his arms. He clutched her to him, his fatigue and hunger falling away. His mouth found hers and it was like coming home. "I thought you were out."

"I was setting the table." She reached for his bag, but he picked it up and handed her the shopping bag.

"For you."

Her smile was tremulous. "Thank you."

With one hand on the small of her back, he urged her inside. "You're welcome."

"I'll show you where you can wash up; then you can eat. Pork tenderloin."

"You don't seem surprised to see me."

"I'm not," she said. "After I called for the tenth time LaWanna finally told me you were on your way, but having trouble. I told the concierge to expect you." She touched his face. "You didn't have to come, but I'm glad you did." Her hand fell and she shook her head. "What you did with Carter and Elizabeth was nothing short of a miracle. You helped even after I said I didn't need your help."

He took her hand. "No matter what, I'll always be there for you."

"I think that may be starting to sink in." She took his arm. "Come on and eat."

"I had planned on taking you out to dinner." He washed up at the sink, then hung his jacket on the back of the chair.

"I'd much rather be at home with you."

Lucian agreed. He watched as she lit the two white taper candles on the glass-topped table. "I like your place." Her home was an arresting mix of Southern flavor and New York savvy. The golden yellows and earthy greens wrapped the apartment in quiet beauty.

She beamed with pleasure. "I'll give you a tour later and drill you about how you pulled my chestnuts out of the fire." She placed his plate in front of him. "Help yourself. I've already eaten."

Lucian blessed the food, then dug in. It was delicious. "You could give Sandy lessons."

"Thank you." Miranda picked up his empty plate and went to the sink. "Mother didn't like cooking, so I helped Grandma Pearson. She taught me."

Lucian suspected there were a lot of household chores that her mother had left to Miranda. He said nothing, simply helped her clean up the kitchen, something he had never thought about doing before. His mouth quirked.

"What?" she asked, putting away the last dish.

"Never thought I'd enjoy washing dishes." His hands curved around her waist and he drew her to him. "But I've got a feeling that it has a lot to do with the woman I'm helping."

Her hands rested on his chest. "I thought I could do everything, be everything by myself. I found out I was wrong."

"Any problem is easier if you're not alone." He brushed his mouth across hers. "A bit of my grandmother's wisdom."

"Sharing is not one of my strong suits," she confessed.

"I wouldn't go so far as to say that," he teased.

She laughed, then sobered. "Thank you. I don't know what I would have done without your help."

"If you'll let me, I'll always be there," he said softly.

Sadness mixed with fear crossed her face. "Lucian, I don't know if I can give you what you want, yet I want you to stay anyway."

"I'm not going anywhere."

She visibly relaxed. "That's not exactly true." She took a couple of steps back. "Race you to bed."

He didn't catch her until she was on the turned-down bed, laughing at her victory. "I won. I won."

He stared down at her a long time before he slipped off his shoes, unbuttoned his shirt, then knelt on the bed in front of her. "Do you know how incredible you are? You have so much to give."

"I wish I could see me with your eyes."

"One day you will. I promise."

He kissed her as if she were fragile, as if she were the most precious thing in the world. Miranda felt the punch of desire as he came down on the bed on top of her. Her hands splayed on the muscled hardness of his chest, felt the warmth. "You definitely tempt a woman."

The words were barely out of her mouth when her tongue flicked across first one nipple, then the other.

Lucian sucked in his breath. "Miranda." Her name was a ragged whisper.

It was all the encouragement she needed to love him as completely as he loved her. She was determined that he feel the same intensity. "Too many clothes."

This time she was the aggressor. She didn't stop until their clothes were scattered on the floor. "Now." Pushing him down on the bed, she straddled him, sucking in her breath as she felt his hard erection pressing against her woman's softness.

"Honey, you're killing me."

She scooted up a bit, drawing a hiss from him. Her hands once again on his chest, she stared down at him. She'd take every precious second with him. "Prepare yourself to be thoroughly loved."

The intensity of his eyes made her feel both weak and powerful. "That's all I ever wanted from you."

The words went straight to her heart. Few people in her life had cared about her unconditionally, wanting nothing from her except love. Leaning over, she began kissing him on his forehead, working her way down to his mouth, where she nibbled and teased before going to his chest and abdomen. Her hand measured the hard, thick length of him, bringing him off the bed.

"My turn." Instantly she was on her back, his mouth making a greedy foray over her body; then his mouth was on hers again. His hand swept down her quivering body to find her wet and hot. He stroked her there with the same erotic rhythm of his tongue in her mouth, driving her to the breaking point.

"Lucian," she called to him, and he answered, sliding into her slick, welcoming heat. She felt the rightness of it as her body clenched around him; holding him, then he began to move.

Eagerly she met the thrusts of his body and made demands of her own. He met each one until they went over together, locked in each other's arms.

Miranda couldn't imagine being happier. She'd been smiling nonstop since she'd woken that morning in Lucian's arms. They'd made love again, then taken a shower together. Leaving him in the bedroom to finish dressing, she had gone to the kitchen to cook breakfast. He had to leave shortly to go to the airport.

She'd miss him, but knowing they'd talk daily and that he would return next Friday helped. They'd have the entire weekend. And when he returned to Dallas, she was going with him. He'd asked her in a weak moment in the shower when he had been doing delicious things to her body, and she hadn't been able to say no.

She was sliding the pancakes onto the plate when he entered the kitchen, looking so tempting she wanted to gobble him up. "You're going to turn heads at the trunk show," she said, not at all pleased by the thought.

Sliding his arms around her waist, he said, "The only head I'm interested in turning is yours."

She smiled. "Good thing I believe you, or you'd have to go to the airport on an empty stomach."

"About time." He kissed her on the cheek, then reached for the chair to seat her when the doorbell rang.

"I'll not expecting anyone." She lifted a dark brow and smiled. "Do you by chance know who it might be?"

A dimple winked in his handsome face. "Why don't you answer it and find out?"

Smiling, wondering what Lucian had sent her this time, she started for the door. Last night, after making love the second time, she'd finally gotten around to opening the gift-wrapped box he'd brought of chocolate, orange, and amaretto truffles tied with a gorgeous orange bow.

Opening the door, she stared in shock. "Mother."

Chapter Eight

"HELLO, MIRANDA. Don't look so surprised," her mother said, entering the apartment. "I thought I'd save you the trouble of sending me the check and pick it up." She sighed dramatically. "Although I wish you had gone to Italy for my statu—"

Lucian stepped out of the kitchen. "Good morning, Mrs. Collins."

Mrs. Collins stared at Lucian a long moment, then abruptly turned to Miranda, anger sweeping across the older woman's face as she took in her daughter in a silk robe with obviously nothing underneath. "Who's that man?" she demanded.

"Lucian Faulkner," Lucian answered, stepping forward to extend his hand. Miranda, with a shell-shocked look on her face, hadn't moved.

Miranda's mother ignored him and his hand. "Miranda, I can't believe you're stupid enough to throw your life and career over for some man who just wants sex."

"Mother, please," Miranda finally said. "Please try to understand."

"Understand that you're throwing away everything that you've worked and sacrificed to achieve?" she said tightly. "It's a good thing I came over here so I could stop this."

"Like you did in college," Lucian said.

She whirled toward him, her anger increasing. "So you're the one! You won't ruin my daughter's future. Get out."

"Mother, calm down."

She turned on her daughter. "Don't be blinded because the sex is good."

Miranda gasped. It was all Lucian could do not to forcibly show her mother the door. "Miranda knows I care about her." He wanted to go to Miranda, but didn't know if that would make her mother's attack more vicious.

Mrs. Collins glared at him. "I'm sure you've pledged undying love and devotion, but it won't last, and in the meantime it will destroy everything she's worked for."

"Are you worried about Miranda or what her career can do for you financially?"

Miranda's mother sharp intake of air cut through the room. "How dare you say such a thing to me? I've sacrificed everything for her."

Name one thing, he almost said, but he realized it would only hurt Miranda. She was obviously torn. He crossed to her and stared deeply into her troubled eyes. "Don't lose faith in me or what we have." He kissed her lightly on the cheek. "See you Friday at the trunk show."

"No, you won't," her mother answered. "She wants nothing more to do with you."

"I'll see you Friday." Lucian picked up his overnight case and left, hoping that history wasn't going to repeat itself.

"How could you be so gullible?" her mother asked the second the door closed. "Are you listening to me?"

Miranda turned from the door. "You're wrong about Lucian, Mother."

"I can't believe we're having this conversation," she said. "Have you forgotten the hell your father put us through? How embarrassing it was to have to leave our beautiful home and go live in a cramped two-bedroom apartment? We lost friends, everything."

"Naturally, I was confused and upset at first, but Grandma and

Grandpa Pearson made me feel welcomed and special," Miranda said.

"They loved you because you were mine, and their only grand-child." Her mother's mouth tightened. "But you could put my parents' entire apartment in the master suite of our house on Long Island."

Miranda started to say that was probably true, but she'd never felt as happy there as she had in her grandparents' home. She left the thought unsaid. Perhaps she'd been too young to understand. Her father had been busy with his electronic company and her mother with her "me time," as she called it.

"I wish they could be here to see I've succeeded." Her grand-mother had taught Miranda to sew. She was the first one to recognize her talent and encourage her. Her grandfather took money he could ill afford to buy her material to work with. Both her grandparents had died when she was a freshman in college. The only reason Miranda and her mother had been able to make ends meet after their deaths was because of the money from the life-insurance policy they'd left.

"You won't have your success long if you have an affair with that man instead of paying attention to your company," her mother warned. "You know how fickle the fashion industry is. One bad show and you're history."

"If not for Lucian, I might have been heading in that direction al-ready." She told her mother what had happened with Elizabeth Bass and LaMier's. "He wants what's best for me. He helped when he didn't have to."

"To get you into bed. But soon you'll be just another woman, while he goes on his merry way," her mother said bitterly.

Miranda realized she'd never change her mother's mind. She had transferred her anger toward her adulterous husband to Lu-cian. "Mother, I have to get ready for work."

"Miranda, don't throw away your life on a man who only wants to use you."

"I don't want to discuss it anymore." Miranda went to the door. "We start on the new design today."

"Then I won't keep you. If you could write out the check, I'll be on my way," her mother said.

"Of course." Miranda went to the secretary in the great room and quickly wrote out the check. Ripping it out, she gave it to her mother, who was now smiling broadly. At least in this she could make her mother happy.

"Thank you, Miranda. You're such a good daughter." She briefly hugged her, then hurried to the door. "Good-bye."

She tried to be a good daughter, but a good daughter wouldn't keep remembering what Lucian had asked her mother. *Are you worried about Miranda or what her career can do for you financially?* He was wrong. Some people just showed their love in different ways.

The doorbell rang again. Probably her mother wanting to give her one last piece of advice. She opened the door.

"Delivery for Ms. Miranda Collins."

Miranda stared at the large box, then signed for the package and closed the door. She quickly went to her desk. Carefully she cut the outer wrapping of craft paper to reveal a corrugated box. Opening it, she pulled out packing bubbles to reveal a jar of chocolate-raspberry syrup, chopped pecans, and cherries.

Next time we'll try to finally make the sundaes, but I wouldn't count on it.

Lucian

Would there be a next time? Picking the box up to discard it, she noticed it remained heavy. Placing it back on the desk, she dug deeper to find a box of vanilla buttercreams. A cardboard circle kept the ecru bow from being crushed.

I couldn't resist adding these, just like I couldn't resist you the first time I saw you.

Lucian

Miranda plopped down in her chair, both notes clutched in her hand. Once again she had to make a decision, and this time there would be no going back.

Miranda had avoided talking to Lucian since he'd left New York. Instead of calling, as she had in Dallas, she'd sent thank-you notes for the chocolates that he'd sent daily. When he'd returned from his jog Saturday morning he'd found a message on his answering machine. Her voice had been brisk and businesslike. The event at Elizabeth Bass's home had been a success. The visiting dignitary wanted both of the outfits Miranda had modeled.

There'd been no mention of them as a couple. He'd called her at work and at home. If he managed to get her on the phone she was always too busy to talk. It was almost an exact repeat of her brush-off when they were in college.

"Worried about tripping over your feet and embarrassing yourself?"

Lucian glanced around to see Devin and four of the other bachelors from the *People* spread already on the sidewalk in front of LaMier's. "I'll leave that up to you." He got out, then went to the limo pulling up behind them to help his mother and grandmother out. His father and grandfather slowly followed. Only their love for their wives and grandson could have gotten them here.

"It won't be so bad, Dad, Granddad," Lucian told them. "You can see firsthand how the catering is handled."

"Seems a high price to pay for what we have to sit through," his grandfather said, gray-haired and handsome at seventy-eight.

"You tell him, Dad." Lucian's father was a carbon-copy younger version of his father. At fifty-five his black hair had just begun to turn gray.

"Would it help to know that the waiter has special instructions to serve you scotch and lobster salad?" Lucian asked, knowing they were his father's and grandfather's favorites.

"Smart boy you have there, son," his grandfather said.

"Just like his grandfather," his father said.

His mother, beautiful as always, shook her head. "If you two could stop patting each other on the back, we have a fashion show to attend."

"I'm more interested in seeing the designer," his grandmother said. Like her grandson, Devin, she never minced words.

"So am I," Lucian said, taking her arm. "Let's go find her. Devin, please check to see that the caterers have everything in place."

"You got it. But afterward, models, here I come."

Miranda felt a prickling sensation and knew before she turned that she'd see Lucian. She didn't expect to see the two couples with him. She recognized them immediately.

Acting as if he were used to the hustle and madness of models getting ready, Lucian led his parents and grandparents around a rolling rack of clothes. "Hi, Miranda. I'd like to you meet my parents and grandparents."

Still in somewhat of a daze, she shook their hands. "I'm pleased to meet you."

"Not as pleased as I am to meet you," his grandmother said.

"A showing is always exciting," Miranda said.

The robust woman waved the words aside. "I'm talking about you."

Miranda blushed.

Lucian's mother stepped forward. "We're hoping that you'll join us afterward for dinner."

Miranda moistened her lips and tried not to look at Lucian. "Thank you, but I'm not sure."

Lucian's mother gently touched Miranda's unsteady hand. "Please think about it. We'd all like to get to know the woman who inspired such a unique idea for a new collection of chocolates."

Miranda's head whipped up and around toward Lucian. "You told them?"

"He certainly did," his father said. "Couldn't stop talking about it."

"Or you," his grandfather added. "Although I can see why." He nodded his gray head. "Boy always did have good taste and a sharp mind. Got both from me." He winked at his wife, who blushed. "That's why it was easy to leave him in charge."

Miranda knew her mouth was open and snapped it shut. She'd never met a more open or likable group of people.

"Caterers all set." Devin strolled up with four broad-shouldered, handsome men. "We're ready for duty."

Someone whistled. Miranda wasn't sure if it was her man-hungry hairstylist or one of the models. She couldn't blame whoever it was. Together the men were quite impressive.

"Ms. Collins, is everything ready? The women saw the models and are becoming a bit restless."

Miranda turned to see the store manager and Winston Carter, CEO of LaMier's. *Talk about pressure and a golden opportunity.* Introductions were made.

"I'm looking forward to this and the continuing association with A Chocolate Affair," Mr. Carter said.

Lucian's father and grandfather flanked him. "We appreciate the opportunity to showcase the best with the best," his father said.

"The only way to go is first-class," Lucian's grandfather agreed. "Shall we take our seats?"

Lucian's father and grandfather enjoyed a good time, but they were also shrewd businessmen. "Ready, Miranda?"

"The men haven't practiced," Miranda said, worried.

Lucian tenderly palmed her anxious face. "They could escort and charm women in their sleep. Take a look."

Miranda turned to see the men surrounded by a cluster of women. "We go on first."

Lucian extended his arm. "Let's show Devin and the others how it's done."

There was such a reckless challenge in his voice and in his face that she laughed. "Let's."

Miranda had a ball. From the moment she looped her arm trustingly through his, the butterflies in her stomach settled. The customers enjoyed the imported chocolates, the stylish clothes, and the gorgeous men. Two women almost came to blows over the last dress in their size. Devin and one of the other bachelors stepped in to separate the two. When it was finally over, the store manager had a huge grin on her face, and Mr. Carter was in the corner having an intense conversation with Lucian's father and grandfather.

"You have set the standard by which all other trunk shows will be judged," Lucian said, sliding his arms around her waist.

"Lucian," she said, looking around to find his mother and grandmother beaming at them.

"Yes?" He nuzzled her neck.

She fought to keep her thoughts clear, then saw something that snapped her spine straight.

"Miranda, may I see you?" her mother asked sharply.

Lucian stepped to one side, but he didn't release Miranda. "Mrs. Collins."

"Miranda," her mother repeated.

Miranda's heart clenched. This was the moment she had known was coming, and dreaded. "All right. Everyone should have cleared out from the back."

"Don't do this," Lucian pleaded.

"I have to," she whispered.

Smiling triumphantly, her mother followed her into the back. "How arrogant of him to think you'd choose him over your own mother."

"Were you this bitter before Daddy asked for the divorce?"

"Realistic. You'll do well to be the same."

Miranda was already shaking her head. "I can't live without love. I tried."

Her mother frowned at her. "What are you talking about? Get your bag and let's go."

"No." Miranda whirled, and Lucian was there.

"I love you, Miranda. I want you to marry me."

Rude laughter filled the room. "You can't possibly think she'd throw away everything for you."

Lucian came further into the room and held out his hand. "I signed a contract for space in the Dallas Market Center for you to have a design studio and showroom in Dallas. You can commute back and forth to New York as long as you feel it's necessary."

"You wasted your money. Miranda, let's go."

Lucian's hand didn't waver. "The swan chicks hatched. They're waiting for you to see them. I've stocked up on chocolate-raspberry syrup. The pastry chef should have samples for the M collection by next week. How about Saint-Tropez for our honeymoon?"

"The man sounds delusional. Come on, Miranda. We're going."

"Where?" Miranda asked, not moving.

"Home, of course," her mother said, sounding irritated. "I'll drop you off on my way."

"I almost forgot. Tonight is your bridge night."

"Why are you acting so strange?" her mother wanted to know.

"Giving up someone you love is hard." Miranda picked up her purse.

"You'll get over him," her mother said dismissively.

"I won't have to." Miranda took Lucian's hand and held on as tightly as he was holding hers. "I love Lucian. I always have and always will. I never knew I could be as happy as I am with him. For the first time since Grandpa and Grandma died, I know how it feels to be loved unconditionally."

Her mother stared at her in disbelief. "He only wants to use you."

"He only wants to love me, Mother. I know that with every fiber of my being." Miranda took a deep breath. "I want you in my life, but I can't be the way you want me to be. I won't shut Lucian out of my life to please you. I don't want to grow old and bitter as you have, collecting things, afraid to love anyone, even your daughter."

Her mother's eyes widened in shocked outrage. "I kept you from throwing away your life and this is the thanks I get? You turn on me?"

"Lucian is my life," Miranda said quietly, her hold tightening on his hand.

"He'll leave you with nothing," Miranda's mother predicted.

"You can't leave your heart." Lucian pulled Miranda closer to him. "I started falling in love with her the moment I first saw her. This is forever."

Miranda gave Lucian a watery smile, then turned to her angry mother. "Mother, please be happy for me."

"You've made your choice, so there's nothing left to say." Miranda's mother stalked from the room.

"Mrs. Collins," Lucian called. The older woman stopped, but she didn't turn around. "Family is important. You'll be family soon, and Miranda loves you. I'd like to see you at our wedding, the birth of our children. The door will always be open."

Mrs. Collins continued without looking back.

Lucian pulled Miranda closer, felt her tremble. "I'm sorry."

She swallowed, then lifted her gaze to him. "I'll just have to believe that one day she'll understand that love doesn't have to hurt. It takes the Collins women a long time to see what's in front of them."

"You're a rare woman." He picked up her left hand, kissed it, then slid a five-carat canary-yellow diamond on her finger. "And I'm keeping you."

Tears filled her eyes. "It's beautiful. I love you so much and was so scared I'd lose you."

"You don't have to worry any longer." He rocked her in his arms. "I'm not going anywhere. You're my sweetest addiction, my one guilty pleasure."

She smiled up at him. "And you're mine. All mine." She kissed him, thinking of the chocolate-raspberry syrup at her apartment.

♥ ♥ ♥

National bestselling author Francis Ray is a native Texan who lives in Dallas with her husband. A graduate of Texas Woman's University, she was twice nominated for the Distinguished Alumni Award. Ms. Ray has thirty books in print. Her awards include the *Romantic Times* Multicultural Career Achievement award, Emma award for single title and novella, Atlantic Choice Award, The Golden Pen, and finalist for the Holt Medallion Award. You can visit her at www.francisray.com.

A Good Man Is Hard to Count

by MARYANN REID

Part One

THE BEDROOM WAS DARK, except for a thin thread of light coming from an open window. The scent of dampened skin and coconut-scented candles, now flattened pieces of wax, clung to the walls. Chyno's rhythmic motions were on cue with Maxwell's sexy tune coming from the living room stereo. A cool summer breeze washed over the bed as Chyno's hardness danced inside Savannah and she sang the words to herself.

Music always brought Savannah to another dimension as the sound of the words made love to her. Many a night she slept alone to the Quiet Storm, but tonight she had welcomed company. But Chyno didn't know the words to any of the good songs.

"Take it slow, Chyno," Savannah moaned, sprawled on her back with 230 pounds of Chyno on top of her. She grabbed Chyno's wide back, slick with sweat, and knocked a candle to the ground. She walked her fingers down to the slope of his tightened behind. Her small hands couldn't even grasp one of his cheeks.

He turned his skilled hips in a circular motion, his pelvic bone gently pressing into her. This heightened the tension she was aching to release.

Savannah kept her eyes on the broken ceiling fan, rolling them back with each pant. It was a signal that she was about to release, and she needed to get on top to do that.

But Chyno held her down. "I'm getting it the way *I* want it tonight," Chyno said, moving away her wet hair, glued to one side of her face, with his teeth. When she looked into his green eyes, he closed them, shutting her out of whatever he was experiencing. The sweat from Chyno's bald head trickled down and stung her open eyes. But she kept them open. Though she was moist and throbbing down below, she needed something more.

He seemed to know of her needs, and his mouth wandered down to her luscious pit. She reveled in the feel of his affectionate tongue and his sculpted shoulders flexing as he nestled his face deep inside her. His licks and delicate sucks creamed the apex of her thick black thighs. But still she ached for the release she wanted so badly.

As if he read her mind, he climbed back on top, slid right in, and rocked her body to the top of pleasure mountain that night. Not caring if the cops came knocking, she howled louder than a wolf at the moon. When he was through he traveled down to her dark crevice and licked his juices off. The last time a man did that, he almost killed her later. She knew what the gesture meant for a man, but she was too spent to bring it up. And he was too good to complain about it.

On Monday morning Chyno was gone, and she put another yellow sour stick in her Man Jar. Chyno was a Dominican construction worker she had been sleeping with for the past three weeks. He would come by about once a week with a trucker's appetite and an aim to please. She gave him the color yellow because his toasted skin reminded her of fried plantains. They met on Easter weekend. She was walking by his construction site and he helped her cross a broken-up Dekalb Avenue. He was the only one wearing jeans overalls, a white hard hat, and no shirt. What caught her attention first, however, were his green eyes and chiseled jaw. He looked like a model or a Hollywood actor. And the way his beautiful greens drank her in, in her peach summer slip dress, made her nipples salute him. Not long after meeting Chyno, she met

Jacques, a Moroccan lawyer, while she was lunching with a friend at a Harlem restaurant, Native. He was small by her usual standards, only five-foot-ten and 165 pounds, but highly intelligent and attentive in bed. He would come into town every few weeks on business, and feed her body eleven inches of French cordon bleu. And with that, she gave him the blue sour sticks in the jar. And up until recently there was Sohn, a sommelier at the Tribeca Grill. He was Asian, and the sex that lasted only as long as it took to eat a sour stick.

Savannah relinquished her thoughts when she marched up the steps and through the black steel door of I.S. 738 in Brooklyn. "Good morning, Ms. Savannah," said Mr. Thomas, a fellow teacher. She smiled and passed him to go into her classroom. They'd had a "flirting thing" since her first year teaching art at the school; it was the only thing that made her feel sexy during school hours. Chasing after ten-year-olds was like playing a part-time mother. As soon as she unlocked the door to her classroom and turned the lights on, the school bell rang. It meant that she was late. She usually arrived twenty minutes early to straighten out the desks and sweep, but her mind was still singing Maxwell songs. Seconds later, a swarm of boys and girls flew into class toting colorful book bags, the latest sneakers, and elaborate hairdos. Some tripped over one another, while others covered their mouths and giggled. Savannah sighed, because there was just no way to get them serious about art first thing in the morning.

"Take your time. You can't draw with a broken arm if you trip and fall," Savannah warned.

She walked up and down the rows with a stern look, holding her attendance book to her chest. The students listened, especially the boys, and slowed down their pace. Even at the young age of ten, most of the male population was putty in Savannah's hands. One by one, she called each row for attendance, and so began the routine she had performed every morning for the last three years.

Right before noon the kids went out to lunch, and Savannah washed the boards to prepare for her next period to come in. She was only a few hours into her morning, but she was already tired. When she stretched her arm to wipe the top of the board, a muscle in her lower back pulled. She was still feeling the effects of Hurricane Chyno. She smiled to herself at the cost of getting some part-time loving these days.

"Need me to rub that for you?" Her classroom door closed. It was that familiar voice again.

Savannah removed her hand from the small of her back and rolled her eyes. She wished Mr. Thomas would get it over with. He was practically in love with her, she thought. The notes in her mailbox, the chocolates on Valentine's Day, and the steady glances in the teachers' breakroom. He should slide up behind her, grip her hips, and bend her over. He was too timid for Savannah.

Savannah slowly twisted her body around so as not to aggravate her back any further. She walked to the door and locked herself away from prying student eyes. This was her job, and if any students caught her open flirtation with Mr. Thomas, it could lead to the start of a rumor mill that would ruin her reputation. "Mr. Thomas, unless you are giving that massage right now, I have no use for it." She loved putting him on the spot.

Mr. Thomas grinned like a Cheshire cat. He was about forty-five years old, six-foot-three, thick, solid build, tight, curly black hair— and white. But that just made the pot a little sweeter to Savannah, because she didn't discriminate. And she loved the way Mr. Thomas salivated over her.

"Hmmph, I didn't think so," Savannah said as she bent down in front of him to pick up her bucket. Her fitted orange linen pants framed her round behind like a portrait. No matter what she wore, her butt was always the main attraction.

Mr. Thomas eyed Savannah from the curve of her behind to her neatly French-manicured feet. "You are the only teacher I know who can wear three-inch stilettos in a classroom all day," Mr.

Thomas said, his eyes glimmering. "You look especially beautiful today. You have a glow or something."

Savannah sighed again, and gathered her bundle of thick black hair into a knot behind her head. "Thank you, Mr. Thomas. You have a glow, as usual," she said, glancing below his belt. She counted the time to when the students would return from lunch. She sat on the edge of her wooden teacher's desk and parted her lips. They were shiny with a fresh coat of burgundy lip gloss. She stared at him, but didn't say anything. It had been a fantasy of hers to have an older white man's face locked between her thighs. From what she heard, they were the best at giving head. And older, because she liked feeling young and delicious.

"Well," Savannah finally said. Mr. Thomas seemed to wake up from his own fantasy. He wiped the corner of his mouth. "I'm about to eat my lunch. Talk later?"

"Can I feed you?" he asked, stepping closer to her. Savannah inhaled his Old Spice cologne as he came over, resting his brown-speckled hands on her bare shoulder. Her skin, still sensitive from Chyno, erupted in goose bumps and sent an electric shock inside her white cotton panties. She uncrossed her legs and Mr. Thomas situated his body between them. He outlined her ears with his lips, losing his nose in her hair. His expert tongue flicked the inside of her earlobes. She thought he was trying to show her he could handle his business down south, too. She leaned her neck to the side, exposing more of it, and unfastened the top button of her yellow cardigan sweater set. She didn't touch him, but let him feel her. He circled her poking nipples with his finger. Savannah felt his bulge press against her panties. She leaned back as they rubbed up on each other like the kids did behind the steps after school. Mr. Thomas's light tapping motion was enough to make Savannah marinate like a slow roast.

Then the bell rang, and she and Mr. Thomas hurriedly straightened themselves up. He went back to his side of the hall, and Savannah was left to wonder just what would have happened if there

were more time. Nothing, she thought. Because Mr. Thomas was
just a tease, and so was she—with him.

After two hours of lesson planning that afternoon, when she got
home Savannah filled a flute with a flat champagne. It was the
almost-empty bottle of Krug Rosé that Jacques had brought over
three weeks ago. She kicked her bare feet up on the antique coffee
table and took a noisy sip. Her eyes darted to her Man Jar on the
wicker nightstand, which could be seen from the living room. She
sauntered over to it, holding her drink. She took a final sip of champagne and sat down on the bed. She could still smell Chyno in the
air. She opened a window and sat down again, staring at the jar.
There was only one red sour stick in a bottle of plenty of yellows
and blues. The red sour stick represented the last black man she
had slept with. Parrish. She had deliberately left it in the jar for the
memories. The rest of them got lost between him, her, and a night
of kinky "good-bye sex," when she used all his red sticks. He was
leaving to move back to DC, where a new job at a law firm awaited
him. That night, Parrish wrapped lengthy sour sticks around her
toes, fingers, and breasts. Parrish broke one in half and inserted
part of the sweet candy inside her, then sucked it out. The sugar-
coated outside left speckles of sweetness on her skin. For Parrish,
she tied several sour sticks around his hardness and nibbled each
one off until it was finished. The best part was the sugary sweet
taste it left on his foreskin, which was even sweeter mixed with his
own juices. But now she missed not only Parrish, but that extra
grip, thrust, or command that black men had in the bedroom. It
was important to her to keep things balanced, and variety was her
joie de vivre. Unlike her girlfriends, she didn't believe her man had
to be black, just available, working, and respectful. But she didn't
want a man right now anyway. Even at twenty-five, single for three
years, she liked not having to watch a three-hour football game so
some guy could realize how lucky he was to have her. When the

champagne turned flat and her tickle had been pickled, it was time to call "next."

Savannah stopped counting her sex partners at ten, and that was long ago. When a woman reached ten, she thought, she should start from one again. It was her way of erasing the dozens of men she had had the displeasure of hearing complain about their wives, girlfriends, kids, jobs, etc. The last time she had a boyfriend was the time she loved so hard, she almost died. Not physically, but spiritually. Everything that she had known to be good at that point had turned bad. *Derrick.* He left her permanently altered after a volatile three-year relationship in which he promised her bliss and marriage, only to leave and marry someone else. He'd been married for four years with two kids. It would have been three, because she was pregnant then for a short time. Savannah lay on her back, closed her eyes, and exhaled. Alone, because her father had kicked her out long before, Savannah had lived a life where she met men at clubs, moved in with them and a few weeks later, moved out. She even tried a stint at stripping while in college. That didn't get her anywhere, except into a hell of a lot of trouble. But the sex . . . In bed at night, she still got wet at the memories of the ménage à trios, the hedonistic acts at the "locked-door" parties, and the quickies in the Red Lobster bathroom, where one guy had an urge to eat her following a dinner of oysters. How could she ever be satisfied with one man after all that?

If it weren't for her father's intervention she would still be swinging from a pole. Before his death, he got her a job at the school where he taught for sixteen years. She liked this new life, where she was in control and paying her own rent. Back then, she relied on men to call the shots and set the tone. The Man Jar helped her maintain control over her emotions and keep track of her men, and acted as a lovely condiment to sex, too. As a colored sour stick increased in number, she knew the relationship was coming to an end—no more surprises.

Savannah flashed open her eyes when the phone rang. She picked it up on the first ring.

"Hey, *chica*. Are you up for a margarita or are you tied up with one of your men?" Giselle said, her only friend left from her "wilder days." She was married now.

"Girl, if you had called here a few nights ago, I may have been tied up—literally. Chyno was here. And I am still tired," Savannah bragged.

"Well, it ain't easy fucking two men at the same time!" Giselle laughed. "If I were single, I'd help you with that problem."

Savannah had to laugh, too. "It's not at the same time; I give my little girl time to breathe. Don't get it twisted. I'm single, and I don't need to explain myself."

"Honey, ain't nobody asking you to. I may be married, but I still like fucking. Except with Trey, all he like is getting head. And you know I get dizzy doing that."

Savannah didn't say much, but she thought Giselle married Trey for all the wrong reasons—like a ring and health benefits. She couldn't see herself stuck like that ever, especially with a man who was all about getting his. "You gotta breathe through your nose. Stop acting like you hadn't had more than enough practice before you got with him," Savannah jibed, turning the TV to *Jeopardy*.

"Anyway," Giselle huffed, moving away from a past they both didn't like talking much about anymore. "So can you walk? Or are you just, like, totally handicapped by big-ass Chyno?"

"I am still sore, but it's only out of bed when I feel the pain and tiredness. When we was sexing, I didn't feel anything but good all over," Savannah said, twirling the phone cord around her thumb.

"Sounds like somebody has some details to share. How about we meet at SugarCane at about five P.M.?"

About a half hour later, Savannah and Giselle were sitting at the Caribbean restaurant's bar nursing their first mango martini. The

restaurant doors were open like a sidewalk café, and the sidewalk was already packed with an afternoon crowd waiting to get in.

"So what is up with you and Chyno? You've been seeing lots of him lately," Giselle said, tossing a handful of braids over her shoulder.

They were seated next to a group of women who seemed desperately on the prowl to Savannah. That was just not her style.

"Yes, three times a week is a lot for me." Savannah's eyes smiled behind her bangs. "I think it's the way he touches me—so soft and gentle, but lately he's been getting rough, like he's trying to stake his claim or something. He licked his cum off me, too."

"Oh, no. That is sooo nasty." Giselle grinned, fanning herself. One of the women next to them laughed like she had heard them.

"It's not nasty, but it's his way of saying that I belong to him. It's like some primal territorial thing. Some men make you call their name; others"—Savannah adjusted the shoulder strap to her orange, thigh-high summer dress—"like to lick their own cum off your skin."

"So I guess he's getting kicked to the curb," Giselle said, rolling her eyes. Giselle playfully winked at the bartender and he winked back.

"I'm thinking about it. He's already called me twice. Next thing I know, he'll be popping up unannounced. Trying to make the situation all his, like he's in control of it. This is my party and *I'm* kicking folks out," Savannah said, as a waft of air blew her dress past her thighs. She parted her legs, enjoying the summer breeze.

"Is that why you still use that silly jar?" Giselle grimaced.

"It's not silly. It helps me keep count of all the men I'm with and keep my emotions in check. It's not easy separating love from sex. I don't trust myself to keep how I feel under wraps, so the jar is kind of like my overseer, making sure things don't get out of control."

"But how?"

"When I meet a guy, I give him a color and put a stick in for each time we have sex. As the jar fills up, I get to see which color is get-

ting too prominent. That is usually the guy whose time has come to go. We may be having too much sex, and the timing is always right."

"Right?"

"Yeah, because by then I start feeling somewhat attached. I notice when they don't call, and I'm not supposed to."

"So what happens with the other sticks? Let's say there's a guy in there who ain't been getting none?"

"I don't have that problem! The jar usually fills up. Two packs of sour sticks, which is about ten, usually does it."

Giselle squinted her eyes as if she were finally getting it. "I just hope you are not holding yourself back from a good man. Chyno really likes you, but you can do better," Giselle said, with the wisdom of a married woman.

"That is what I mean. I'm always keeping my options open. If Chyno could stay like he was, or be like Jacques . . . He and I can be in bed for hours . . ." Savannah said, swaying her body back and forth to the reggae music. Again Savannah caught one of the women next to them listening.

"Really?" Giselle said, as the next round of mango martinis and a platter of coconut shrimp were laid in front of them.

"I can lie with Jacques for hours while he sucks on my toes, plays with my hair, licks me from my nipples to my pussy and back again. I'm like a big old chocolate smorgasbord to him. And sometimes we don't even get to the sex."

Giselle just nodded with her straw hanging from her open mouth.

Savannah took that as sign to go on, but this time she was more discreet. "Like last time he nibbled on my ass, licked the inside, and turned my cheeks red. You would have sworn I was hiding gold up in there." Savannah picked up a shrimp from the plate. "And you know I like my booty played with, because it's the short route to the pussy. And when he clapped both my cheeks together, I just got all moist from the vibration to my—"

"Okay, okay," Giselle said, holding her hand up. "I officially hate you. Last time Trey went that far down, he was looking for the remote."

Savannah and Giselle both cracked up.

"That's why I can't be bothered with that one-man, marriage thing. I need more." Savannah frowned, sipping her martini.

"You need stability. . . ." Giselle whirled around in her chair to get a better look at the front door.

"And you need some dick," Savannah teased Giselle. "Did I tell you Jacques is coming into town tomorrow night? He's having a car take me to his hotel suite at the W and he will be my man toy for the evening. Oh, what are you and Trey doing tomorrow night?"

"Spades," Giselle said flatly, biting into a shrimp.

"I rest my case," Savannah said, as they both clinked their glasses.

Savannah was just about to tell Giselle about Mr. Thomas when Giselle suddenly became distracted.

Standing at the entrance of the restaurant was a vision of chocolate-brown man in loose-fitting black slacks and a short-sleeved gray shirt that did nothing to cover up a set of bulging arms. He scanned the room before walking toward the bar.

Savannah gave him the once over. The group of women next to her exploded in whispers about him. He was at least six-two, with a well-kept mustache and goatee. His entrance exuded a quiet strength. He pulled up a stool at the end and straddled his long legs around it. With his elbows parked on the bar, he signaled to the bartender with a nod.

"Who is *that*?" Savannah asked, her eyes dropping down to the tent shape between his legs. There was a slight bulge gathered to the left of his thigh.

"That is what we all want to know, honey. I was with some girls from my job, and we've spotted him here a few times—alone. He must be the new face in the 'hood. I heard he's a fireman. . . ."

But Savannah wasn't listening to her friend when she heard the brother order a gin and tonic. His voice had a deep, authoritative tone to it. As he spoke the muscles in his jaw moved, and his juicy lips curved up when he smiled at Savannah. When the women next to her saw that, they sucked their teeth.

"Girl, did you see that look he gave you?" Giselle nudged Savannah. "You gotta bottle up whatever you have and sell it."

"He could hose me down anytime." Savannah waved at him innocently. "Preferably with his tongue." And he gracefully nodded, holding her gaze. He was a man of few words, but his body language was saying plenty, and Savannah was all ears.

A bouquet of white roses greeted Savannah when she arrived at school the next morning. Savannah didn't even have to read the card to know who sent it.

I still want to feed you.
                                                        —Mr. Thomas

Savannah thought his brief one-liners were cute and got her imagination working, but she didn't need the drama of dating someone at her job. She cut up the note, just like the many others she had received from him, and threw it in the trash. The last thing she wanted was a nosy student starting rumors. She didn't mind being Mr. Thomas's secret fantasy, as long as it was kept secret.

Later in the morning, while the children drew and painted paper sunflowers, she thought about the fireman. What she wouldn't do to at least find out where he lived. She already knew she was going to fuck him; it was just a matter of when.

"Ms. Avery, do you like my sunflower?" asked Tiahnna, a tiny Puerto Rican girl.

"It's purple. It looks stupid!" shouted the boy behind her.

Tiahnna covered her face with the drawing, embarrassed, as some of the kids laughed.

Savannah knelt down beside Tiahnna's desk and the whole class silenced. She showed Tiahnna's sunflower to the class. The kids looked up and at one another.

"I didn't say all the sunflowers had to be yellow. Are all roses red?"

"Noooo, Ms. Avery," the class said in unison.

"How boring would it be if everything were the same color? So before you put your markers away, add something to those flowers to make them stand out!"

The kids went back to work, trying to make their flowers unique.

"Thanks, Tiahnna," Savannah said, and handed her paper back to her, as a few kids gathered around the girl with a new appreciation for her work of art. Savannah took special interest in this moment because when she was a student she had also been the different one. She had been embarrassed when she developed more quickly than the other girls. It was her fifth-grade teacher who'd helped her define herself as extraordinary, and since then she had never been anything plain.

Chalk and streaks of Magic Marker stained Savannah's pink tank top. She couldn't wait to get out of her clothes and into something slinky and sexy to meet Jacques for the evening. She took her time getting ready. She didn't want any distractions and erased two "hook up for the weekend" messages from Chyno. If she had it her way, she didn't plan to leave Jacques's suite until sunrise. She soaked her feet in a milk-and-honey footbath for fifteen minutes while she watched *Jeopardy*. Then she took a forty-five-minute shower in which she scrubbed her skin with an olive-and-sugar exfoliant, shaved her bikini area until it was a small patch of hair above her budding clit, and ran a bath with baby oil to soak her body for ten minutes. Afterward her skin looked good enough to eat off of, and that was exactly what she had planned.

There was a nearly finished bottle of Hanae Mori sitting on her vanity dresser next to her pewter jewelry box. She sprayed some on her chest and behind her thighs. A delicate set of red lace thong panties and bra waited on the bed to adorn her body. She slipped into those carefully, making sure not to snag the intricate lace patterns. She didn't go through all this preparation because Jacques was so important. She just enjoyed any chance she had to make herself feel special and sexy. If she took her teacher 'tude home with her, she thought she'd end up looking like those shriveled-up lunch ladies at the school. She smiled to herself about Mr. Thomas. She was more seduced by his desire for her than she was by him. He wasn't someone she had romantic feelings for, but his advances were a boost to her tattered self-esteem. There were still bits and pieces of her past life with men that chipped away at her every so often.

As she walked around her tiny bedroom, the motion of her thong against her skin was making her moist already. She loved the feel of the thin strip of chiffon down her ass. As a cover, she threw on a fitted leopard-print shirt dress that fell just under her thighs. Fastening each button, she caught a glimpse of herself in the oval-shaped vanity mirror and realized her hair was undone. She was paying so much attention to the rest of her body, she forgot what a comb and brush looked like. Without much ado, she let her black weave tumble down to her shoulders, sprayed on a curl activator, and shook her wet and wavy tresses loose.

In the kitchen she unwrapped a fresh pack of blue sour sticks for Jacques. He already had six in the jar, and she added another one, then put the jar away. Then she heard the car horn outside. Jacques had sent a car to pick her up just on time. She grabbed her bag and her keys and dashed out the door.

As Savannah walked down the long, narrow hall of the W Hotel, she saw Jacques waiting at the door of his room in black silk trunks and a robe. She looked him over for a moment as she got closer to him. He wasn't the handsomest man; fairly thin, demure, with thick, bushy eyebrows that connected. But he was kind. And he made her feel important and desirable, even if it was only every four weeks. That was the only reason she had more than one man: Each one made her feel a certain way. Chyno made her feel safe and protected. There was a man out there who could be all she ever needed, but she thought, with her issues, that he'd probably slip through her fingers like water.

"Ahhh, my cocoa princess," Jacques said at the door in his heavy French accent. "Come in, come in."

Savannah entered the room, spun around, and stood there for him to absorb. He then inched toward her and they embraced. He didn't waste any time trying to find her pouting lips, but Savannah turned her face away.

"I just got here, let me at least take off my shoes," she said, as she slipped off her red pumps. She examined the luxurious suite, with its camel leather couches, plush cream-colored carpeting, and cathedral ceiling.

"Your toes are so flawless. I could make love to them alone," he said, kneeling by her bare feet. He planted kisses on the backs of her knees and thighs. But Savannah was hungry for some food instead.

She took him by his hand and brought it to her face. "We have all night. Now behave," she said, tapping the tip of his nose. He blushed. She knew what he liked. His type was definitely a pleaser who liked taking orders, and she had an extensive list this evening.

"Or you will spank me like last time." He laughed. Savannah enjoyed watching his face light up. She thought it made him look handsomer, and younger than thirty-five. Then an image of the fire-fighter brother she had seen at SugarCane crossed her mind. He, too, had a brilliant smile that showed off shiny, bright teeth.

"Did you hear me?" Jacques said, kissing the space between her breasts.

"Oh, yeah, like the last time," she said, blinking quickly, and playfully poking his side. She looked over in the next room at a table full of silver platters of food and chilled bottles of champagne. "But the last time we didn't have all this food."

"Well, it's just some champagne, fruits, cheeses, and other treats. I also made them bring up a special order of Buffalo wings, just for you," he said, uncovering the elaborate chicken-wing platter.

"Now we are talking!" Savannah said as she grabbed a wing and passed one to him.

He put it down. "Come on, I want to eat *you* first. Let's get in the Jacuzzi."

He flung his robe to the floor, stepped out of his boxers, and walked to the Jacuzzi stark naked. Savannah licked some sauce from her fingers and took a deep breath. *For a slim man, he has some nice buns.* She watched him descend into the swirling water. It was something she forgot, because they saw each other less and less lately.

Her unbuttoned shirtdress cascaded to the carpeted floor. She walked toward Jacques as if she were holding a precious, delicate diamond between her thighs. The spanning view of the city was immaculate from the Jacuzzi room. The lights from the city looked like tints of gold. She stood at the edge of the Jacuzzi, play-modeling for him in the red lace set he had bought her as a gift.

He clapped. "Lovely—I knew that size would be perfect on you," he said, holding her thighs as she dipped her feet in the water. "May I?" he said, his hands on her panty line.

Jacques proceeded to slide her thong off and tossed it to the side, after he inhaled the crotch. "Mmmmm, let me taste," he said, as Savannah arched her back and stretched her legs open as she sat on the Jacuzzi's edge. He flicked his tongue inside the folds of her lips and directed the pulsating water to run down the sides. He turned the water to cold, to numb any feeling she had. Then Jacques covered her fleshy mound with his entire hot mouth and she literally melted on his tongue.

"Aaaaawww," groaned Savannah, as she twisted her body in a moment of pure primal delight. Jacques pulled her thighs toward him and completely covered his face. Savannah lay back, still twisting around at his unimaginable skills. She just couldn't stop moving, as if something possessed her. Her clit twitched with every movement of Jacques's tongue as if it were talking back to him. Then he spit on it. She loved that erotic feeling that came over her each time he did that. He sucked it off, and she couldn't help but reach down and taste herself. She had to have some of what was driving him just as wild.

"I just want to consume all of you," he said, dragging her into the water. He pulled off her bra.

"Suck these titties good," she panted as she played with herself. He lost his face inside her bouncing C cups, making her nipples hard as black pebbles. He bit and gently suckled them like a baby, sending Savannah into an orgasm that nearly knocked her silly.

Then Jacques crept up from behind and lifted her ass up.

"There you go." She laughed, pleased that she could rest on her stomach while he entertained himself.

She lay on the side of the Jacuzzi. Jacques squeezed her ass cheeks together, talking to them in French, which he used when he got overly excited. She couldn't understand the words, but she understood his fascination. She poked her behind out farther and tried to relax as he stuck his nose, face, and tongue between her cheeks. He bit and slapped it a few times so hard, she jumped. It was all a part of their game.

"Slap this big black ass harder. That's all you got?" she asked, shoving her behind up against him. "Let me show you how someone gets slapped."

"Oui, oui, oui," Jacques said.

"Yes, yes, yes. Now bend over that chair over there," Savannah said, as she watched Jacques crawl, wet and dripping, from the water.

"Good," she said, as she dug in her bag for her leather whip wrapped in silk. "Get over there now!"

Savannah bit her tongue to hold in her giggles. It was always funny seeing Jacques like this. She wondered what he got out of it, but didn't laugh, afraid of ruining their fantasy moment.

Savannah lifted the whip high into the air and let it come down hard on Jacques. He flinched. She did it again. He flinched some more. His light brown skin was red and raw. Getting down on her knees, she rubbed his blotchy red behind and took a good look at it. She could see his sweet balls and his massive hardness dangling from the other side. She massaged the back of his balls, her mouth ready to explore them.

"So are you ready for more?" she whispered in his ear. She stroked his hardness with her hand and smeared the juice coming from his slit into her fingers.

He nodded, keeping his head down. She cracked the whip on his sore behind a few more times. "There, now you see how it's supposed to burn. Now I am going to swallow your dick whole and suck it like a straw. Sit by the Jacuzzi."

Jacques happily obliged and crawled his way to the Jacuzzi.

"You forgot my toes today," Savannah said, sticking her feet out and digging them in his face. "Suck them first."

And Jacques did just that, sucking her toes like they were chocolate syrup. "Okay, enough," she said, and she descended into the bubbly water.

Savannah massaged his thighs as he kept his eyes closed, waiting. He was as hard as a cucumber, dripping at the tip. Unlike Giselle, Savannah loved giving a man oral gratification. It gave her the ultimate feeling of power and control. A man's penis in her mouth seemed natural to her in all its glory. She poured some warm water on his hardness and outlined the mushroomed tip with her tongue. His eyes still closed, Savannah flattened her tongue against his balls while the tip of his hardness poked at her for more attention. She worked her way back up and sucked his entire length into her mouth to the back of her throat. Jacques had lots of length and girth, and with practice she had been able to deep-throat it without gagging. Moving her head in and out, she kept her breath warm and her tongue light against him. He ran his hands all over her hair, encouraging her as she sucked on him.

"You look so sexy. Let me see your face," he said, pulling her hair away from her. But Savannah knocked his hands off her and said, "I suck the dick while you sit. Now relax." And with that and few more slurps and gentle strokes of her mouth, Jacques exploded his liquid cream on the side of the Jacuzzi. She just was glad he didn't get any on her.

About an hour and a short nap later, still naked, Jacques and Savannah made their way to the food and wine. Jacques fed her strawberries, pieces of Gouda cheese, and chicken wings with champagne. He ordered her not to lift a finger and to keep her eyes closed. It wasn't until about three A.M., when Savannah heard the crinkly sound of a condom wrapper, that they finally had sex. She was so exhausted, but she just wanted to get it over with. It lasted just five minutes of mostly Jacques yelling French expletives at her. Maybe that was why she liked the hours of foreplay more. When it was through, she went back to sleep for four hours. She showered and left, not wanting to get too comfortable with him. He called her a car. She thought comfortable partners had comfortable sex, which to her meant she might as well be married. Instead she went home and slept all day Saturday. She dreamed of being saved from a burning building by a burly black firefighter. And she wondered if her dreams could become a reality.

Savannah didn't wake up until well after noon on Sunday. Her house was a mess from leaving it since Friday night and sleeping most of the prevoius day. The sheets she slept on were the same ones on which she had sex with Chyno. As she lay in bed, she felt tired—not physically, but emotionally. With each man she had to be a different woman, and it was getting hard to keep up with. She just wanted to be herself and stop controlling everything. There was a part of her that was bad, she thought, and felt unwanted because of her troubled past. Even though she wanted to be loved more than anything, she was afraid of how much that would change every-

thing around her. But her brain was too tired for analytical prod-
ding. She stumbled to the kitchen and swung open the refrigerator
door. There was a pack of molded Swiss cheese, week-old milk, a
bowl of wilted salad from McDonald's, and a rotten banana on the
bottom shelf. She slammed the door shut. She wished there were
someone around she could send to the store. It was steamy hot outside, and she was in no mood to fuss with soccer moms and their
busy toddlers at the local supermarket. But she had to. Like everything in her life, if she didn't do it, it just wouldn't get done.

Savannah pinned up her hair and threw on jeans shorts, a
black tank top, and shades. Packs of people coming out of the
local church down her street blocked the intersection. She had to
dip and dive between wide-brimmed hats, hefty pocketbooks, and
little children running around. Some people looked at her with
their noses turned up. She felt somewhat envious when she saw
couples her age, arm in arm, walking together. The last time she
had been in a church was when she was baptized at ten years old.
Her grandmother always told her that was ten years too long, and
that was plenty of time for demons to take over her soul. Maybe
they did, she thought. Maybe she'd never be a "good girl" or
"good wife." She was always reminded of how bad she had been
since then.

At the Pathmark, Savannah picked up boxes of Corn Pops ce-
real, Lean Cuisine frozen meals, fresh bread, a few packs of steak,
potatoes, an already prepared rotisserie chicken, and macaroni and
cheese. The line wasn't as long as she had expected, and she was
out of there in no time, hustling up the street with two heavy, drippy
bags of food. As she waited to cross the crowded intersection, a car
raced down the block and pulled up in front of her. Savannah
quickly kept walking.

"Excuse me, Ms. SugarCane," said a voice she had heard once
before. "Still like mango martinis?"

Savannah nearly dropped her bags when she turned around. It

was him. She didn't know whether to run or to act like he had the wrong person. She looked like something someone dug up.

"Hi," Savannah said as she looked on. Ignoring another car beeping at his double-parked vehicle, the man walked over to her. She fidgeted with her sunglasses to keep the direct sunlight from driving her crazy.

"I'm Clinton. I think we *almost* met at SugarCane about a week ago," he said, extending his large brown hand. He was dressed in white linen pants and a cream-colored shirt, looking especially cool on this hot day. Savannah wondered if he was just coming out of the church like the rest of them.

"Oh, that's right," Savannah said, "I *almost* forgot." *Damn right, I did.*

"Sorry if I startled you, but I told myself that if I saw you next time, I'd approach you . . ." he said.

"Savannah. Nice to meet you," she said, adjusting a bag on her hip. Her underarms were damp with sweat, and she had just remembered she forgot to wear deodorant.

"Mind if I help you with your bags? Do you live far?" he asked, already taking them. Savannah liked his assertiveness, and she felt it was nice of him to ask.

"I live just a few blocks away. But if you insist." She was relieved that she didn't have to walk any farther, moving around like a tipsy curvy in the heat.

Clinton placed both bags on the backseat, and some of the sauce from the chicken dripped onto his shirt.

"Oh, my God," Savannah said, covering her mouth.

Clinton looked down at his shirt and grinned. "It's seen worse than some chicken grease. Don't worry about it. I'll send you my dry-cleaning bill." He smiled as he opened her side of the door.

As she waited for him to hop in, she felt awful, but he handled it so well. If it had happened to her, she knew she would have been pissed-off.

"So this is the part where you tell me you really live in Long Island, right?" He smiled, again.

Savannah laughed. "No, I just live on Willoughby and Myrtle. It's not that far," she said. "All you have to do is turn on—"

"Vanderbilt and go straight down," he said, completing her thought. He revved up the engine. "I live on that street."

Savannah's heart skipped a beat. "Really? Well, I live on the corner of Myrtle."

"So do I." Clinton kept his eyes on the road and didn't once look at Savannah's exposed legs in her cutoff jeans shorts. She wanted him to look, and now she was even more insecure. She must really look tore up, she thought.

"Okay, where exactly?"

"One Seventy-five Willoughby," he said, turning the corner to their street.

"Get out!" Savannah said, slapping her thigh. "You're lying."

"Well, one of us is. And it ain't me," he said with a belly laugh.

"What floor?"

"Eleventh," he said.

"Seventh." Savannah's stomach turned.

"I knew you looked familiar when I saw you that night. There is this one other girl in the building who looks like you. Each time I see her she's with some new guy," he said, looking at her sideways.

Savannah clammed up and looked out the window. "Wow, must be some new girl who moved in. I haven't seen her."

"Hmmmm," he said, as he parked his car in front of their building.

Clinton took the bags out of the car as Savannah opened the door to the building. She didn't know if it was good or bad that he lived so close.

Clinton and Savannah took the elevator to her floor. There was little room between them, and Savannah could feel the heat radiate from his body, or maybe it was hers. Since he had told her he lived there, her forehead had broken out in a sweat. She stood in front of

Clinton and could feel his eyes looking down at her back. She was relieved when the elevator doors flew open.

"So here I am," Savannah said, turning the key to her door.

"Mmmm, the chicken in one of these bags sure smells good," he said, putting her bags down beside her door.

"Yes, it's the rotisserie chicken. It's my dinner today." She wanted him to come in just as much as he did. And as fine, handsome, and ebony brown as Clinton was, she would be kidding herself if she thought she could turn down his advances.

"Mind if I come in? Just for a few minutes. I can help you unpack," he said, his eyes softening.

"Sure." Savannah stepped to the side, and let him walk in with the bags.

He walked to the kitchen and immediately started to unpack. Her place was still a mess, but where the kitchen was situated he couldn't see the rest of the apartment. Savannah slipped off her shades and did nothing but watch him. She was sort of in awe of this man who had just appeared in her life out of nowhere. One minute she was looking at spoiled cheese, and the next minute she had a handsome fireman in her apartment putting away groceries.

"Would you like something to drink?" Savannah asked, proud that she had a respectable-looking refrigerator now.

"Thanks," he said, and leaned against the kitchen counter.

Savannah prepared him a glass of iced tea. She broke off a slice of Italian bread. "Would you like a piece?"

"Yeah." He smiled and took the warm piece of bread from her hand. Its warmth seemed to travel from his skin to the bread, down to her arms.

They both chewed their bread silently, focused on each other's moving mouths.

"So," Savannah said uncomfortably, forcing her eyes off his luscious lips and big, brown eyes. There was some moisture from the summer heat forming along his hairline, which was a low-cut fade.

She wanted to lick the sweat off. And she'd never been the domestic kind, so she didn't know what else to do. "Do you want some chicken?"

"What's that?" he said, pointing to her Man Jar in the kitchen cabinet. He chewed on his soft bread and studied it.

Savannah wondered if she should tell the truth or lie. "They're sour sticks. I like collecting all the colors."

They both stood, quietly eating, as he finished the last of his iced tea. Savannah felt foolish for telling him she collected sour sticks. "Thank you," he said, putting his empty glass in the sink. "And if you ever need anything, I'm in eleven-E."

"Same here. Thanks for the ride," Savannah said, bewildered that he didn't try harder to stay.

At the door he turned around and asked, "Why don't you have more reds in your jar? That's the best flavor," he said, his eyes softening again.

"I'm working on it." She smiled and slowly closed the door.

Part Two

SAVANNAH HADN'T SEEN Clinton for an entire two weeks. In between she had seen Chyno twice, or as much as she could see of him in the dark. But she didn't walk Chyno in and out of her building, as she usually did. She didn't want to be caught with any other man until she knew what was going on with Clinton. He obviously had been spying on her, and they both knew that he had been talking about her when he mentioned a girl in his building with numerous men. She wanted to keep her profile low, but it was hard, because Clinton wasn't stepping up. She thought they would at least have had sex by now after those flirty moments in her kitchen. Considering he lived in the same building and she thought it would make seeing each other effortless.

She studied his schedule as much as she could. He was off Wednesdays, Thursdays, and Fridays, because his car would be parked on the block when she returned from school on those days. On the other days she'd hear him zoom off sometime after six A.M. She wanted him to come to her, but something told her he was waiting for her to make the next move.

On Thursday evening, Savannah met Giselle at SugarCane. It was Savannah's idea, just in case Clinton would pop in.

"Why do we need to buy ten-dollar margaritas so you can see this man again? You can just go up a few flights and ring his door." Giselle said, frowning as she looked at the extensive drink menu.

"Maybe I need to be drunk to do that?" Savannah rolled her eyes at Giselle. Just because Giselle wasn't getting any action, she didn't have to rain on her parade, she thought.

"You don't have to be drunk to do anything. Not *you!*" Giselle said, waving her finger at Savannah. "If it was all about getting drunk we could have bought a cheap-ass bottle of E & J and some Coke, like we used to do way back when."

Savannah sighed. Giselle was always good at calling her out when she was faking. "Okay, well, I'm hoping he will be here tonight. It was a Thursday when we saw him here last."

"Yep, but now you know he lives in your building. Go upstairs and act like you have a broken pipe or something. I can't believe you." Giselle laughed. But when she saw she was laughing alone, she put her hand on Savannah's knee. "You really like him, don't you?"

"Me? Please, I don't even know him. And imagine, he lives in my building and we haven't even fucked. That is a definite sign that I don't—"

"You do!" Giselle covered her mouth in awe. "That's why you're acting all flaky. If I know you, you have no qualms about taking control of situations with guys. Now you have one who can possibly see your dirt. Ain't God good?"

"Shut up, Giselle." Savannah laughed nervously. "I do like him. I mean, there's just some quiet vulnerability about him. And the way he helped me with my groceries and . . . and . . . I don't know. Maybe I'm just making all this up."

"Girl, listen to me. All them men you sleep with cannot compare to one man who can take care of you, protect you, and make your toes twist in bed like cheese curls. One man, Savannah. What is so hard about that?"

Savannah just shook her head. She was always overly concerned whether a man liked her or not. Since Derrick, she was afraid to let any man pursue her, so instead she'd pursue and dismiss them before they could. She didn't want to put herself out there to get rejected. But she did have a need to be wanted, to be desired in more ways than just the sexual. She was tired—tired of trying so hard.

"I just don't want to mess this up," Savannah said.

"It hasn't even started!" Giselle said as the bartender set down their drinks. "Give it time to develop. Just fall back and see what he's working with."

"That is what I've been doing. Trust me, I've had plenty of fantasies about showing up buck naked at his door at three A.M. But I just couldn't. And this is from a woman who can do that with a man like Jacques, who I rarely see and am not really into."

"See, that's it. That's why I know you are into Clinton. You just don't think he will like what he sees when he gets to see it. Savannah, you really are one of those women who are aggressive, and you like sex. Don't change that to make some man like you. But don't think that is all you have. You know what you gotta do."

On her way home that evening, Clinton's car was still parked outside. Maybe he was home all night, she thought, doing what good men like him did. Liquid encouragement urged her to ring his bell. It was only ten P.M. But she wasn't drunk enough. She searched her brown suede pocketbook for her keys and turned the latch on her door. She looked down and picked up a brown package that lay by her feet.

Red is my favorite flavor. Talk to you soon. C.

Inside the bag was a package of red sour sticks.

Soon? Soon? When is that supposed to be? she thought. *Soon* was a word she liked to use with men, and usually she meant, *I'll call you when I feel like it.* And to leave a pack of red sour sticks? She flung the package on the table, dropped her bag to the ground, and slammed the door behind her. She didn't bother with the elevator. She raced up the four flights to his apartment. He wasn't going to start playing head games already, she thought. She was the player, not the played.

Savannah knocked impatiently on his door. She smelled her breath with her hand and there was a slight liquor odor. *He's gonna think I'm not only drunk, but crazy, too, coming up to his apartment like he owes rent.*

Savannah turned around. Then the door opened and she heard, "Savannah?"

Clinton was standing at his door, rubbing his eyes. It looked to her like he had been asleep. Alone, she hoped.

"What's up with the red sour sticks?" she asked.

"Do you want to come in?" Clinton pulled his black cotton robe around his waist. Savannah could see his massive chest peeking through the open slit.

She walked toward him and peered at his apartment from the door. Everything was pitch-black, with a stream of light coming from a back room. From what she could tell it looked cozy and smelled nice, like vanilla. She not only wanted to come in, but stay, too.

Clinton opened his door farther. "Hey, I saw your place; you can at least see mine."

Savannah walked into his apartment, a larger version of her own. The walls were painted white, with a wicker basket on the table full of mail, and a large fish tank taking up half the wall in the living room.

"This is nice," she said, unusually reserved.

"Look, I got the sour sticks because you needed more red. Are you mad?"

"What do you mean?" Savannah asked defensively. There was no way Clinton could know what she really did with that candy, she thought. "I like candy like anyone else. I was meaning to get the red ones anyway."

A smile danced across Clinton's lips, but his furrowed forehead announced how confused he was.

She wanted to change the subject to a topic she was more adept at handling. "Can I see your bedroom?"

Clinton's smile stayed pasted to his brown, luscious lips. "I didn't see yours."

"Do you want to?"

"I never thought about it," he said.

Savannah rolled her eyes and walked to the door. *Here he is again actin' like it's all about him.* "Okay, well, I gotta get up early in the morning. We'll talk *soon.*"

"Wait a minute," he said, walking behind her. Her back was pressed against his living room wall. *Yeah, I knew he wanted this.* Savannah searched his expression with her eyes, and it spoke of everything she was feeling. She closed her eyes and felt the warmth of his lips cover her own. His tongue pressed against her lips, parting them some more. Savannah wrapped her arms around his broad shoulders. She ran her hands down his firm, solid ass and realized he wasn't wearing any drawers. The thought of his hardness just hanging loose and ready wet her panties.

"Mmmm," Clinton said as he kissed the groove between her neck and collarbone. "Now can I show you my bedroom?"

Savannah pulled her body away from him. She just couldn't. She didn't want it to go down like this with Clinton. Even for her, it was too soon. She wanted him to like her before he liked anything else on her.

"I gotta go," she said, and brushed past him. Clinton watched her disappear out the door.

At three A.M. she heard two knocks on her door. There was no question in her mind that it was Clinton. She lay on her back and promised to open it if he knocked again. But thoughts of ignoring him ravaged her brain. *Knock. Knock.* All she could see was his chest and those sexy, thick lips of his canvassing her body like a paintbrush.

She slid out of bed, half-naked, and draped the soft peach cotton sheets around her. She turned on her stereo to her favorite slow-jam station and unlocked the door. Before Clinton entered, she dashed to her bedroom and waited in the dark under the covers.

His shadow appeared in her bedroom doorway. "Savannah, you in here?"

She used the remote and turned the music up a little louder and couldn't believe her ears. "Juicy Fruit" by Mtume was playing, and that used to be her jam from her junior high school days.

Clinton stood at the end of her bed with a quiet, confident posture.

Please don't say anything, Savannah thought. She had always wanted to be taken this way in the dark by a "stranger."

Clinton peeled off his charcoal-colored sweatpants and white wife-beater shirt. He climbed into the bed beside her, and the heat from his skin seeped through hers. The cool metal from his gold chain sent goose bumps down her back.

"Shhiiit," he said with a deep, entrenching moan. He pulled up on her ample, arched behind and cupped her breasts in his hands.

Savannah sang the words to the song as Clinton grew harder against her back. She turned over and hummed as she took a good look into his sleepy, smiling brown eyes. She spread her legs more to give him full entry.

Their tongues teased each other.

Then his head dipped under the covers.

"Ohhhh!" Savannah shouted as she felt his hot tongue wedge between her throbbing lips. He squirmed his body to get better access to her wet middle. Savannah bent her knees all the way back as he held her thighs around his face as if he were eating the hell out of a succulent watermelon. He licked and sucked her until she came.

By now, there was no song that could compete for Savannah's attention. Clinton rolled over on his back and rubbed his dick. Savannah stared at it as if he were daring her to suck his impressive piece of work. He massaged it slowly in his hand, beckoning Savannah to give him the same treatment he gave her.

Just when she was about to, he gripped her hips and sat her on him. With little effort, she managed to take his hardness all the way inside her. She rode him hard and long. She finally got him, she thought. His eyes were rolled back, and he bit his lower lip as beads of sweat rolled down his forehead. *Good, take that.* She squeezed her thigh muscles and sucked his hardness deeper inside her. Clinton moaned, "Damn!" Savannah kept pumping away, breathless. By now most men would be asking for mercy, but Clinton just kept moving with her.

"Stay still," she murmured, pushing his chest down.

Clinton smiled at her with his eyes closed. "Baby, I think you finally met someone who can hang as long as you do."

Savannah rested her chest against his, and he slapped her behind several times. He stuck his finger inside her ass as she continued riding him on top. She had never felt such a sensational and unusual feeling at the same time. He dug his finger deeper inside, pushing her pussy hard against him. *Damn,* Savannah thought. *He's fucking the shit out of me.* Not exactly what she had planned, because he was the one who was supposed to get whipped.

An hour later, Savannah lay weak and spent beside Clinton. He was up and alert, eating out of a bag of Doritos.

Savannah stayed quiet as Clinton chuckled and laughed at an old rerun of *Seinfeld*. A feeling of insecurity crept up on her. What if she wasn't good enough in bed? He was supposed to be asleep, she thought. And did he even come? All she could remember was having multiples, and that had never happened before. But she felt incomplete. There was something that she had to do. Something she was good at, and was sure would turn Clinton out—at least for the rest of the morning.

As he munched on his chips and laughed at the television, Savannah slowly slid back under the covers.

"Savannah, you gotta listen to this part. This is the scene where Kramer . . . Kramer . . . *Shiiit* . . ." Clinton dropped the bag of Doritos to the ground.

Savannah licked him like the lollipop they sang about earlier. With each inch of him in her mouth, she lost herself in the crinkly hairs between his legs. She immersed herself in his aloe scent and relished the tenderness of his skin on her tongue.

"Baby . . . baby, oh, damn." Clinton said those words so many times, Savannah looked around just to make sure they were still alone.

Finally, when she was through putting on her best performance of the evening, she stayed up and watched the early-morning news as Clinton lay asleep with his head nestled in the crook of her arm. Just as things were supposed to be.

At noon the following day, Clinton and Savannah were still to-gether. While he slept, Savannah had unwrapped the red sour sticks and slid one out and into the jar. Wearing only panties and a bra, she stared at the small jar on her kitchen counter and won-dered how many sticks it would take until she tired of Clinton. But she couldn't picture that. The head she had given him was the kind reserved for a boyfriend, and she hadn't had one of those in years. As she put the jar away, out of sight, she felt a warm hand slide down her arms.

"Good morning—or should I say good afternoon?" Clinton said with a heavy laugh, and squeezed her into him.

"Oh," Savannah said, putting the jar in the cabinet. "I didn't want to wake you, but I've got some things to do soon." She felt bad about lying, but figured she'd make it easier for him to leave if he wanted to.

"Anything you need help with?" he asked.

"No. Thanks." Savannah pulled out a pan and some butter. "Like grilled cheese?"

Clinton nodded and folded his arms across his bare chest. "Why did you put only one sour stick in when I bought you a whole pack?" He held the jar in his hands.

Savannah flinched. "I wasn't finished putting them away."

Clinton didn't respond, and it left an uncomfortable silence between them. Then he asked, "Am I supposed to be red or something?" He laughed nervously.

"No," Savannah sighed with frustration as she flipped the sandwiches. She was tired of his questions, and didn't understand when firefighters got so smart anyway. "It's just something I do. Some people like sorting M&M's and I like sour sticks. Ready to eat?"

Clinton gave her a sarcastic smile that said he was determined to get to the bottom of her candy fascination.

Over the next two weeks, Savannah and Clinton exchanged nights at each other's apartments. They ordered in food, rented movies, and secluded themselves behind closed doors, where they explored each other's bodies until the break of dawn. By now Clinton had acquired eight sour sticks, which left little room in her jar for more. The crowded jar was a sign that it was time to clear out the clutter.

On Friday evening on her way home from school, Savannah couldn't wait to see Clinton, who said he had a special evening planned for them. She scrambled around her lingerie drawer looking for the perfect outfit. Lace? Fishnet? Silk? There were too many sexy numbers to choose from. She decided to just go naked, with a cheetah-print robe and some furry red high heeled slippers.

She combed her shoulder length black weave until it was smooth and soft. On her lips she dabbed a red glossy lipstick that complemented her dark skin. Her nails were still fresh from a French manicure she'd had a week ago. As she massaged her body with her favorite man-snatching perfume, Hanae Mori, the phone rang. She dashed around the room for her cordless but couldn't find it.

"Savannah, I'll be there by eight o'clock. You'll be pleasantly surprised tonight," Clinton said on the machine, and it clicked off.

Pleasantly surprised? Savannah thought there were no more surprises left. Clinton had showed her enough surprises in the bedroom to have his own "How to Please Your Woman in Bed" manual. Like last Saturday, when he showed her "the clitorator." He flattened his pink tongue on Savannah's clitoris and vibrated it, bringing her to a shivering orgasm. But as she thought back, the biggest surprise of all was that he liked to talk to her. They talked about everything from the latest movies to current events after sex. She felt relaxed and easygoing with him, and neither was in any rush to leave the other's side.

At exactly eight P.M., the bell rang. Savannah slipped on her red, furry heels and sashayed her way to the door. She fastened her cheetah-print robe around her, leaving a little space for just enough cleavage to show.

When she opened the door, her eyes grew wide at what Clinton had on. He wore a two-piece khaki-colored linen suit and held a fresh bunch of roses. She couldn't believe it. They were going out, not staying in.

She pulled her robe closed to cover her breasts. "Come in," she said, taking the roses and holding her head down. "Thank you."

Clinton grinned with his hand in his pocket. "Maybe I should have said something earlier. But I wanted it to be a surprise."

She looked at his handsome, freshly shaven face and his brilliant smile and just couldn't get mad. It sure was a surprise, she thought. And she felt cheap and silly for settling for just the sex, when he was obviously willing to give more. But it was what she was used to, she thought, and she could have settled for less.

"I'll go get ready. Give me about fifteen minutes." Savannah smiled and put the roses in a cheap vase she had in the kitchen. As she stood in her bedroom, she cried to herself. Was he taking her out on a date? She hadn't been on a real date in over a year. What if he asked her about her past, her personal life, what would she say? she thought.

She rummaged through her closet for something suitable for the evening. She pulled out a white jeans skirt and a green camisole blouse with gold hoop earrings. But she kept her purple thong on, because she had a feeling it would come in handy later.

La Traviorta was a quaint Italian restaurant on Montague Street in Brooklyn. It was a picturesque, humid summer evening with warm, calm winds. They were seated at a table in the back, away from the hustle and bustle at the bar. Savannah didn't feel completely out of place, as the restaurant was packed with other couples enjoying a relaxing evening together. The hardwood floors and hanging chandeliers gave it a touch of living room intimacy. She worried that she was underdressed, or that her bad table manners would show.

After the waiter took their orders and filled their glasses with a fine Italian red wine, Clinton zoned in on Savannah's anxiety.

"Are you okay with the place? I picked it because I hoped we could take a walk by the Promenade later."

Savannah guzzled down her wine, leaving some at the bottom of her glass. "Sure, this place is nice. I just can't wait to get back home and eat my favorite meatballs." She laughed, nudging her feet between his legs under the table.

"Come on, Savannah." He gave a smile that reached his eyes. "I want us to do different things. I want to get to know *you*."

"Like what? You know where I work, where I live; you know every inch of my body inside and out. What else is there? Please don't get serious on me, Clinton." Savannah sipped the last of her wine and bit down on her bottom lip.

"Well, isn't there anything you want to know about me?"

Savannah looked inside herself, because she had tons of questions. But that would only make him want to ask her too.

"Talk to me," he said. "I gotta be more than some good dick." He laughed.

"You *are*, Clinton. That's why I don't want to mess anything up."

"Why do you feel you would mess anything up? Savannah,

you're not a bad person. . . ." He caressed her chin. "Don't be afraid to talk."

"Do you have any kids?" Savannah asked him, swirling her wine in her glass. She sipped it slowly, knowing that she would need this and more to get through the evening.

"None that I know of." Clinton chuckled. But when he got Savannah's angry stare, he straightened up. "I don't have any. But I want some. Preferably after I get married. Do you have any kids? Just because you live alone doesn't mean you don't have any."

"I . . . I mean, no," she said, shaking her head. "I would rather wait till I'm married too."

"So where did you grow up? What did you do before teaching?" he asked.

"I grew up in Brooklyn," Savannah said, as she pretended to be interested in the couple across from her who were locked in an animated conversation. She didn't want to give Clinton any eye contact. Maybe he'd take the hint, she thought.

But he stayed quiet and just looked at her, as if he were waiting for more. He looked willing to hear anything she was ready to dish out, she thought. And there was just something about him that she trusted, that made her feel safe. She took another swig of wine.

"Clinton, I didn't grow up with a regular childhood, I turned my life around. I used to dance, drink, and do things that I can't stand to talk about. So please don't make me. I just thought you should at least know that much," she said as she closed her eyes. She didn't want to see his expression. It might make her want to take back her words.

His fingers intertwined with hers, and he squeezed them hard enough that an indescribable energy emanated from them. It was a warm, soothing feeling that made her eyes well up. He brought both her hands to his mouth and kissed them.

Midway through their dinner of shrimp ravioli for Savannah and chicken breasts wrapped in proscuitto for him, she realized how special a man Clinton was. She thought his demeanor would change, or he would have berated her with more questions or, worse yet, judged her. It was still the same between them, but only time would tell.

"Sorry that I was a little unprepared earlier this evening, but I am glad we had a chance to do this," Savannah said, inhaling his subtle Drakkar cologne as they strolled down the Brooklyn Promenade.

"How would I look not taking you out? I mean, what turns me on most is a woman who can keep me interested in and out of bed. I wanna see what you're working with besides what your mama gave you," he said, smiling at her with dreamy eyes.

"Oh, okay." Savannah lightheartedly cut her eyes at him. "Good to see there's more than one head on you, too."

Clinton playfully grabbed her from behind and swayed her from side to side. "Always got a comeback. But I like a little spice on my plate."

"Be careful what you ask for. Spice burns." Savannah laughed again. She was having a good time playing around with Clinton. It was refreshing to be with a man who wasn't too sensitive or intimidated by her snappy remarks, she thought.

"Tell me, how is a fine firefighting brother like you single?" Savannah asked as she and Clinton walked hand in hand. "Because as long as I lived in that building I never saw you. I know you had to be holed up with someone, somewhere."

"I have been—in a fire station with fat Italian dudes farting all night," Clinton said, shaking his head. "But seriously, my last situation was, like, two years ago. That ended because I cheated, honestly. She wasn't the woman for me. And I wasn't the man for her," he said, as they both stopped to look at the city lights across the twinkling night water.

"You cheated?" Savannah grimaced. She knew she wasn't one to judge, because she had cheated in the past, too. But Clinton just didn't seem like the type, and those were the ones she had to be careful of.

"We had an off-and-on relationship. Sometimes I didn't know if we were on or not. And she . . . Well, let's say she wasn't a saint herself. It took me a while to trust women after that."

"So she cheated on you, too?"

"Yeah, actually, she cheated first. It just wasn't someplace that I wanted to be," Clinton said, turning to face Savannah. "I want to be here with you, for however long you keep me." He flashed a grin.

Savannah's stomach bubbled with anticipation. She reached up and planted a wet, long kiss on Clinton's waiting lips. Several couples passed and looked on as their lips locked. Savannah felt as if she were in a scene from a movie.

"Come here," Clinton said, taking her hand. "Let's find a spot just for us."

They walked all the way down to the end of the Promenade, where an enclosed circle with benches awaited them. Behind the water fountain was an area covered by trees and leaves. Savannah couldn't wait for what Clinton might have in mind.

There was another couple seated in the area on a small bench to the left of them.

They ducked behind the water fountain, and Savannah leaned over a park bench. The cool night breeze sent a shiver up her thighs as she hiked up her skirt. Clinton positioned himself behind her and gently pulled her panties down to her knees.

"Arch your back, baby," he whispered in her ear. She poked her behind out and hiked up a leg on a bench. Clinton humped her gently and massaged her pulsating pussy until his fingers were damp with moisture.

"Stick it in," Savannah moaned, feeling scandalous.

Clinton spread Savannah's ass cheeks and entered her with an urgent but gentle force. Keeping her hands against the park bench for resistance, Savannah bit her tongue to keep down her sounds of pleasure. Clinton pumped inside her as he nibbled the back of her neck.

"You like this, baby? Tell me you like it," he said as his pace picked up.

"Yes, I love it—harder, please, make it hurt." Savannah's eyes rolled back and she swallowed her joy. Clinton got rougher and faster, holding her head down. Her knees began to shake and buckled beneath her. Her hands were raw and red from holding on to the bench, but she wasn't letting go. Within minutes she and Clinton came together, then pulled up their clothes and fell down into each other's arms onto the bench.

The next morning Clinton had an idea for them to go to the Barbecue Food Fest at Madison Square Park. She thought they would discuss what had happened the night before, but she caught herself. That was just one way that Clinton made her feel different, made her care about how he saw her. With a man like Clinton, she thought maybe the Man Jar had seen its last days. But she'd rather wait.

They stood in line under the hot, summer sun for a Kentucky-style barbecue beef brisket. Savannah playfully massaging his shoulders. She looked at the cooks slicing the juicy mound of beef to shreds and couldn't wait to sink her teeth in.

Clinton eagerly placed their orders for barbecue and beer. They walked to a shaded spot under a tree that seemed to be waiting just for them. Clinton pulled a green-and-white-checkered tablecloth from his backpack. "I bet you didn't think a man could be prepared for these sorts of things," he said, unfolding it.

Savannah grabbed the other end as they settled it down on the green grass. "Right. I don't know too many men who walk around with tablecloths in their backpack. But I like it. You don't have to try to seduce me anymore, Clinton. You already got me in bed."

"Now, why do you have to be so cynical about everything? Can't I just be doing this to be nice and useful, or did you want to sit that pretty ass on some dog waste?" He sat down and patted the space next to him.

"True. Well, this is nice," Savannah said, cuddling into his embrace.

She rested her body against his as they both ate their pieces of barbecue, feeding each other from time to time. Some sauce was on Clinton's lip, and she tackled him to the ground, her body on top of his, and licked his lips clean. No one seemed to notice as they rolled around on the grass, even rolling under an empty stand for Texas-style barbecue shrimp. She felt carefree, as if it were just the two of them. She thought that if being in love was like this, she was more than ready.

Couples strolled the perimeter of the park for the next delicious bite as they listened to the jazz band playing on the other side of the park. Clinton snapped his fingers to the beat of Miles Davis's "Kind of Blue." Savannah had several of Miles's CDs and that song was her favorite of all. The rise and fall of the tempos reminded her of her up-and-down life, just like a seesaw. Kids played with one another on the grass, including one who nearly knocked over Clinton's food. This made Savannah upset, because the boy's parents didn't even apologize for him, but Clinton played it cool and laughed it off.

"I gotta ask you something," Clinton said, lying on his back, looking up at the clear, turquoise sky.

Savannah lay on her back as well, staring at two serene gray birds on the branch looking out at the bevy of excitement before them.

"Will you come with me to my sister's baby shower tomorrow? We don't have to stay all day." He wiped some barbecue sauce from Savannah's lips.

She covered her mouth as she chewed. Again, something unexpected. "Yeah, I guess I can."

Clinton gulped down his beer as they both clapped at the wonderfully orchestrated jazz band.

Savannah somehow felt that they were both just going with the flow, something she wasn't used to. However, his invitation was a good sign that they were heading upstream and not downstream. And she just had to leave it at that—for now.

After they finished their beef brisket, they ventured off to a small café in the Village for dessert and homemade root-beer floats. They sat for hours until closing as they joked about their day and their gluttonous appetites for food and sex. Savannah had such a good time with Clinton that she found herself content with just being in the relationship, other than trying to define it.

Savannah and Clinton made love several times until the wee hours of the next morning. When she woke up in Clinton's bed, she heard the crackle of bacon on the stove and smelled fresh coffee brewing. She wanted to go back to sleep, afraid waking up would disturb all the good vibes she was feeling. But before she could think about that too hard, Clinton walked into the room with two trays of lightly toasted bread, fried eggs, and crispy bacon.

As they ate in quiet contemplation of their day ahead, she thought about yesterday. That was the most she had ever done with a guy in one day out of bed. Going to a man's family gathering was something she hadn't done either. She wondered how Clinton's family would be—if they were snobby, down-to-earth, fat, skinny, tall, short. She hoped, how ever they were, that they would just like her. She needed them to accept her and make her feel included. Besides, Giselle was never much for having female friends. The thought of actually making some new ones excited her, even if it was just for the day.

Clinton dressed in a pair of loose-fitting jeans and a white buttondown shirt. Still lounging around in his oversize navy-blue FDNY T-shirt, Savannah admired the way he took his time fastening each button with care and examining himself from side to side. He was a man of style and distinction, she thought. The special attention he gave her body, he gave to himself, and she respected that.

"Are you gonna keep staring at a brother all morning?" Clinton said, kneeling down by her side of the bed. He planted a wet one on her lips.

She dragged her body up from the bed. "Is this your sister's first child?"

"It's her second kid, from some dude no one in the family has met. As much as I tried to tell my sisters about the men out here, they still put all their trust in them. They get knocked up and let down. I feel for them," he said, closing his eyes for a moment, then opening them.

"Everybody makes mistakes, Clinton. I'm sure your sisters probably thought they had someone good while it was going on."

"I guess, but they're my little sisters, and I feel somewhat responsible, you know. But I didn't meet any of those guys, because they never came around. If they did, they probably would have thought twice when they saw a big brother like me watching 'em."

"But they are grown. I'm sure you are a still a good example to them of what a good man is. Sometimes we women know something ain't the best for us and we still go through with it. Like Chaka Khan said, 'be it right or be it wrong.' "

"True. God knows, I certainly was in some messed-up situations because it was giving me something to do," Clinton said. "She had her first child a few years ago when she was twenty-three. You both are practically the same age. I just wish she were as smart as you are when it comes to men." He kissed her forehead.

"Me, smart?" Savannah huffed. "I never thought of it that way. But you may be right," she playfully boasted.

"I'm sure you and she will have lots to talk about," Clinton said as he dabbed on some cologne.

But Savannah wasn't so sure about that.

Clinton's sister Tiffany lived with their mother in a small two-bedroom apartment on Flatbush Avenue. When they both arrived, the apartment was decorated exquisitely, with green and pink baby decorations hanging from every corner. Even the cake frosting was pink, with green marzipan flowers. The paper tablecloth had the baby's name written all over it: Dejá Tiffany Daniels.

"Oh, hello!" Ms. Daniels said when she opened the door and her arms. "So you finally get around to coming to see your people."

"What'sup, Mommy," Clinton said, giving her a big bear hug. "This is Savannah, my girlfriend."

Savannah's mouth tightened.

"Hello, dear," Clinton's mother said, looking into Savannah's wide-open eyes.

"Oh, hi, Ms. Daniels. Nice to meet you," Savannah said, offering her hand.

Savannah had learned to tell a person's sincerity by the type of handshake she received. Ms. Daniels's was weak and light. Her touch felt as though she were afraid of contracting the flu or something, Savannah thought.

Ms. Daniels ushered them both into the kitchen, where foil-covered pans of food lay around ready to be served. The comforting scent of fresh bread baking filled Savannah's nose and boosted her appetite.

"Here you go, babies. This is some freshly squeezed limeade. It's so hot out there, I know you must be parched," she said, handing over two cool glasses to Clinton.

"Ms. Daniels, the decorations look wonderful. Did you do all this?" Savannah had to come up with something to ask. She didn't want to seem too quiet or rude.

"Child, no. Tiffany's friends did all this, and they should be coming in any minute now. Deidre and 'em went to the store to get some more ice." Again Savannah noticed that Ms. Daniels gave her no eye contact and directed her words to Clinton, even though it had been her question.

Savannah sipped her juice and mentally reviewed her outfit. She was dressed conservatively in an aqua-blue knee-length skirt, a gold belt, and a matching sleeveless top. She had wanted to wear pants, but for some reason Clinton had convinced her to wear a skirt.

Suddenly Savannah heard the chatty voices of several females and the click-clacking of their heels in her direction.

"Mommy, did you call Nicole to make sure she gonna get Tiffany here on time?" asked a young woman dressed in fishnet stockings, a black miniskirt, and a red tank top.

"Deidre, I already did. Don't be so rude, and say hello to your brother and his lady friend," Ms. Daniels said.

Lady friend.

"What's up, big bro. Where you been hiding at?" Deidre asked with a smirk and her hands on her hips. "Oh, never mind." She shot a look at Savannah and sashayed her way to the refrigerator.

"Deidre, this my girl, Savannah," Clinton said.

Savannah made a note to herself to ask him what the deal was with his family. To her, they were awfully odd.

Deidre turned around for a split second, then went back to packing away the ice. "Hey, girl, how you." She didn't even turn around.

"I'm fine. The decorations and things are lovely." Savannah took a generous sip from her limeade; she only wished she had a drop or two of Grey Goose to lighten her up.

Deidre totally ignored her. "Clinton, I had told you I was gonna bring my friend Jameeka. She is dying to meet you. I told her all about my big, handsome, firefighting brother who lives on the good side of Brooklyn."

Clinton shook his head.

Savannah blasted him with a look, but Clinton shrugged as though he didn't know what she was talking about.

"Jameeka? Your friend who got more baby daddies than the state of Louisiana?" Clinton put his empty glass down on the red-and-white-checkered tablecloth.

Savannah could tell by his flared nostrils that he was pissed-off.

"Oh, so when you have a thing against baby mamas? You think you better than some folks cause you ain't go no kids? Practically every woman has a child these days. I have two, so what you sayin'?" Deidre spun around on her heels as if she were ready to throw blows if she had to.

"I'm saying you are being ridiculous. Are you drunk?" Clinton glanced at his mother, who nodded her head yes.

"Girl, how many kids you got? Don't these niggas be tripping out here?" Deidre said, smiling at Savannah for the first time this evening.

"I don't have any. Sorry." Savannah wasn't sure why she apologized, but she felt her response was not something Deidre expected.

"That figures," Deidre slurred. "Of course you would be going after some uppity chick who probably hate kids. I bet she *had* a kid."

That struck a chord in Savannah. She wanted to jump out of her chair and pound Deidre to a pulp. "Excuse me; I have to go to the bathroom."

When Savannah walked out, she didn't know where to go, and opened two or three closet doors before she found the bathroom. All she heard was Clinton's loud voice overpowering Deidre, whom he was undoubtedly putting in her place. Savannah sat on the toilet seat and cried. There were just too many feelings boiling up inside of her. She wondered if she should tell Clinton about that one time she was pregnant many years ago. That information she had promised to reveal only to her husband, and not one man before that. She stayed in the bathroom until the voices calmed down.

When she walked out, Clinton was waiting for her on the other side.

"Sorry, baby. My sister is a drunk. She's sorry. I just didn't think she would be like this at her own sister's baby shower." Clinton put his arm around her.

"It's okay; nobody's perfect." Savannah smiled up at him. His arm around her made her feel safe and sound, a feeling she had longed for all her life.

They walked out into the living room, where some women were seated on the black leather sofas. Savannah thought the baby shower chair looked absolutely glorious with a green-and-white-frilled canopy. Deidre introduced them all to Clinton and Savannah. She gave Savannah a feeble smile that said she was sorry, but Savannah didn't return one. She was too busy scanning the room for this Jameeka. And she knew exactly who she was before she was introduced.

A woman in deep-red lipstick, a tube top that read SUCK THIS and a skintight jeans skirt sat way in the corner with her eyes fixed on Clinton, who was the only man. Savannah studied her physique, which was top-notch stripper quality. Her legs were svelte, shiny, and toned, as were her shoulders. Her breasts looked round, and the cleavage went on for days. Damn, why did she listen to Clinton about what to wear? she thought.

"And this is Jameeka, y'all. She new in town. Jameeka, this is my brother, Clinton," Deidre said, grabbing his hand from Savannah.

Clinton politely shook the girl's hand, she clearly didn't have any idea what was happening. "And this is my girlfriend, Savannah," Clinton said, signaling to Savannah to come over and shake hands.

"Hi." Savannah held in the pain Jameeka inflicted on her hand with a crushing grip.

"Hey, girl," Jameeka said with a plastered smile. "You better keep an eye on him. You know how women love them a man in uniform." She laughed, and so did Clinton, on edge.

Just then, Ms. Daniels ran out of the kitchen to signal Tiffany's arrival.

Clinton dimmed the lights, and everyone held their breath in the dark. Jameeka was standing on the other side of Clinton, too close for Savannah's comfort.

"Surprise!" The lights from cameras flashed all around the room, as almost everyone rushed to Tiffany's side and escorted her inside.

"I can't believe this," Tiffany said repeatedly as she sat down in her special chair. "I thought you guys were planning this next week-end."

Diedre turned the lights back up. "It's a surprise—hello, you ain't supposed to know," she said, running her hands through her short, cropped haircut. "Oh, this is Clinton's girl, Georgiana."

"It's Savannah," she said, and shook Tiffany's hand. Her grip was firm, and as gentle as her smile.

"Welcome. Now what did my brother do to get a girl like you?" Tiffany said, but before Savannah could respond, the girl's attention was diverted elsewhere.

But that sounded more like it, Savannah thought. She could get to like Tiffany, but definitely not Deidre. And that was probably the root of all the looks and comments. They weren't used to seeing Clinton with a woman like her, who was smiling especially wide.

Tiffany happily opened her gifts, grinning happily at the wrought-iron basinet Clinton bought her. Savannah thought that was a fine choice, too. Several of the other gifts were sexy lingerie pieces, though Savannah had no clue why a pregnant woman would need those. She thought it was tacky. But the hearty soul food of baked chicken, greens, and sweet potatoes was served immediately. It was followed with generous slices of white and chocolate cake. Savannah stayed close to Clinton, who didn't mind staying close to her as well. She picked up that he wasn't entirely comfortable with his family. He was the different one who made something out of his life the best he could. They seemed to admire him, just as she did.

Clinton got up to fill their glasses with more limeade, and Savannah stayed behind purposely. As soon as Clinton rose up, Jameeka was hot on his heels. Savannah knew her modus operandi. She used to do it before, scheming against women with desirable men. She understood what it was to be a woman wanting a man. Some other chick would have demanded to leave already, she thought, but not her. She had to see how Clinton reacted by himself with women like Jameeka to really see what she had.

Jameeka took the pitcher of limeade from Clinton and filled both of the glasses as she smiled in his face. He smiled back, too, as they exchanged words. Clinton leaned over and whispered something in Jameeka's ear, and she laughed. Savannah's heart nearly jumped out of her throat. Clinton had to know she was watching. Then Jameeka rubbed Clinton's flat stomach and jokingly held her heart. Savannah didn't mind. She was a woman being a woman, she thought. And it turned her on a bit to see another woman flirt with him. She didn't feel scared, as she normally would. But then Clinton reached into his pocket and handed her something.

Jameeka dragged herself behind him as she held Clinton's camera in her hand.

"Come on, baby, let's take this picture," he said to Savannah, setting the drinks beside her and encircling her body with his arms.

Savannah beamed with the happiest smile she could muster and prayed that Jameeka would catch every inch of it.

After the photo was taken, Jameeka said, "Here you go," and dumped the camera in Clinton's hands. She grabbed a handful of chips and walked toward a group of women who were engaged in a lively discussion about whose baby daddy was seen at the club.

"Hmmph," Savannah said, behind him.

"What's up with you? She took a great picture; look at this," he said.

And Savannah thought she had too. She was expecting her side to be cut off.

Clinton took several more pictures of them by themselves, them with Tiffany, and some with his mom. Savannah didn't know what his picture fascination was, but she wasn't complaining. If she couldn't be physically in Clinton's life forever, at least a part of her was.

Before she left, Clinton's mother came up to her and said, "Sorry if you were made to feel uncomfortable earlier. It's just we ain't used to Clinton bringing somebody around. You must be really special to him."

And that made her evening picture-perfect.

*   *   *

In the morning, Savannah and Clinton lay naked in her bed watching C-SPAN. She remembered that she hadn't checked her answering machine since the night before. The red flashing light showed that there were seven messages for her. She wanted to ignore them, but figured the longer they lingered, the more they would make Clinton suspicious.

"If you could be anything in the world, what would you be?" Clinton asked her out of the blue.

"Hmm. Maybe a world-class Alvin Ailey dancer who travels the world, flirts with Italian men, and eats provolone cheese for dinner," Savannah said, scratching her head.

"Why am I not surprised? I can see you and those lovely legs doing your thing across a stage. Of course, in a legit fashion," he said, grabbing a bottle of Sprite that sat on her wicker nightstand.

"Definitely. But maybe one day my kids will make me proud," Savannah said, turning down the volume on the TV. "What about you?"

"I don't know. I don't have anything specific, but I always wanted to live a beach lifestyle. To me, that's living. The only problem I would have is getting sand in my car."

Savannah silently agreed, because she, too, had always loved the warm weather, and even flirted with the idea of moving to Miami Beach one day. It meshed well with her hot-blooded attitude and sex appeal, she thought.

When Clinton went to the bathroom, she took those few moments to play her voice-mail messages. She set the machine on low and erased them one by one. As she listened and erased, she realized they were mostly hang-ups, until she got toward the end. There were consecutive calls from Chyno and one from Jacques.

"So you gonna leave your yellow man hanging? My girl is gonna be out of town for the whole weekend. I want to come by and blow that back out like I did the last time. . . ." Beep.

"It's Jacques. Oops, I have something in my mouth. Let's see. An S,

a A, a V, a A . . . Savannah, nice and tasty. And I can't wait to eat. . . ."
Beep.

Savannah felt the need to throw up as she disconnected her phone from the wall. She heard the toilet flush, and composed herself. She quickly dried her eyes before Clinton came back into the room. Every part of her felt disgusting, like a whore. None of those men cared anything about her, and she had shown she cared even less about herself. She had never felt more grateful to be with a man like Clinton than she did now.

"What's up?" Clinton said, strolling back into the room. His face was twisted with discontent.

Savannah turned on her side, away from him, facing her small chrome stereo system. "Nothing. I think I want to get some more sleep. Come lie down."

"Who the fuck are Chyno and Jacques?"

Savannah froze like a stone. Clinton had eavesdropped on her.

"What kind of bullshit messages were those on your machine? How many niggas are you fuckin'?" Clinton's eyes narrowed at her as he stood at the foot of the bed, as he had that first night he came down.

"Look, these are guys from before we were together. I just have to tell them to stop calling," Savannah said, sitting up in the bed. "Now please lie down next to me."

"How many men are lying down next to you, Savannah?" Clinton stood there with his arms folded and his legs spread, like a sergeant ready for an inspection.

"Clinton, I had a sex life before you. I was seeing a few dudes and—"

"So what color are they?"

"What?"

"All of sudden you got hearing loss?" Clinton pierced her with a look that could kill. And it almost did. "No wonder why that jar is filled with every color of the fucking rainbow."

"Clinton, wait," she said, throwing off her covers and running

Part Three

—

ABOUT A MONTH had passed with no sign of Clinton except for his car. Wherever he was spending his time was far away from her, she thought. She spent last weekend with Chyno and the weekend before with Jacques, but even those trysts were losing their flair and excitement. She couldn't even climax with them, which was always a dead giveaway. Her mind was on Clinton's slow hand and loving gaze. They made love, compared to the sex she had with other men. It was the kind of lovemaking that made people lose their jobs, pay their bills late, and stay in bed for days. He made love to every flaw and every physical asset. It was an experience she had never had in bed, and it made her feel free, without a care.

The last day of school came and went with no particular fanfare. Usually she'd have a drink with Giselle to signal the official beginning of her summer break. But Giselle and her husband were having their own problems. To give her mind a positive distraction, Savannah signed up to teach summer school. And so did Mr. Thomas, who had never taught summer school before. She wondered if he signed up because of her.

At the end of her Wednesday art class, she cleaned up the tiny bits of construction paper from a summer collage project. She rubbed glue and glitter off the desks and swept up the dust balls under the closet. Usually this was a job the kids would do, but she wasn't in any rush to get home.

behind him. "Wait, it's not like that! I told you I ca
jar."

Clinton grabbed his clothes, slipped on his pants an
headed to the door. "Yeah, and I need a woman, not a li
mind games. I hope one of your friends can give you
need."

"Well, whatever!" Savannah spat behind him. "I ain't
you. I'll be a'ight," she said, her throat holding back her urg
out loud.

Clinton turned around and huffed. "Just wait until tonight.'
he disappeared down the steps.

Tonight wasn't a night she wanted to be alone. She closed
door gently and connected her phone back to the wall. She waite
And waited. And waited some more for Clinton to call. But h
didn't. At eleven P.M., surrounded by a bedful of used Kleenex, she
tried his number, but got no answer.

Inside, she beat herself up for not ending those situations right
away and letting them fester until they stank up her new relationship. Perhaps he was expecting this from her, she thought. And it
wasn't about the candy, but she knew Clinton was angry at her for
lying to him and treating him—and men—like conquests. She
thought she had been kidding herself that she could handle a real
relationship. They only bring her pain and disappointment, as they
always did. She didn't expect to hear from Clinton again, though
she desperately wanted to.

That night she dreamed of being trapped in a burning building.
And there was no sexy firefighter there to save her.

"Well, well, Ms. Avery taking over the janitor's job, I see," Mr. Thomas said, as he walked in her classroom and closed the door behind him.

Savannah flashed him a look that showed she was not in the mood today. She swept faster, hoping to make him back away from her. Instead he just walked around her to her desk.

"Mr. Thomas, is there something I can do for you? If not, I'm pretty busy," Savannah said, looking at him in his jeans and white guayabera shirt. She had to admit to herself that he was looking handsome. He always reminded her of a younger Tom Selleck.

"Nothing much, just wanted to stop by because I haven't seen you since school ended. You're looking sexy in those heels, Ms. Avery." Mr. Thomas sauntered toward her in a confident, macho kind of way that made her feel he was gonna pick her up and whisk her away.

"Look, Mr. Thomas," she said, holding the broom with one hand. "Thank you, but I'm pretty tired today. The class lasted longer than it should have, and the kids hardly had any supplies to get the project done. . . ."

Mr. Thomas took her broom away and grasped her hand. "You smell good enough to eat," he said in her ear.

His scent was clean and fresh, and he caressed her back gently. Savannah leaned against his body on the closet door, bringing them close enough that their noses touched. His hands were up her fuchsia cotton dress, wandering around her ass and touching down between her thighs. She liked how it felt as she directed his hand to squeeze her ass a bit harder. They didn't kiss, but let their tongues dance around each other, firmly pressing into each other. Now he was the one against the wall, and Savannah humped him like an anxious little boy. Mr. Thomas's face turned red, and his hardness poked at her enough that she had to look down to make sure it was still in his pants. She ground up against him, unbuttoned the top part of her dress, and plucked out one of her breasts. He sucked on it like he was sucking the tastiest juice.

"Come on, let's get in the closet," Mr. Thomas said, kicking the door open.

That was when it hit Savannah. Her body may have responded, but her heart and mind belonged to Clinton. Suddenly his hands felt wet and cold. "No, no. I can't. As a matter of fact, all this is just wrong. Mr. Thomas, please leave," she said, buttoning her dress back up. She couldn't keep behaving this way for temporary satisfaction that led to long-term frustration.

Mr. Thomas's face turned beet red, and he held his hands up. "Okay, sorry, Ms. Avery. I just lose myself when I get around you. I'm sorry."

"Mr. Thomas, we're both a little crazy. Let's just act like this never happened. See you around," she said, smiling. They shook hands, and Mr. Thomas left holding a binder to cover a part of him that was noticeably not ready to leave.

Savannah plopped herself down on a student's desk. She had to get back with Clinton. She wanted a real man in her life who could not only make her toes curl, but listen and take care of her. There was no way, she thought, she was going to let Clinton slip away. He hadn't called, but something told her he was keeping an eye on her. And she felt it was time that she balled up her pride and paid him a little visit.

Savannah had invited Giselle over for the evening for pizza and to catch up on their separate dramas. They would usually meet at SugarCane, but Savannah figured if she wanted to get new results, she had to start doing new things besides hanging at bars.

"So girl, tell me about Mr. Firefighter. I bet he is swinging one long hose!" Giselle said, adding a third slice to her already thickened waist.

"Well, he is in the double digits. And he's nice." Savannah didn't know where to begin, but Giselle knew her well enough that she didn't have to fake. "I think I fucked up, though."

Giselle stopped chewing.

"He heard the phone messages from Chyno and 'em . . ." Savannah said, filling her glass of white wine. "And you know the type of voice-mail messages *I* get."

"Savannah." Giselle finally let go of her pizza to throw her hands up over her head. "He is a working man with city benefits. Do you know he can retire in ten years and still get paid, plus keep his medical and dental?"

"Sorry, Giselle, I may have forgotten those minor details," Savannah said, rolling her eyes. "I could care less about that bullshit. I liked him for making me laugh, making me feel good, special, like I am a good woman."

"You are a good woman. You can't look to no man to make you feel that way. They can take it from you at any time. You have to give it to yourself. Don't beat yourself up for being you. But are you going to call him, drop by his place, or go to his job to make peace?"

"Hell, no! I am not showing up at any man's job or tying up his phone lines. He knows my number, and he hasn't used it."

"Of course not—his ego is hurt. It looked like he was opening up to you, and then he finds out you are getting wide-open with other men!"

Savannah sighed as she nursed her glass of wine. "I know what I have to do. I have to let him know that I do care."

"Good, you need to go pay him a visit, for real," Giselle said.

Savannah nodded at the clock atop her television, which read ten P.M. It was a Thursday and he was off. She peered out her living room window and saw his car parked. It made her feel better. As soon as Giselle left, she was going to clear up any misunderstandings.

"Well, now that we got that out of the way, I have a question," Giselle said, taking a gulp of wine from the nearly finished bottle.

"What is wrong with you!" Savannah laughed at Giselle's antic.

"Girl, you know Trey and I have been having issues. I don't know what I want anymore. When I married him, I thought could grow to love him, but it's the same. We act like an old married couple. We rarely do anything together anymore," Giselle said, cutting her eyes at the TV. "Girl, marriage don't fix what's broke."

Savannah thought that Giselle was finally learning her own lessons. She didn't want to have a life like hers. That was why she had to be sure about Clinton, because when she married, she wanted it to be for the right reasons. "You two just need a good weekend away. Trey works a lot of hours. See if you both can work on something," Savannah said, folding her legs to get comfortable.

"He mentioned something about counseling. That's for white folks, though," Giselle said. "Right?"

"Wrong. It's for people who are serious about getting through the rough times together. I know you want to do it, Giselle. You have been married for a while now; give it a go," Savannah said, almost hearing her own advice.

Giselle fidgeted with her hands. "I guess. Maybe we can start all over. I want to get this right before we have kids."

"See, that's what I'm talkin' 'bout. That don't sound to me like a woman who wants to leave her husband."

Giselle sucked her teeth and grabbed her bag. "Look. I gotta run before Trey starts blowing up my cell. But thanks for listening. I know what I gotta do," she said, smiling, and walked out.

Savannah covered her face with both her hands. Marriage wasn't something that she was obsessed about, like most women, but to her Giselle was a good example of never being satisfied. She wondered how much of Giselle was in her.

As Giselle disappeared down the block, Savannah walked the several flights up to Clinton's apartment. That would give her enough time to think, she thought. As she reached the last step, she heard male laughter and the sound of heels.

She ducked at the bottom of the steps to see if her gut feeling was true. Clinton was walking from the elevator into his apartment with a woman holding a bag that looked like take-out food. Savannah's brain told her to run up those steps and give him a serious tongue-lashing. But her legs couldn't move. She couldn't run down to her apartment either. The woman was dressed in tight jeans, and an even tighter red tube top, and she couldn't keep her hands off him, whispering in his ear as he searched for his keys to the door.

That was all she needed to see to know that she was wrong all along. He probably had several women, though he had come off to her as if he were single and free. Who did he think he was, berating her for having male friends, she thought, while he had his own friends with benefits? Savannah walked down the flights of stairs to her apartment and sat by her window. She couldn't sleep all night and stayed up watching old movies on TV and crying in intervals. She was at her window when the young woman walked out into the night all alone at four A.M.

After school on Friday afternoon, Savannah headed straight home. She opened the candy jar in the kitchen and took out all the blue and yellow sour sticks. It was time to get rid of them, she thought.

Sitting in her kitchen, she analyzed the jar and wondered if she would ever have any use for it again. It represented a part of what was her past. But its emptiness also showed the baggage that she chose to release. She took the jar stuffed with sour sticks and dumped its contents in the trash, leaving only the red ones.

About a week later, Savannah was now ready to talk to Clinton. He was outside washing his car with a male friend. Savannah studied them for what seemed like an hour. Clinton wore only a sleeveless ribbed T-shirt and knee-length khaki shorts. She was in awe of how handsome he was, all wet and shiny from the water and sweaty from the day. Each time his arm wiped the hood of his car, he would bend over showing his bulging biceps. His friend wasn't half bad either, she thought, but there was no comparison to Clinton's hunky physique. She timed how long it would take Clinton to reach his apartment when he was done.

When she called his house, he picked up on the first ring.

"It's me," Savannah said, her fingers trembling on the phone cord. "Long time."

Clinton sighed as if he were relieved to her from her, too. She wanted to tell him how much she missed him and needed him. But she sensed he had plenty of sweet words to say to her.

"I'm moving," Clinton revealed.

"Oh." Savannah's sulked on her brown futon sofa. This was the part where he was supposed to profess his love, she thought. "Is it because of me?"

"My lease is up next month and I'm not renewing it. Just thought you should know." His deep voice sounded shaky, as if he were trying to sound a way he didn't feel.

All Savannah heard was silence on the other end. She realized this was her moment, not his. "I got rid of my dirty laundry. I had to face a lot of my issues alone, and I swear I am ready to be whatever you want us to be. I'm sorry, I was just scared. I thought you should know that before you moved. Uhm, so, take care."

"Savannah, don't hang up. Thank you, and I'm sorry, too, if I was a little abrupt. I just don't have time for games anymore. Good-bye." And the line went dead.

She flung her phone against the wall. *So it's like that? Thank you and I'm sorry? Like I was nobody important anyway.* And he was leaving. She didn't understand how he could just move. He was pulling out one of his control cards, she thought. It forced her to get more aggressive if she was really interested in making amends. She would have to do more than make a phone call. It gave them little time. But she just didn't have any more energy to put in all the work.

Savannah tossed and turned all night in bed. Each hour she looked at the clock and calculated what Clinton could be doing at that time. It was three A.M., the time they had first had sex. She thought back to that early morning and inhaled what smelled like Clinton's sandalwood cologne. It was almost as if he were in the room. She wet her fingers and slipped her hands inside her green chiffon panties. Massaging between her thighs with gentle strokes, she thought of Clinton's hands exploring her secret garden in the dark. She flicked her clitoris with her thumb until it swelled up and became sensitive to any touch.

"Whew, I need you," she whispered as she rolled over on her stomach. Leaving her hand beneath her, she gyrated her hips on it until a pressure built up inside. She wanted to release it and be done with it, but she just couldn't. She was pushing herself too much, and slowed down. She slid one finger inside her and stroked it in and out as if Clinton were watching her. This really worked, because she was never one to masturbate alone. Flipping onto her back, she fondled her breasts, too, until she damn near saw an image of Clinton at the foot of her bed. Tired and exhausted, she threw her head back on the pillow, blowing hard to catch her breath.

It wasn't more than a half hour later when she heard a knock. *Knock. Knock. Knock.* Sleepy-eyed and nearly bumping into her nightstand, Savannah looked through the peephole.

It was Clinton staring back at her.

"Yes?" she said, trying to act as though she were still upset. But before he could answer, she flung her door open. "I was asleep."

"Cool. I was trying to sleep, but couldn't and . . . well, you know."

Savannah walked back to her bedroom and left him standing at the door. She didn't care how she looked with her behind cheeks sticking out of her grandma panties and a dingy T-shirt. According to him, they were officially over, so she didn't know exactly what he was trying to do. But she decided to fall back and watch.

Clinton slipped in the bed next to her. "I wanna work this out," he said in her ear. He smelled like fresh soap and not like a man who had just left work.

"I do, too. Missed you." She gathered the peach-colored covers over her body and curled up in a fetal position on her side of the bed.

"I missed you even more," he said, his fingers walking their way up to her hardened nipples. He pinched them firmly and squeezed them between his fingers, just as she liked it. She wanted to push him away, but it would probably be the last time they ever had sex. He massaged her shoulders and nestled his nose on the back of her neck, moving her long ponytail to the side.

"I missed *this,* too," he said, reaching down to fondle her throbbing, fleshy pussy. *"Shiiit."* He clutched her ass cheeks in his hands as Savannah rolled over on her stomach. "And *this.*" He spoke in a low voice in her ear, his thick lips sucking on her lobes.

Tears were trapped in Savannah's eyes. She wanted to lie there and be made love to, letting him have his way with her. She turned to face him, and his eyes drank in every inch of her. He kissed the edges of her eyes, which were damp with tears. Then he pulled up her white tee and gently pressed both of her C cups together, sucking one nipple after the other. The muscles in his dark-chocolate shoulders rippled as he situated himself on top of her. His face moved back and forth, as if he were drinking out of two water fountains. An electric shock ran down her legs to her thighs. He bit down on her nipples gently, and the pain registered only as pleasure to Savannah.

"That was just an appetizer; now it's time for dinner." He slipped her panties off and smelled them. "I can't wait to eat." He smiled.

Savannah spread her legs like an eagle's wings and served it up.

Part Four

In THE MORNING SAVANNAH was sprawled on her stomach as Clinton massaged baby oil over freshly showered skin. He smeared her dark brown thighs with oil, massaging from the slope of her behind to the plateau of her back.

"Ahh, this is too good," Savannah murmured with her face buried in the pillows. "What is it that you can't do, Clinton?"

He laughed and worked his strong, long fingers into her shoulders, sending her off into another doze. But it was midmorning, and their whole Sunday was ahead of them.

When Clinton was through, Savannah nestled her smooth, naked, shiny body in his arms. He nibbled behind her ears and asked, "Will you move with me?"

Savannah brushed her long hair away from her face and turned around to see him. "Say that again?"

"You know my lease is up. And I still want to be able to see you all the time," Clinton said, smoothing down her fake tresses.

"But what about my place? I still have another six months. And you haven't exactly said you want us to be exclusive." Savannah couldn't believe that she was talking this way. Clinton just had something that made her want to be his, but she wasn't willing to lose her ground. She didn't want to end up like his sisters, with babies and no man, no commitment.

Clinton grunted. And that sent shivers down Savannah's thighs.

She loved that deep man-grunt he made; however, it was also a sign of his dissatisfaction. He flipped the channels on the remote, and rubbed his newly growing mustache a few times, as he thought to himself.

"A man ain't always gotta spell things out, baby. I want to be with you. And if I'm asking you to move in with me, ain't that enough?"

"Come here; I want to show you something." Savannah hopped out of bed naked and took Clinton's hand.

She walked him to the kitchen and pulled down the empty jar.

"I got rid of all my baggage because I don't want any more. I don't want anything that is halfway done. I had this because I was scared of being walked out on. It was my way of making sure I got rid of men before they got rid of me. This may sound like a game to you, but for me it was serious as heart attack. Does that sound like a woman who would be okay with enough? I have to have it all or nothing, Clinton."

Clinton grabbed the empty jar from her and examined it. If you ask me, you need to get rid of this jar as soon as possible."

"Not until I have a good reason to."

Clinton held his hands up in surrender. "Okay, okay. I don't want it to seem like things are as easy as I say. I told you what I wanted, but I understand if you need some time to think. Besides, I got some things I want to tell you, too."

Savannah grabbed an orange juice from the refrigerator for each of them. And she grabbed a seat, knowing she would need it.

Clinton stayed standing against the kitchen counter. "When we was apart for a bit, I did have sex with other people. I also know you were spying on me that night from the bottom of the steps."

"And?" Savannah asked, unapologetic.

"And I also saw you with some guys. I'm just gonna assume that we both handled our business with other folks and now all that is over with, right?"

Savannah nodded. She walked toward him and caressed the black coils of hair across his chest. Getting down on her knees, Savannah slid off Clinton's blue-checkered boxers. His hardness stood before her, knocking her gently across the nose. She massaged his carved thighs until she reached the sack of tender flesh dangling from his legs. Carefully holding his length in her hands, she licked up and down the shaft.

Clinton pulled the hair back from her face to get a better look at her, while she sucked his magic rod into her mouth. Her head bobbed back and forth as she slurped and sucked him until his knees weakened.

"Savannah, baby," he groaned, spreading his legs. "You look so sexy doing what you do. *Damn.*"

That drove her to suck him in even further, because she did feel sexy as hell—and powerful. With every inch of him in the hot alcove of her mouth, he pulled her face closer into him.

"I'm gonna cum any minute, oooh." Clinton gripped the back of her head as she kept her mouth wet and supple and cradled his mahogany dick. She didn't want to move. She wanted to consume every ounce of his liquid cream.

Clinton ground his teeth, and he exploded a warm creamy substance down her throat. Savannah gripped his sweat-drenched thighs as she kept on massaging him with her lips. Her mouth glistening with his juices, she crawled down to reach his balls and gently kissed and licked those with her tongue.

Blessed with the ability to retain his hardness, Clinton joined Savannah on the cold kitchen floor and entered her with a force that made her body shake like a rattle. He practically had her under the table as they slid across the kitchen floor covered in sweat.

Clinton pummeled her body with all eleven inches of grade-A satisfaction. Clinton sucked Savannah's salty-sweet nipples, causing her to call out his name.

"Clintooon, Clintooon . . ." she whispered as she pulled his ass deeper into her source. *"I love you."*

"I love you, too, baby." Clinton kissed Savannah's trembling lips and pulled out with expert precision.

He dripped cum all over Savannah's quivering breasts and stomach. And all she could think was how sweet it was.

"Hey, girl!" Giselle waved to Savannah as she sat outdoors at Scopello, a small Italian restaurant on Lafayette Street. It had been weeks since they talked, and they both had too much to catch up on and not enough time.

"Two house reds," Savannah said, holding up two fingers to the young waitress. She slipped on her shades to avoid the relentless sun and smiled in Giselle's direction. There was definitely something different about Giselle, including what looked like some recent weight gain hiding beneath a long, blue summer dress.

"Whoa, that four train was so packed and sweaty this evening. The air conditioner was broke, and folks had the nerve to smell funky, too." She laughed, sitting down across from Savannah.

Savannah adjusted the strap to her cheetah-print halter top. "Well, it's not their fault. There were plenty of times I wore deodorant and still ended up smelling a little musky."

Giselle laughed again. "I'm talking musky to the umpteenth, girl! Anyway, nothing was gonna stop me from seeing you today."

A timid busboy appeared and set two ice-cold glasses of water before them. Giselle anxiously sipped hers as she watched the after-work crowd zoom by on a humid, August afternoon.

"So how did your talk with your hubby go?" Savannah said, playfully tilting her head to the side.

"It went good. He told me he was feeling the same way about us, but he doesn't want to lose me." Giselle grabbed her glass of red wine from the waitress and sipped it noisily. "And I don't want to lose him either. It's just hard when you start off on the wrong foot. Make sure you get it right with Mr. Firefighter before you go any further. Da hell with his good health benefits."

Savannah laughed and bought the glass of red wine to her lips. "Hmmm, well, I got that part covered. We stayed in bed for hours the other night. I'm telling you, I don't know what he has over me. I can't think of anything else but him."

"I have never seen you like this. Not even with that scum Derrick. Mr. Firefighter seems to be doing more than putting out your fire; he is sparking some new flames in you, girl!"

Savannah gently patted her forehead, which was damp from the humidity. "It's just a little scary. I don't want to give my power away to any man, like I used to. When you do that, they shit all over you."

"But this guy don't sound like that. He sounds like one of those good men who slipped through the cracks. You betta get him, girl, before someone else does."

Savannah covered her laughter. "See, it's that type of stuff. I didn't have to get him; he got *me.*"

"Sounds like you got it all figured out then." The waitress returned and laid down their salads.

Fanning herself with her hand, Savannah said, "Maybe, but I know he is gonna want more." Savannah sprinkled some pepper on her salad. "His lease is up, he is moving, and he asked me to go with him."

"So when are you leaving?" Giselle shoveled the salad into her mouth and looked at Savannah, bewildered.

But Savannah said nothing.

"Girl, I said don't be messing this up. That man is showing you a commitment. You better go take care of your biz."

"Giselle," Savannah said, slamming down her napkin. "My business is me. It's protecting my interests. I am not living with no man without a ring. Until I am married, it's me for myself."

"Fine, fine," Giselle said, shaking her head as though Savannah were a hopeless case.

"Just because you moved in with Trey before he married you doesn't mean it's like that all around. At least you were engaged. I need something. I have made some major changes in my life, and I know I want all those things: some stability, some sense of normalcy with one man. And he knows that."

Giselle's frown slowly turned into a sympathetic smile. "I just want to see you happy, whatever you decide. Talk to him. But just remember—instead of talking about the life you want, sometimes, you have to just live it. If I tried to think through everything, I'd be still dancing in that club because I was afraid of getting disappointed again. Plus, some of the best things are unplanned," Giselle said, dangling a fry from her mouth. "I'm pregnant! Six weeks, girl."

"Congrats!" Savannah yelled over the loud sounds of police sirens. "No wonder why you looking all happy and all. I want to be the baby's godmother," Savannah said, squeezing Giselle's hand.

"Oh, no, the last time you said the Lord's name was on your back. No, thanks."

Savannah couldn't argue with her. They both laughed hard with their mouths full, turning heads from the nearby tables.

"This is the three-bedroom apartment on Seventh Avenue that approved me. It has beautiful bay windows, and it's closer to your school," Clinton said, showing her the pictures in his digital camera. They lay snuggled under his black silk sheets.

Savannah clicked through the photos and fell in love. The apartment was sun-drenched, with an island in the kitchen that faced the living room. The bathroom had one of those old-fashioned circular bathtubs and a separate shower. If it were possible, she thought, she'd jump right through the camera and into the gorgeous photos.

"So what do you think?" Clinton rubbed her shoulders as she lay across his chest. "I know you like it."

"I do. Um, I think you will really be happy in it. It has everything, like the apartments in one of those home magazines." Savannah pretended to sound excited, and not torn, as she felt.

"I guess you're not ready yet?"

"I'm not, Clinton; I just don't—"

"Savannah, I am ready for a real relationship. I am a grown-ass man and would like to wake up with my woman every morning. It's about time you really started acting like we're a couple."

"How have I not acted like we're a couple?" Savannah sat up in the bed and rolled her eyes so hard her head hurt.

"All I'm saying is, every time I try to get close you pull back," Clinton said, his thick brows slanted in concern.

Savannah sank into the bed. "Seventh Avenue is just a ten-minute bus ride from me. It's not like you're moving out of state. I will be there with you whenever you need me—and when you don't. I want to do this right, Clinton," Savannah said, rubbing his chest. "You know I love you."

Clinton sighed heavily, and Savannah felt the thump of his heart through her hands. "Let me just say this," he began, with his dark, handsome eyes peering into her soul. "Before I met you, getting married was out of the question. And now you've made me want to get married. But I'm tired of playing by your rules all the *got-damn* time."

Savannah tried to remain cool, but her insides were jumping all around. They had been together only four months, but she already felt a part of him. And that was why, she thought, she had to take her time. To her, keeping her own space was her only leverage. If she had learned anything about men, it was that they had all the power in the relationship, and very little before. It was up to her to keep hers until he showed her that he wouldn't abuse his power later.

"I never really thought I would want to get married, either. But I'm not about to just throw myself at your feet because you mentioned the word *marriage* in our future. Life still goes on, and I have to look out for me," Savannah hissed. She didn't mean to sound so defiant, but she felt that Clinton was trying to give her an ultimatum.

Clinton grunted, and she was familiar with his sound of frustration. He was a man used to getting his way, but she didn't blame him. He was loving her the only way he knew how, and she was doing the same with him.

"Well, if it's like that, I'm gonna look out for what I want. I already made my offer. And I see you made your decision," Clinton said, getting out of bed and slipping on some gray sweatpants and a T-shirt.

"Clinton! Where you going?" Savannah flew out of bed behind him, but he shrugged her off him.

Savannah watched him search for his keys and slam the door. She couldn't help feeling that she was rejecting him, and prayed he didn't think that, too. She walked back to her bed and wondered if she was just making things worse. *What if he just gives up on me?* she thought. She lay back down in the bed, and the heavy weight of loss rested on her chest, which heaved up and down as she fought back tears. The bed that had been warm and toasty a few minutes ago now felt cold and hard. She fantasized about needing him to feel her with those big, brown hands. She had a feverish urge to have him in her mouth and suck in all his essence. She wanted to reassure him, make things right. But he was gone. She dozed off with dreams of him making love to her and whispering sweet, nasty nothings in her ear.

Four hours later, she woke up to a tender, soothing voice.

"Savannah," Clinton said, stroking her hair. "I want to show you something."

She rubbed the sleep from her eyes, and pitter-pattered to her kitchen. "You decided to come back?" she asked, looking at Clinton standing there with a bag.

He opened it and handed her a red pack of sour sticks, "This flavor will never run out."

"I do want us to eventually move in together. I know this is gonna work." She wrapped her arms around his neck and hopped her naked body on him.

Clinton pulled down the jar from the cabinet, and a sly smile grew on his lips. "I couldn't agree with you more."

A few minutes later Savannah was covered in the sugary taste of slim red sour sticks and in the sweet, new possibility of a love that was all hers.

♥ ♥ ♥

Maryann Reid, a graduate of Fordham University, has written for *Black Enterprise* magazine, and her novella *Single Black Female* appeared on usatoday.com. She lives in Brooklyn, New York. She is currently working on her next novel.

Her Web site is at www.maryannreid.com.

Chocolate Kisses

by RENEE LUKE

To my editor extraordinaire, Tina Brown.
To the Playground, for fun, love, and support.
To my agent, Sha-Shana Crichton, for finding Chocolate Kisses *a home.*
To Stacey Lynn Riemer, who is much more than my critique partner—she is my best friend.
And finally,
To my husband, LA Luke, who is all the hero I'll ever need.

Chapter One

TONIGHT'S THE NIGHT!

Tugging in a breath, Nicole Davis studied her reflection in the mirror. "Now or never," she said, wondering if the dress she'd chosen to wear made her intent apparent.

"Lord, I hope so," she whispered, smoothing her palms down her hips, feeling the softness of the persimmon silk covering her body. She knew apprehension would make the words difficult when it came time to tell Marcus why she'd called him over tonight.

Not that Marcus's coming over to hang out on a Saturday evening was an unusual occurrence. Rather it was one that happened with weekly regularity, in combination with the Monday-Wednesday-Friday-morning workout regimen they shared at a nearby gym. Hell, she'd known Marcus since her senior year at California State University, Sacramento, a long six years ago, and had developed a close bond of friendship with him.

But last Saturday night she had worn a pair of faded jeans and a plain T-shirt, not a silk dress that clung to her body, revealing more curves than she knew she had. Even her cleavage looked larger, accentuated by the plunging line of the material and the wisp of cloth hugging one shoulder. Last Saturday night they were friends; tonight she wanted them to become lovers.

A butterfly tremor of anticipation ran the length of her spine. It wasn't like her to set out to seduce a man, but tonight she put aside pride and took a chance, because if she wanted Marcus—and she did—she'd have to make her move before he left town for good.

Nicole bit down on her bottom lip to keep it from trembling. Shaking off her unease, she grabbed up a feather brush, dipped it into Honey Dust, and lightly brushed the shimmering, sweet-scented powder across her chest and up the slope of her shoulders.

She liked the way the powder made her caramel-toned skin glisten, reflecting the soft golden rays of more than a dozen candles. She'd spent almost an hour arranging them around her bedroom, then setting them aflame.

Although she'd been expecting it, the sound of the doorbell startled her. Her breath hitched in her lungs. *It's just Marcus.* Despite her intense physical attraction to him, she'd never been nervous in his company before. Nicole took a moment to smooth back her hair, which had been washed, pressed, and curled that morning.

Walking out of her bedroom, she flicked the wall switch, lighting the room with only the small flames of many flickering candles. Padding barefoot, she passed the kitchen as she made her way to her front door.

Entering the living room, she grabbed the remote control and turned on her stereo, glad she'd remembered to remove Jay Z, replacing him with the more sensual songs of Keith Sweat. The fact that her favorite CD was now considered old-school gave validity to this scene of seduction.

Next month she'd turn thirty. She didn't have a man, hardly ever dated, and was downright lonely, not to speak of horny. And, with the announcement that Marcus had accepted the job offer that would move him three thousand miles away, this was the perfect—and quite possibly the only—opportunity to indulge in such a fantasy with him.

She was a woman with needs, and damn smart enough to know that unless she solved the problem herself, no one was knocking at her door.

The doorbell rang again, causing Nicole to laugh.

He was ringing the bell!

Sucking in a calming breath, Nicole opened the door with a smile, hoping Marcus wouldn't see the nervous twitch of her lips.

Marcus stood on the top step, lounging against the bricks decorating the front of her Spanish-style house, his wide shoulders silhouetted by twilight and the artificial illumination of the streetlights. Her gaze moved across loose-fitting khakis and casual black button-down shirt that hugged the sharp contours of his sculpted body.

His full lips lifted into a smile. His midnight eyes sparkled in welcome. She'd always thought his smile was sexy as hell, but now the sight of it virtually stole her breath away. The straight line of his clean-shaven jaw framed his face. *Damn gorgeous.*

His left cheek was chiseled with a single dimple that deepened when he smiled. Nicole resisted the urge to run her finger across his indented cheek, just to feel the texture.

"Hi," she said, holding on to the edge of the door to keep her knees from knocking together.

"Hey, Nic. You going out?" His eyebrow arched as his penetrating gaze swept over her.

"Nope," she replied. *It's Marcus, girl; you can't be nervous.* "Come on in." Nicole stepped aside, keeping the solid wooden door between them.

Marcus's foot hesitated on the threshold before he stepped across and entered the foyer. Nicole closed the door as soon as he had passed and followed behind him, walking down the narrow hall that opened to the living room. Keith Sweat pulsed from the speakers. Marcus swung around to look at her, his eyes narrowed, his features showing he misread what he'd walked into.

Nicole could see his uncertainty. He tilted his head to the side, obviously confused. His dark gaze shifted farther down the hall, where the flicker of flames cast shadowed movements across the carpeted floor, spilling pale light into the dim hallway.

"You have someone here, Nic? Do you want me to go?"

"Only you, Marcus."

He shrugged, then lifted his hand. "I brought a couple movies," he said, showing her the two DVDs he held.

Nicole reached out and took hold of the movies, her fingers lingering on his skin for longer than she'd intended. With reluctance she pulled away, immediately missing his warmth. "I've been wanting to see these movies. But not tonight, okay, Marcus? I was hoping we could talk."

"Yeah. Sure. What's going on, Nic? Is everything okay? Did something happen?"

Drawing a deep breath, Nicole gathered her courage for a moment, knowing this was the time to put up or shut up. If she had any hope of getting what she wanted, she had better speak up, and do it now.

"Nothing is wrong." Nicole grabbed his hand again, her palm brushing against his as she intertwined their fingers. "Come in here." It took only the slightest tug to get him to follow her into the kitchen. She set the DVDs on the counter and released Marcus's hand.

Moving to the fridge, Nicole withdrew a bottle of white zinfandel and a Bud Light. She tried to ignore the heat of Marcus's dark eyes as they followed her movements back to the counter, where she poured a glass of wine, then popped the top of the beer. She handed the beer to Marcus, careful not to allow her fingers to brush against his.

She was nervous enough about asking Marcus to change their relationship into a mutual yet more physically satisfying one. Touching him now, before she said what was on her mind could be a serious mistake.

Nicole lifted the glass of wine to her lips. Taking a long, deep drink, she searched her mind for just the right words. *Go slow: explain what you want.*

"Marcus, I want us to become lovers."

The words spilled from her lips in the opposite way she'd planned. Seeing the shock on Marcus's handsome features, she rushed on. "I mean . . . nothing would change between us. We'd still be friends. You know, no strings attached."

Marcus neither moved nor said anything. He simply leaned against the counter, his feet shoulder-width apart, his arms hanging by his sides. One hand held the untouched beer. The other was a fist. Though he schooled the emotion and surprise on his face, Nicole thought she saw a frown dance about the corners of his sensual lips.

As well as she knew him, she had no idea what to expect. The longer it took him to reply, the more worried she became. The self-doubts resurfaced, all of her old insecurities nipping at her heels.

Biting down on her bottom lip, Nicole swallowed back her moan of dismay. She'd been a fool to suggest this, despite how badly she wanted him. With her heart racing, she lifted the glass and drank another full gulp. Over the clear rim, she took a long look at Marcus.

His clean-shaven head glistened. She longed to run her hands across the smooth, dark skin reflecting the under-cabinet lighting. Her gaze dropped lower, lingering where his brown skin disappeared into the black collar of his shirt. The tic of his pulse in his neck matched the rhythm of her own.

A muscle in his shoulder bunched and drew her attention. His bulging arms pressed against the material of his shirt. Nicole ran her tongue along the edge of her bottom lip, thinking of how those strong arms would feel around her. Realizing she'd been staring, she quickly slid her gaze away, heat covering her cheeks.

Still, Marcus didn't respond.

Clearing her throat, Nicole spoke, her voice just above a whisper. "Marcus?"

"Did you want to start tonight?" His rich voice split the silence. Lifting the beer to his mouth, he drained almost half of it, his dark eyes never leaving hers.

"You're interested?" she choked out, surprise and delight resounding through her.

"Do I look interested to you?" he asked, lowering his beer to the level of his crotch and tilting the bottom toward the apex of his legs. He grabbed her hand and pressed it to the expanding bulge beneath his pants.

Feeling Marcus's swelling flesh caused most of her doubts to vanish. She knew she was blushing, yet her eyes seemed frozen to the spot where her fingers encased the khaki cloth surrounding his erection. She was unsure what to do or say next, yet her hand lingered, Marcus growing thicker beneath her palm.

"Are you sure about this, Nic?"

She yanked her hand away and stepped back. Her gaze snapped up to his. For a long, drawn-out moment they simply gazed into each other's eyes, searching out the friendship that had been so much of the past six years. This was Marcus, her friend and confidant. This was a man who was both physically attractive and yet humble and caring. Her tension eased.

"I'm sure, Marcus," she replied, flashing a smile. "I know it seems odd, but I've been wanting this for a long time."

"What prompted your asking?"

"You're leaving."

His brows furrowed.

"But there's more, too. Time? Need? Desire? I just feel like I am missing something—intimacy with a man. You're my best friend. I love being with you and talking to you. I thought maybe you could satisfy my other needs, as well. Once you're gone"—she paused to swallow what felt like a marble in her throat—"the chance will be lost."

"And nothing would change? We can still be friends after? You'll still be able to look me in the eye and meet for our workouts? You won't have regrets?"

"I've thought a lot about this. I know we can still be friends or I wouldn't have asked. Will you have regrets?"

"Hell, no."

"Well, then, neither will I," Nicole reaffirmed.

Chapter Two

TRYING TO HIDE HIS OVEREAGERNESS, Marcus turned and placed his half-emptied beer on the counter behind him. He closed his eyes. *I haven't had enough beer to be drunk.* He'd dreamed of making love to Nic, but with his leaving, he'd thought his fantasies would never come true. Now she was offering him a chance to make them a reality.

Despite his incredible attraction to her, this was Nicole—sweet, caring, sensitive Nicole. Yeah, he wanted her, but more important, he liked her and definitely didn't want to hurt her by leaping into the sack without making sure she was certain.

Turning back, he swept his gaze over her. She was beautiful, dressed in a pinkish slip of cloth that did little to hide her ripe breasts and showed the sensual slope of her hips. Her supple legs stretched almost a mile to the floor, to where she'd not bothered with shoes. He smiled at the pink dots of polish adorning her toes.

"Come here," he said, his tone huskier than he'd intended.

Without hesitation Nicole stepped in his direction. He took hold of her, guiding her fingers up his chest to drape over his shoulder. Her other hand splayed across his abdomen, sending a jolt of awareness to his cock like a bolt of lightning. Her thighs brushed against his as she settled into the juncture of his legs, shooting a pulse of blood to his erection.

"I think you're too sensitive to have sex just for sex, Nic," he said, cupping her cheek in his palm and turning her face up to his. He ran his thumb over her lush bottom lip.

"I can," she insisted, as her pink tongue peeked between her lips to touch his thumb.

Marcus growled in the back of his throat at her sensual gesture, then dipped his head and lightly brushed his lips across hers. She was softer than he'd imagined.

In the space of a heartbeat the kiss changed. Marcus slid his tongue along the seam of her mouth, tasting the cherry of her lip gloss and feeling her faint tremor before she opened for him. His tongue slipped past her teeth and into the sultry depths of her mouth. Along with a trace of mint, he was met by a rush of feminine sweetness that sent another surge of blood to his groin, leaving him rock-solid.

Reluctant to lose control too quickly, Marcus slowed the kiss, allowing himself time to become accustomed to the feel of her.

Nicole leaned into him, deliberately brushing the tips of her hard nipples against his chest. Feeling the rush of desire dampen her sensitive vagina, she did it again. She settled the apex of her legs against the length of his rigid penis, which throbbed to life beneath the barrier of his pants.

Despite worrying that she might be moving too fast, Nicole ground her body into him. He joined her, thrusting forward each time she rolled her hips toward him with so much intensity pulses of need buckled her knees. She sagged completely against him.

Marcus wrapped his arm around Nicole's shoulder and pulled her toward him. His mouth came down hard on hers like molten lava. He drew her bottom lip into his mouth, nibbling on the fullness. His lips moved across her skin, over her jawline, and down the column of her neck, leaving a cool trail of moisture where he'd already been.

With his free hand Marcus cupped the weight of her breast in his palm, rubbing his thumb over her taut nipple until it pebbled into a hard peak that strained against the silk of her dress. *The damn dress.*

He kissed along her collarbone, following the slope downward until he met the swell of her breasts.

"Mmm . . . you taste good. Sweet, like sugar," he mumbled against her flesh.

"Honey," she corrected. "Honey Dust."

"Honey? Mm-hmm . . . I like it."

Nicole shuddered as his arm slipped down her back and his large hand came to rest upon the roundness of her bottom. He softly kneaded her flesh. The music paused as the CD changed songs. A deep, sensual rhythm pulsed through her body when it played again. She could feel Marcus sway to the lyrics and beat.

She moved with him, allowing her head to fall back, giving him better access to her neck. His lush lips moved back up her chest, settling where her pulse throbbed against her skin. When the sharp edge of his teeth scraped against her, fine tremors spread across her skin like a wildfire across an August meadow.

With deliberate slowness he nibbled and nipped at her, kissing and teasing as he began to make the descent toward her breast.

He reached the line of silk draping from her shoulder. His teeth bit into the fabric and tugged the material lower so the seam pressed into the fullness of her breast. Half of one dark nipple peeked over the hem, exposed for Marcus to devour. Nicole felt her nipple harden further in anticipation of the wet warmth of his mouth.

Liquid heat seeped through her panties. Tension wound in the core of her body as Marcus drew her into his mouth and began to suck. His rough tongue swirled and lapped, his teeth grating against her skin.

Growling deep in his throat, Marcus shoved away from the counter, stalking forward while pushing Nicole back. He kept his arm around her and her body pressed tightly against his.

Marcus's hands settled on her waist when Nicole hit the resistance of the opposite counter. His fingers gripped the material of her dress and bunched it in his fist, creeping it up her thighs. The coolness of the spring night air swept against her legs in striking contrast to where Marcus was touching her. Sensation shivered down her spine.

Nicole rested her hands on his upper arms, feeling the muscles tighten beneath her palm as he flexed his hands about her waist, lifting her onto the counter before him. Her bottom settled upon the silk of her skirt rather than the cool tile countertop, the front of the material riding high. Glancing down, she saw that her white lace G-string panties barely hid the triangular patch of curly black hair covering her mound.

Marcus wound his index finger around the narrow strip of satin and lace and pulled it upward, digging it into her folds of skin, brushing it against her clitoris in three quick successions. A tingle began deep within her body, while heat danced across her skin. She sucked a gasp of breath between her teeth as he again lowered his head and sucked her exposed nipple into the humid depths of his mouth.

"Damn, Nic. If you've changed your mind, you'd better say so now. I'm not sure I'll be able to stop if we take this much further," Marcus growled, his lips pressed against the responsive skin of her breast. The vibration of his words echoed through her entire body.

"Don't stop. Please don't stop," Nicole managed between sharp breaths. "You're making me feel so good."

She felt his smile upon her skin as he continued to rub the cloth of her panties against her flesh, the muscles on her inner thighs quivering in reply.

Annoyed by the barrier of his clothing, and wanting desperately to feel his smooth skin with her hands, Nicole moved to the front of his shirt, where a row of buttons acted as a prim schoolmaster. She quickly dismissed the shirt, freeing each button until the edges fell apart and his dark sculpted chest was partially visible.

Her hands dove beneath the cloth and skimmed across his skin. Wisps of ebony hair tickled her palm. Masculine heat imbued her skin, making her dizzy with desire. Her fingernails scraped against his flat, hardened nipples. He groaned. She reveled in his response.

With his fingers he spread the lips of her vagina, allowing his thumb access to circle and press against the button of her clit.

"Ahh, Marcus," she whimpered, her body shuddering.

She heard his throaty chuckle as his tongue left her breast cold, damp, and lonely—begging for the return of his mouth. Instead he settled upon her lips, smiling as he swooped into her, his fingers moving in the same slow, delicious tempo as his tongue.

His finger dipped into her, swirling in the natural spring of moisture signifying her arousal, drawing the silken essence from her core to rub around her labia, into the glistening black hair above.

Wanting to return the treatment, Nicole slid her palms down his defined pecs, across the flat plain of his stomach, over the contours of his straining abdominal muscles, to where a single button and a not-so-daunting zipper secured the waistband of his khakis. With one flick the button popped open, and the zipper slid down with a sigh of relief after struggling to stay up against the strain of his hardened cock begging for release.

Sliding her fingertips down to the elastic waist of his boxers, Nicole broke the kiss. Placing one hand on his chest, she gave a slight push so he was exposed to view. He must have realized her intent, for a slow, devilish grin turned up the corners of his lips.

Nicole smiled when she saw the Oakland Raiders boxers, the ones she'd given him for his last birthday. She'd thought them a funny gift. What else could she give a Raider fan who had lots of souvenirs? She was grateful now for her selection, for they guarded him like a true lineman did the quarterback, and looked stunning in contrast with his brown skin.

Taking the edge between her thumb and forefinger, Nicole pulled the elastic waistband down his narrow hips until the solid length of his cock sprang free. Gasping at the sight of him, Nicole stared at his long, black flesh standing rigid, the head pointing straight at her vagina with undeniable masculine power. The throb of desire beat within her clit with as much force as if Marcus had still been stroking her.

Nicole secured the band of elastic under his tightly drawn balls and wrapped her fingers around his shaft, stroking from the top downward until the side of her hand was met with pubic hair, then reversed up his length. He was so thick her fingers couldn't meet. Veins bulged from his penis, making the journey a massage for her palm.

"You're beautiful," she whispered, fully in awe at the sight of his male body, flawless and powerful, supremely different from her own, fundamentally made for joining.

"So are you." His midnight gaze fixed on her damp, pert nipples.

Nicole slid her hand down, tightening as she stroked back up, drawing out a ball of moisture that looked like a droplet of morning dew on the petal of a rose.

"Ahh. Mmm . . . Nic," he moaned.

She swirled her thumb in his lubricant and dampened the velvet head of his cock until it was slick and ready for entry.

"Hell! We have to stop. I don't have anything." His voice was strained with tension.

"I took care of it." Reaching behind her, Nicole grabbed a ceramic cookie jar shaped and painted like a bouquet of roses. Lifting the lid, she dumped the contents onto the countertops. Silver foil—wrapped Hershey's Kisses littered the tiles.

Marcus narrowed his eyes, staring. It took a moment to realize what he was seeing. Mixed with the silver-wrapped Kisses were at least two dozens foil packets, each containing a condom.

"Do you always keep condoms with Kisses?" he asked, holding back a laugh, though the grin on his face betrayed him.

"No. I bought them."

"For this?" he asked.

"Yeah, for tonight."

He leaned forward and pressed a chaste kiss to her lips. "For how long, Nicole?"

"Maybe a month or two? I lost count. I've been wanting to seduce you for a while."

"Seduce me?" Marcus was shocked and slightly disappointed.
He could've been sexing Nicole all this time; now he was about to
move. Marcus tossed back his head and laughed. "It didn't take
much to seduce me, did it, Nic?"

Nicole shot a glance at his erection. "No, I guess not." She
smiled.

Marcus's dark eyes appraised the countertop. "Why so many?"

"I didn't know what kind you like—what kind you use," she
whispered, now embarrassed by the sheer number of condoms
she'd purchased. "I bought every type the drugstore carried."

"How about this one," Marcus said, plucking a foil packet from
beneath a few Kisses and handing it to Nicole, hoping she wouldn't
notice the slight tremble to his hand. *I'm shaking?*

"Good choice." She took the condom from his fingers and tore
off the side. She stared wide-eyed at the slip of lubricated rubber
she held between her fingers.

Marcus could see her confusion, so he guided her hand to his
erection and used his own fingers to move hers over his cock.

"Like this," he said, slipping the tight latex down his rigid dick.

Nicole was breathing almost as heavily as he was by the time the
circular condom was fully extended. Her hand cupped his balls and
began to massage them. A groan rumbled from his throat, sounding almost like a growl.

She was damn beautiful sitting there on the counter with her
legs spread for him. He settled between her thighs, grinning as she
wrapped her bare feet around the backs of his legs and drew him
closer.

Placing her hand on the back of his neck, she urged him down
to her, closing the distance in the space of a second. He returned
his lips to hers, his tongue slipping into the sultry depths of her
mouth, swirling, mating, undulating.

Marcus settled a hand upon her breast. Smoothing his index finger over the taut nipple, he plucked and rolled, the weight of her firm globe fitting perfectly in his palm. His other hand went to her slick vagina, ready and eagerly awaiting his attention. She closed around his finger as he added one, then two into the folds of her labia, dipping into a pot of molten honey.

Marcus leaned forward, his body urging him, his mind unable to resist. The lure of Nicole's lush body, ripe and hungry, slick, yet tight around his fingers, caused his erection to pulse with lust. When he felt her feet flatten against the backs of his knees and tug him toward her, he lost the last bit of restraint.

He brushed the latex-covered tip of his cock against the welcoming heat of Nicole, panting with the need to delve into her hard and fast. But if he did as his body called, this would be over in a few short, hard thrusts.

He slipped his fingers from her and wrapped them around his dick, brushing it against her clitoris, dipping deeper into the folds of her core. She was hot and wet and sweet, like going to heaven, like coming home.

Unable to hold back, and tortured by the tightening satin flesh around him, he thrust into her so deeply that his pubic hair tangled with hers as she ground her hips into him.

"Ahh, hell, Nic!" he growled through clenched teeth, his lips covering hers. His body began to tighten in need of release just from the feel of her.

"Umm . . . mmm." She shook her head slightly moaning into his mouth. The taste of her breath was feminine and sugary. His body pulsed as her flesh gripped and hugged and tightened around his cock buried deeply within her.

She tilted her hips forward, easing off the counter's edge until he supported her, her supple legs wrapped around his back. He placed his hands around her bottom and thrust forward at the same time he pulled her hips toward him. They met with one hard grind.

Nicole's body shook as he thrust into her hard and fast, pumping in long, languorous strokes, grinding his hips against hers so his pubic hair massaged her clit. Then he quickened, slamming into her in a series of powerful thrusts, his fingers working her breast.

Damn, but he was close . . . too close to slow down. Knowing Nicole wouldn't reach climax as quickly as he was fast approaching, he slipped his hand from her sassy dark nipple, down between them, and found her clit with his thumb.

"Oh," Nicole sighed, a combination of a jagged pant and pure pleasure. Her back arched, the peaks of her breasts stood upright, and her hand splayed out behind her on the counter, scattering the Kisses and nudging her wineglass with enough force to tip it over. White zinfandel splashed on the counter before dripping to the floor.

The scent of chocolate, sweat, wine, and sex permeated the air, a combination so heady it flashed through Nicole's senses like a shot of hard whiskey. Her mind buzzed in anticipation of the crest of climax. Heat scattered across her skin like dry leaves taking to the wind; gooseflesh followed. A soul-deep throb tightened within her core, touched only by the powerful length of Marcus's dark cock. His thumb worked the pearl of flesh that unleashed the sexual need within her.

He came into her one last time, the weight of his body making a firm seal of joined bodies.

"Ahh—Nicole," he growled, breathing heavy with his shoulders bunched.

She felt the convulsions of his body as his cum filled the latex tip of the condom. With Marcus throbbing deep within her, one twist of his fingers sent her soaring over the edge. Liquid heat seeped from her body as each of her muscles clamped down, then released, leaving her shaking with the force of ecstasy.

Marcus wrapped his arms around her, drawing her back to his chest and hugging her tightly, their bodies still one—neither in a hurry to separate. Keith Sweat's deep voice swathed them, acting as a shield from the world.

Marcus smoothed his palm down her back and up again, enjoying the contrast of the cool silk and the warmth of her soft skin. He turned his face into the curve of her throat and pressed a kiss to her neck, still shocked about what had just transpired between them. His Nicole, his friend, sheathed him and fit him like a tight glove designed for him and him alone.

Hell, he had taken her like a man crazed, dying of thirst, and she a fresh sip of water. He had meant to go slow, to bathe her with affection, to love her tenderly, as she deserved to be loved. But instead he'd claimed her in the kitchen, supported only by the edge of the counter and the strength of his erection.

Easing away from her, he framed her beautiful face with his hands, his fingers spreading out into her curls. He gazed into her eyes, the rich color of milk chocolate, her lips swollen and bruised from the intensity of his kisses. "Are you all right, Nic?" he asked, his tone husky. He wanted them to be okay, for their friendship to remain intact.

"Yeah, I am." She turned her face into his palm and pressed a light kiss to his skin. "Thank you, Marcus."

"You're thanking me? Damn, Nic, I didn't intend to be so fast. What kind of man claims a woman standing in the kitchen?" He shook his head in disgust. A shiver of apprehension spread across his skin. Could he have just ruined everything between them?

"The kind I like," she replied in a light tone, laughter bubbling in her voice.

Her laughter offered him a fragment of relief. "Next time, Nicole, I'm going to take my time. Next time I'm going to savor you."

"Is there going to be a next time?"

Marcus paused. *Was* there going to be a next time? He knew Nicole desired it. He sure as hell did. Sexing Nicole had exceeded his wildest dreams. He knew he couldn't resist exploring the possibilities of their sexual relationship before he moved across the country. Tamping down uncertainty, he teased, "We'll see. We shall see."

Marcus eased from her body, wrapped the condom in a paper towel, and shrugged his pants back over his hips. In the past there'd been a moment of awkwardness when finished with a lover, but not now. Not with Nicole.

They righted their clothing in comfortable silence, doused the candles burning in the bedroom before they caught the house on fire, then curled up on the couch and watched one of the movies he'd brought.

Nicole rested her cheek against his arm, still amazed. She'd guessed sex with Marcus would be great; she just hadn't figured it would be wonderful, or that her soul would be as soothed and as sated as her body. But there was a nagging fear he'd been right— sex just for sex might not be what she really wanted. Maybe she wanted Marcus after all. *Don't be ridiculous; he's moving.*

Relaxed against him, Nicole thought about all the changes that would occur when he left. Maybe she needed a fresh start too. She *had* been thinking about putting her house on the market. Her place was small, and now that she was a junior partner she could afford a bigger place—the house she'd always wanted.

When Nicole yawned, Marcus stood and sauntered toward the door. Nicole walked behind him. As usual, he gathered her into a tight hug, holding her a moment longer than on prior nights. Moving away, he opened the door.

Nicole watched him step over the threshold, feeling a bit sad to see him go. Glancing back, Marcus asked, "Monday morning, right?"

"Yep. I'll see you at six A.M." She smiled, then waved as she bade him good night.

With one last glance, Marcus descended the stairs and slipped into the shadowy night. A moment later he was gone. Nicole sighed as she closed the door.

Chapter Three

*N*ICOLE IS BEAUTIFUL.

Marcus gaped at her, hoping his appreciation didn't shine too brightly from his eyes. She stood before him in the open doorway of her home, wearing a white pair of sweat shorts and a pink T-shirt, a small white apron tied around her narrow waist. She looked sexy as hell, while still appearing innocent.

Biting back a grin, he realized she was a perfect match for the bouquet of flowers he held in his tight-knuckled grip, as soft as the pink tulip petals, as lush as the white calla lilies, and as fresh as the baby's breath.

"Hi." She flashed him a brilliant, welcoming smile, then opened the door a bit wider.

Marcus watched as her milk-chocolate gaze drifted over him to the flowers he held by his side. He felt as if he were back in high school, and as awkward as a first date. What would she think of flowers? He'd given them to her before on birthdays and on graduation, or when she got a promotion, but he had never shown up at her house two hours early on their usual Saturday movie night, flowers in hand.

Knowing it was too late to run back to his truck and leave the bouquet hidden there, he lifted the spray of soft shades of pink and white and presented them to Nicole.

"Hey, Nic. I brought you some flowers to celebrate your firm promoting you to junior partner," he said, attempting to make the gesture appear casual.

Her eyes brightened as she reached for the bouquet. "Thanks, Marcus. Come on in. I'll put these in water," she said as she drew the flowers to her face and inhaled. Her nose brushed against the stamen, and a dusting of yellow pollen remained on her rich caramel skin.

Before she could turn in to the shadowed hallway, Marcus stepped into the house and placed his palm against her cheek, immediately realizing how much he'd longed to touch her.

"You got pollen on your nose," he remarked, spreading his fingers into her hair and skimming his thumb across her lips, up to her nose, where he slowly brushed away the yellow dust.

Nicole's eyes opened wide in surprise, but she quickly recovered. "Thanks."

Marcus withdrew his hand, balling his fingers into a fist to keep from reaching for her again. All week long he'd agonized over how to handle his attraction to Nicole. Hell, he'd always been attracted to her, but had never thought to act on it before. Not if it meant risking their friendship. Yet ever since they'd become intimate he could think of little else but getting his hands on that luscious body of hers again.

He'd worried that things might be strained between them come Monday morning when they met at the gym, but she'd entered the weight room in baggy sweat shorts over a tight catsuit that hugged her fit figure and accentuated the fullness of her breasts. As usual, she gave him a welcoming smile and then beat him to the weight machine. All week their morning workouts had remained as they'd always been.

Nicole had been right: She was his best friend, and nothing had changed between them despite their having had crazed sex in her kitchen. Now, as he watched her turn away from him, holding the bouquet of flowers, he had the oddest feeling she regretted what had happened and that he'd best forget about it happening again.

Maybe it was something about the serious look in her rich, dark eyes.

As he watched the sensual sway of her hips as she walked before him, his cock became fully erect, held secure behind his button fly. Adjusting his groin as he walked, Marcus followed Nicole into the kitchen, where she bent beneath the sink to retrieve a vase for the flowers.

Marcus stared at her perfectly round ass sticking up in the air and fought the urge to grab hold of her hips and grind his erection into her. He looked away, the guilt of wanting her eating at him.

His gaze slid back to her ass. Despite the perfect shape of her butt, Marcus knew it was not the possibility of sex that had him coming around, but a genuine liking for Nicole, and a mutual respect.

When Nicole shifted, Marcus turned from her before she caught him staring at her like an idiot, saliva dripping from his tongue. The rose-shaped cookie jar where she kept condoms mixed with Kisses captured his attention. Plenty more remained.

Marcus looked at the counter where he'd taken Nicole, now covered with a cutting board and freshly washed vegetables in a silver colander.

"I was going to make us dinner," Nicole said, grinning at him as if she'd caught him with his hand in the cookie jar, when in all actuality it nearly had been.

"I was thinking we could watch those movies and order a pizza. You don't have to cook if you don't want to," he replied.

"Okay," Nicole said. She brushed a stray curl behind her ear as she stashed the veggies back in the fridge, then handed him a beer. "Which movie do you want to watch first?" she asked, putting away the knife and cutting board.

"You pick."

Nicole untied the apron and dropped it onto the counter. "Can you put in *Spider-Man 2* while I get something to drink?"

"Sure."

*   *   *

Nicole stood still until she was sure Marcus had gone to the living room and heard him fiddling with the DVD cases. Releasing a sigh of relief, Nicole sagged against the tile counter, feeling a rush of desire. He'd caught her off guard. She'd not expected to find Marcus standing on her doorstep hours early, holding a delicate arrangement of flowers. He looked *so* good, his strong legs encased in loose denim, and a black Raiders jersey covering his chiseled chest and muscular arms.

She'd watched him every morning at the gym, trying to decide how he felt about their sexual relationship, fantasizing that he would want to continue it until he moved. After tasting his lips and feeling the solid length of him deep within her, she knew she'd never be satisfied with just one encounter.

A breath of air rushed from her lungs, just a bit more jagged than normal, lust singing through her veins. Until last week she hadn't really realized just how badly she missed sex. Sure, she'd often thought about it, but not seriously enough to do it with a stranger. Marcus was a perfect bedmate.

Taking a deep breath, Nicole lifted the lid to the cookie jar and pulled out a condom packet, shoving it into her pocket before she grabbed a chocolate. She quietly replaced the lid, careful not to let the ceramic tap against itself. Removing the wrapper, she plopped the Kiss into her mouth. She was about to leave the kitchen when she remembered the excuse she'd used to send Marcus from the room and grabbed a soda from the fridge.

In her cramped living room, Nicole found Marcus sitting almost in the center of the couch, the beer on a side table, and his feet propped up on the ottoman with the remote in his hand. He looked so comfortable, supremely masculine, powerfully dominant—arrogantly male. Seeing him with one elbow resting on the back of the couch and the breadth of his body relaxed into the plush pillows, Nicole knew when she sat down that she'd be forced to touch him.

Had he planned that when he sat square in the middle? she

silently questioned, pleased with the possibility. Deciding to use his hogging the couch to her advantage, Nicole put her soda beside his beer and grabbed a loose pillow.

"Scoot over," she said, while swatting the pillow playfully at him. The first shot hit him upside his head and took him off guard.

Marcus smiled a slow, sexy smile, set the remote aside, and propped his other elbow on the couch back, making his intention of staying put abundantly clear. "Make me," he challenged.

Laughing, Nicole swatted the pillow at him again, hitting him on the upper arm. He didn't move, just watched her dance out of his reach after striking her blow. Laughing, she moved forward and hit him again, then retreated in case he decided to come after her.

"I'll make you move." She giggled, swatting him again with the pillow, each successful strike making her bolder.

"I'm still here," he replied, once again challenging Nicole to move him.

"Not for long."

"Mmmm, I am pretty comfy here," he said, wiggling further into the cushions, leaning his head back as if he were about to go to sleep.

Nicole pounced, hitting Marcus across his chest again, but when she attempted to flee she found her pillow ensnared in Marcus's powerful grip. He reeled her in like a fish on a hook. Nicole squealed and giggled, all the while refusing to give up her hold on her end of the pillow. *I have to admit, I'm not fighting very hard.*

"You still going to make me?" Marcus asked.

"Yep," she responded, laughing and tugging, yet eyeing his lap as a good place to sit.

Then, with one hard yank, she tumbled forward, landing sprawled across his thighs. The mood went from playful to charged on contact. Nicole froze for a brief moment. *Is that a hard-on I feel wedged against my belly?*

Drawing up her knees so she straddled his lap, Nicole sat up and removed the pillow that had landed between their chests.

"Do you still refuse to move?" she asked, placing her hands on her hips.

"I think I'll stay where I am," he responded, his tone still playful as he lifted a mocking eyebrow, his lips twitching into a smile.

"Then I am going to have to torture you," she said.

"Oh, yeah? How are you going to do that?"

"Like this." Nicole grabbed the hemline of her T-shirt and lifted it, leisurely pulling it up her body, slowly revealing her naked stomach. Her white lace bra was bared next, before she whipped the pink cloth over her head and tossed it to the floor.

Pressed against her crotch, the hard swell of his cock throbbed with lust. Grinding her hips, she elicited a throaty groan from Marcus.

"Damn, girl, you're gorgeous," he said, his arms leaving the back of the couch as he reached for her breasts.

Before his fingers made contact with the lace of her bra, Nicole grabbed his hands and pushed them back. "Uh-uh," she said, shaking her head from side to side. "No touching. I am torturing you, remember?"

"Do your worst then, Nic. I'm waiting," he said, again taunting her. He replaced his elbows on the back of the couch, his hands dangling down across the throw pillows.

Nicole swayed her shoulders to an imaginary tune, running her palms over her own body, cupping her breasts in her hands, feeling the fine texture of her lace bra and the weight of her breasts straining against it. She smoothed her thumb over her nipple, feeling it grow taut. His erection pressed through denim and sweats to rub against her clit as she danced to the musical beat of her own desire.

She felt moisture soak her shorts, reaffirming her decision not to wear the matching white panties, then the answering throb of want deep within her. She moaned, her inner thighs gripping his jeans-swathed body.

"Will you move now?" she purred.

Marcus's only answer was a movement of his head that made his denial clear.

"Well, then . . ." Nicole put her hand to her mouth, smoothing her thumb across her lower lip. Parting them slightly, she used her tongue to dampen the pad of her fingers, taking more time than needed to make sure they were wet. She then replaced her hand to her breast, the lace becoming transparent as it dampened. She plucked at her hard nipple while biting down on her bottom lip to stifle the moan of pleasure bubbling forth.

Watching the desire darken Marcus's eyes from twilight to midnight, Nicole flicked the hook holding the front of her bra closed and allowed the flimsy straps to slide over her shoulders and down her arms. With both hands she cupped her breasts, kneading her soft flesh in her palms, stroking her nipples until they peaked, then rolling the tight beads between her thumbs and index fingers.

Nicole released her breasts when Marcus trembled between her legs. Leaning forward, she slid her hands beneath the smooth mesh material of his jersey and pulled up the shirt, exposing his abdomen, then farther, until his dark, flat nipples came into view.

Marcus assisted by lifting his arms and shrugging his shoulders. "Kind of you," she murmured as she lifted the garment from his body and tossed it aside.

He nodded his reply as he lowered his arms and reached for her, but Nicole slapped his hands away.

"I said no touching."

"Let me touch you, Nic."

Nicole smiled at the hint of desperation in his voice, though he did what she told him and replaced his elbows on the couch. To further his torture, she ground her hips into his lap in a tight circular motion, her hips undulating against his jeans-clad erection.

"Please . . ." Marcus begged through clenched teeth, his hands balling into fists as he gripped the sofa pillows.

Nicole' shook her head, smiling, enjoying the power she held over him to arouse and torment and tease. Leaning forward, she stroked her palms over his chest. His muscles bunched beneath her hands. Every inch of him was firm under his smooth brown skin adorned with a scattering of curly black hair.

With her tongue Nicole left a damp trail around one dark nipple, kissing and licking her way upward, toward his neck. He smelled like Ivory soap and Polo, like Marcus. Fresh, clean. She could taste his arrogance, yet she controlled him. Is *there anything more intoxicating?*

She nipped at his skin with her teeth. His wild pulse surged beneath her lips in the same furious tempo as her own.

With her hands gripping his shoulders and her thighs against his legs, she rose slightly so that her breasts were level with his mouth.

"Do you want to kiss me?" she asked, shifting her shoulders to brush the peak of her breast across his hot, moist lips.

Marcus licked her nipple, opening his mouth as he attempted to draw her in, but she pulled out of his reach.

Scraping her nails into his skin as she leaned into him again, she said, "I asked if you wanted to. I didn't say that you could."

"Hell, Nic," Marcus growled, gripping the cushion with all of his strength—anything to resist his need to grab hold of Nicole, drag her perfect body up against his, and suckle upon her full, ripe breasts. But he was determined to play out this game of hers, allowing her to take control, damn thankful he'd decided to incite her by sitting in the center of the couch.

Unable to free his cock, he felt his desire pulse against the denim in nearly painful throbs. His nuts drew tightly toward his body as moisture seeped from her sweat shorts, enough that he could feel her damp heat and smell the honeyed scent of her vagina.

His breathing became jagged as he felt his lungs panting for air, control more of a workout than any exercise he had done at the gym. Sweat broke out on his brow. His shoulders ached with the tension of being unable to release the curl of furious desire singing through his blood. *I'm bringing flowers every time.*

Marcus studied the slope of her neck, the graceful fall of her breasts, the shadow of her cleavage, her flat stomach with just enough of a curve to remind him how female she truly was—anything to keep himself distracted while Nicole inflicted agony and pleasure upon his lust-ridden body.

When Nicole lowered, her naked breasts brushed against his chest as her mouth settled on his lips, swallowing up Marcus's groan. He gave over his passion to her control, following her lead as she pecked and nibbled on his lips, then deepened the kiss. Her tongue explored his mouth, mating, swirling, demanding a response from him.

"You taste good," Nicole whispered, pulling away from him slightly and settling her bottom fully on his lap.

His randy cock bucked hard. "You taste like chocolate." He licked his lips, savoring the sweet flavor of where her mouth had been.

"Do I? Hmm, I ate a Kiss from the cookie jar," she replied, a flush covering her cheeks.

"Really? From the cookie jar?"

"Yeah," she said with an innocent smile. Nicole shimmied her way down his muscular legs, her hands caressing his body as they made their way from his shoulders, across his chest, and down his abdomen, to where five buttons kept his erection captive.

With a flick of two fingers she freed the first button.

"And . . ."—she opened the second button—"I . . ."—the third worked its own way through the material, pressed by his hard cock straining the cloth—"got . . ."—Nicole ran her finger down the canyon of his fly, touching and rubbing the trail of pubic hair, her fingernails scraping against him until she quickly loosened the fourth—"one . . ." the final button came apart with the slightest touch of her fingertips, as if magic had released it.

Nicole reached the waistband of his boxers and pulled the elastic down his hips. *Don't stop.* To Marcus's relief, she grabbed a fistful of material, both denim and cotton, and tugged his clothing down to midthigh.

Nicole squeezed her lids shut with a sigh, after catching a quick glimpse of his dark satin skin stretched over his hard, pulsing cock. *I can't remember ever being this aroused,* she realized, opening her eyes. The silken texture of his plum-shaped head was damp with desire, shiny and ready to enter her.

". . . of these," she said, retrieving the condom from her pocket and bringing it to her lips. One hand fondling his dick, the other holding the foil packet, Nicole tore it open using her teeth.

"And I thought you'd brought me a Kiss," Marcus said, sucking air between his teeth.

"Did you want a Kiss?" she asked.

"Hell, yes."

Nicole pouted as she looked over Marcus's hard, lean body. "Is that all, just a Kiss?"

"I want to touch you."

"But you can't. You wouldn't move over, remember?" Nicole smiled at him while gradually removing the slip of coiled latex from the foil packet, the lubricant shining on her fingertips. "What else do you want?"

"A taste of you."

A hot rush of desire built within her. His erection pulsed against the palm of her hand. She stroked down the solid length of him, twisting as she returned. She placed the condom on his cock, remembering how he'd guided her fingers down to put it on, and slowly began to uncurl the latex over the swell of his erection.

"Is there anything else, Marcus?" she asked, her voice just above a whisper.

"I want to make love to you," he growled, his chest rising and falling in quick pants.

"How about if *I* make love to *you*?" Nicole asked, rising to her knees and shifting the material of her shorts out of the way, too eager to bother removing them.

With the condom fully encasing him, Nicole gripped his cock and held it to her, easing open her lips, teasing her clit with his dick.

A quiver ran down her spine. Tension sizzled her inner thighs as liquid fire spilled from her body, surrounding him.

Slowly, taking delight in the texture, savoring the feel of him, as one did a fine wine, she lowered herself onto him, crying out when the sheer mass of him pressed upon her womb.

"Ahh, Nic," he growled, his hands fisting in the pillows, pleasure brightening his smoldering eyes. He held her gaze. "You feel good. Damn good."

Marcus thrust his hips upward, driving into her tight, wet sheath.

"Oh . . . oh . . . Marcus, kiss me," Nicole whimpered, falling forward, her forearms resting over his pecs, her hands framing his face as her lips met his. His tongue slipped between her teeth into the recess of her mouth, lapping and tasting, drinking the sugared sweetness of her like he was a dying man, and she his only salvation.

Marcus kneaded the couch pillow in his fists, his fingers working the material. He allowed her to lead, her hips rotating into him, grinding, lifting, retreating, slamming into him. Riding him. The muscles of her inner thighs tightened as she lifted her body from his, the slick folds of her vagina gripping around his cock, driving him wild.

With a shift of her hips, she brought him back into her in one smooth glide. Still, Marcus kept his elbows on the rear of the sofa, fighting the need to grab her around the waist and drive into her hard, at a speed that would put a quick end to the building orgasm. Lifting his hips, he rose to meet her downward thrust.

"Marcus?" Her voice was husky as she whispered against his lips, her breath fanning warmth across his skin.

"I'm with you, Nic," he reassured her, quickening his motions, adding power to each of his upward surges, tilting so the material of her shorts bunched and rubbed against her clit.

Her body began to tremble in small waves, first with a tightening of her thighs, her hands gripping at his shoulders, her nails biting into his skin, surely leaving crescent moons engraved in his biceps. Her flesh quivered around him, hugging and stroking, encouraging him to go on.

"Marcus," she cried out, her body shaking violently, her back arching. Her vagina convulsed around his cock, every muscle in her body trembling as she collapsed onto his chest. Her slick walls of heaven caressed him with tender shudders.

I'm with you, Nic. With one skyward thrust Marcus joined with her, their bodies becoming one as a wave of sheer pleasure crashed around them. His slack arms banded around Nicole's back, holding her to him, a tangle of sweat-slick limbs, their breathing a succession of jagged pants, their bodies drifting with orgasm.

Marcus felt the connection to Nicole, stronger this time than the last. A web of emotion bound his heart to her. *We're just friends, you fool. I'm moving. I'm leaving her behind with no strings attached.*

When his breathing slowly returned to normal, his body becoming alert again, he realized his cock was still buried deep within her. Biting back a groan, Marcus eased from her.

"You win, Nic. I'll move," he said, trying to renew the playfulness of before.

"Maybe I want to sit on your lap," she teased.

"Anytime."

She got up, righting her shorts, then bent to retrieve her pink T-shirt from the floor. Marcus discarded the condom in a tissue and tugged up his pants.

"Yeah? You don't mind?" She sat beside him, curling her feet beneath her, resting one elbow on his chest, and stared into his eyes. The milk chocolate of her gaze seemed melted in the afterglow of their intimacy and stirred his tenderness.

"Nicole, if you sit on my lap like that, it will be a seat reserved just for you."

"Just for me?" Nicole held her breath while she waited for an answer. Did Marcus mean he wouldn't be dating, or had his comment been a mere slip of the tongue?

"Nic, I think it's best if we do this exclusively. I mean, like you said, there are no strings attached. If you want to go out on a date, hey, no problem. But if you want to have sex with someone else, then *we* probably shouldn't."

"I agree. And you can date, too," she said. She pushed aside the mixed feelings, not wanting to think about them at the moment, maybe not at all.

"Yeah, like I date so often," replied Marcus.

"Well, you could. You never know who you'll meet once you move."

"Until then, I'd rather watch movies with you." Marcus extended his arm, draping it around her shoulders, and tugged her closer to him.

She snuggled into his warmth, glad for the affection after the passion they'd just shared. It felt good to have his muscular arm around her body, holding her to the contours of his naked chest, his heartbeat ticking against her cheek. She sat still while Marcus flicked the button on the remote, turning the TV on. Previews started.

Nicole allowed her lids to drift closed. Thinking of Marcus, she inhaled deeply. She enjoyed the smell of his musky scent, his flavor lingering in her mouth. When the opening sequence of the movie began, she opened her eyes.

Marcus smiled, then bent forward and pressed a tender kiss to her lips. To her surprise, he lingered, his slow kiss conveying affection and tenderness. It was a kiss of lovers who were more than friends. A bolt of fear spread through her body. She couldn't let it take that turn. Nicole turned her head away, ending the kiss.

"Forget the movie. I am hungry. You mentioned pizza. Would you mind ordering some while I jump in the shower?"

"No problem. Is pepperoni all right?" He rolled to the side, releasing her.

"Yeah, and black olives." Nicole slipped from beside him and got to her feet. She could feel the heat of his stare on her back as she retreated.

When she reached her bedroom, she closed the door and leaned against it to keep her legs from buckling. Gulping down several deep breaths, she made her way to the bathroom and started the shower.

Damn, she hoped Marcus hadn't been right when he claimed she was too sensitive to have sex just for sex. She liked him, yes, but she knew that. She was getting what her body desired, and in turn giving him the same. What was wrong with two consenting adults meeting each other's needs? He'd be leaving town soon, so what was wrong with taking pleasure from him while she had the chance?

Nothing!

She tossed her shirt and shorts to the hamper and stepped into the shower.

Warm water cascaded down her body, washing away the sweat and what remained of sex from between her legs. It soothed with caressing wet fingers, cleansing her, reviving her, easing her worry and doubt. *Short-term lovers is all.*

Leaning back against the wall, she closed her eyes and allowed the water to pour over her, remembering the way he'd called her gorgeous. He hadn't seemed to notice the faded stretch marks from when she was a little heavy, before she'd started working out. Marcus was the first man with whom she didn't feel insecure about her body. She liked that feeling.

The water began to chill, reminding her how her body would cool once Marcus moved. *Damn job offer,* she swore as she shut off the water.

Nicole dried and dressed in clean jeans and a plain shirt, then left her room to search out something to appease her grumbling stomach. She found Marcus in the kitchen rummaging through the fridge. A white square box sat on the counter, with the scent of pepperoni perfuming the air.

"That was fast," she commented, lifting the lid and grabbing a slice, choosing to ignore all the warning bells ringing in her head.

Marcus turned toward her and extended a beer. "Not really. You were in the shower for about half an hour. You all right?"

His voice was so soft and caring, a lump of emotion lodged in her throat. Swallowing it back, she answered, "Of course. It felt good, is all. Sorry to keep you waiting."

"Hey, no problem." He moved forward, put his own beer on the counter, and grabbed a slice of the pizza.

Carrying their drinks and plates to the stools at the end of the counter, they sat down and began to talk of work and friends. They discussed changing their workout to include more aerobic activity and adding a protein supplement to Marcus's diet. The combination of powerful sex, a hot shower, and a full stomach forced a yawn from Nicole.

"Hey, I think I'm going to skip the movie. I have to help my cousin move in the morning and I'm pretty tired. I think I'll head home and crash," Marcus commented, getting to his feet and placing his dish in the sink.

Stifling another yawn, Nicole followed him toward the door. "I'm tired, too. It's been a long week at work. I have some briefs to review, but I'd rather curl up with a book. There are a few I bought months ago but haven't had time to read."

"They work you too hard at your firm." He stopped walking. "You need a little time off."

"I love my job, Marcus. I protect the rights of battered women. They need me."

"I know, and you're good at it." Marcus brushed the back of his hand over her cheek. "You make a difference."

"I hope so," she whispered, taking a breath and stepping toward the entry.

Marcus opened the front door, but paused before leaving. He pulled Nicole into his embrace, holding her to his chest, as was their customary parting. Nicole hugged him, feeling his strong arms around her shoulders and his broad chest against her cheek. For the space of a heartbeat, they clung to each other.

Then slowly, as Marcus eased away from her, he placed a quick yet tender kiss to the corner of her mouth.

"See you Monday morning." He stepped out the door and did not look back.

Nicole lingered in the doorway, watching his retreating form, her fingers hovering over the spot on her face where he'd kissed her. That one small, gentle peck seemed to mean more than all of the previous kisses. *I'm not falling for him.* Slowly, she closed the door.

Chapter Four

"SHIT."

Nicole buried her face in her palms, sucking a deep breath into her lungs. *This is a mistake.* Maybe one of the biggest mistakes she'd ever made, but damn, she wanted him. She wanted Marcus, and the ache between her legs sure as hell wasn't going away until she had him.

The warning bells were getting louder with each passing day. She'd started this affair for the sole purpose of getting laid, but now she feared it was more. Much more. With Marcus accepting the job in Atlanta, she'd at first thought her timing was perfect—the no-strings would be easy to maintain.

"What's wrong with me?" she murmured. She'd made it through four years of college and then law school, filled with enough dedication to spend many nights writing briefs, tediously poring over evidence files for hours, and had rarely lost her concentration. Now her body seemed to be in complete control of her mind. Every free thought spun right back to Marcus and her need to see him, to be with him, to have him hot and hard, deep inside of her.

Inhaling a second deep breath, Nicole lifted her head and opened her eyes to the dim interior of her overpacked garage. Turning the key in the ignition and pressing her thumb to the button on the garage-door remote, she knew she had to see Marcus. She gripped the steering wheel as she watched the metal door slide up, trying to think of some excuse for going to his house.

Glancing at the clock on her dash, she read the illuminated green numbers: 11:05, seven long hours before he was due to arrive for their ritual movie night. Nicole smiled. Since their first time, the last four weekends had been a lot less about watching movies and a whole hell of a lot more about having sex.

"And damn good sex, too," Nicole stated. *A girl doesn't always want it at the same time of the day.* Putting the car in gear, she eased out of the garage.

Nicole slid on her new pair of sunglasses, adjusted her seat belt, and looked both ways before she pulled into the light traffic. She listened to the deejay's deep voice pump through her speakers, giving her just the excuse she'd been looking for—to borrow Mary J.'s newest CD. She knew Marcus had it. He'd been telling her how great it was since their Wednesday-morning workout.

Feeling better about going over there with a reasonable explanation, she glanced at the rearview mirror, then changed lanes, making the turn leading to Marcus's condo. Less than ten minutes later she pulled into his condo's parking lot. Nicole checked her makeup in the rearview mirror. She thought about the condoms, which were already becoming more difficult to find, hidden in the Kisses in the rose cookie jar. Slipping the square packet from her purse pocket, where it had been stuffed between real estate brochures, she then slid it into the side slot of her car door.

Feeling heat lick across the skin on her cheeks, Nicole knew that showing up with condoms stuffed in her pocket would mean only one thing to Marcus: She'd come for sex. And although she truly had, she felt a little embarrassed to admit it. Hell, she couldn't even wait until tonight. She was a junkie, and she needed her fix.

Nicole left the car without looking back, flicking on the alarm as she mounted the stairs to his second-story place, glancing once toward his covered parking spot to make sure he was home. She smiled when she saw his shiny black truck.

A bit self-conscious of her figure, Nicole shifted her hips, running her hands over the thin cotton of her summer dress, adjusting the thin straps so the sloping neckline showed little more than the shadowed valley between her breasts.

Taking a calming breath, she pressed her finger to the silver button of the bell, then held her breath as she waited for Marcus to appear. A second later the door was pulled open. He stood just inside the entrance, holding the edge of the door with one hand and a folded newspaper in the other.

"Hey, Nic. What are you doing here?" His eyes were round with surprise, but his wide mouth turned into a pleasant grin.

"I was out and I thought I'd drop by and say hi." She felt her throat go dry. "Hi," she said as she lifted her hand and gave him a small wave. *Why don't I just scream, "I came to screw you"?*

"Come on in." Marcus stepped back, giving her room to pass and allowing the springtime sunshine to filter into the dim interior of his condo. Golden droplets of light sparkled upon his naked chest.

Her attention was drawn immediately to what he was wearing, or the lack thereof. Wide, muscular shoulders, contoured pecs marred only by flat, brown nipples. Her gaze adored the line of hair creeping from his tapered abdomen beneath the waistline of his boxer shorts. Nicole bit back a groan as she lifted her eyes back to his face. She didn't miss the fact that the bulge beneath the thin layer of his shorts began to rise.

"I don't want to bother you," she said.

"No bother. I've got on ESPN." He lifted the paper. "I was just checking the stats on a few college players who will be getting drafted today." He waited for her to enter before he closed the door and walked toward the kitchen. "Do you want a cup of coffee?"

"No, thanks." She sat down facing Marcus as he moved around some boxes stacked in his open floor plan. Seeing his packed things took her aback. It was the first real proof she'd seen of his leaving. A knot tightened in her belly.

Nicole cleared her throat. "Do you have plans today?"

"Not really." He poured himself a cup, then glanced back at her. "You sure you don't want anything?"

Nicole thought she heard the hint of suggestion in his tone. *Hell, yes.* She wanted something, all right. Though it was steaming hot and a rich shade of brown, it wasn't coffee. The response made her nipples hard. It was Marcus, walking about mostly naked and supremely male.

She swallowed down the lust causing her throat to go dry. "Nah, I'm fine."

'"Yes, you are," Marcus said, appreciation thick in his tone. He came back to his glass table, turned a chair backward, and sat down, straddling the back. Resting his bare arms over the top, he made sure the cup of coffee didn't tilt.

Lust bloomed to full glory. Moisture wet her panties beneath the cotton of her summer dress. Her gaze drifted to the leg holes of his boxers, gaping wide open with the spread-thigh position he'd taken. The condo was too dim, and shadows hid the promise of pleasure behind his baggy undergarments.

Shaking her head, Nicole shoved aside the wanton within her and decided that spending time with Marcus could possibly cleanse her of her ever-present desire to have him sink inch by oh-so-ever-long inch inside of her. Moving from the arm of the couch, she slid into the seat beside him and glanced down at the spread of newspapers he'd scattered on the table.

Her gaze caught on the want ads and the listings of open houses being held that weekend. *That's where I need to be,* she thought with a repressed sigh. Why should she wait to start shopping for her new life? Her dream house was out there, waiting for her. Roving over the paper, her eyes traveled to the sports section.

As a player's agent, Marcus had high stakes in who got drafted and in what round. "Any prospects?" She shifted the paper so she could read a list of names, some of which had been circled with red ink. She recognized a few of the names from sport shows and magazines.

"Yeah. A few. I met with Jay Evans a few weeks back. I think he should go early in the first round." Marcus shrugged. "He'll sign with me once I've moved. Wants the name Dynamic behind his agent, and the prestige the firm holds."

"That's the player we had dinner with last month?"

Marcus nodded.

There was silence for a moment before Nicole went on: "I guess most of the big-name players don't want an agent who works on his own in a cow town like Sacramento." She didn't mean it as a question, but hearing the regret in her voice, she attempted to distract herself by glancing down at the paper. "Jay's hot."

"Hot?" Marcus asked, arching a dark eyebrow.

"Er, a good player."

Marcus smiled. The midnight shade of his eyes sparkled as if full of stars. "He's good, all right. I haven't seen a young kid with feet or hands like his in a while. I can't wait to see what he gets done in the NFL."

"So now you wait and see what number he gets drafted?"

"Pretty much. Once I'm his agent, it'll make a difference in the contract we negotiate. I'm waiting on a call. Once it comes in, we can go get some lunch if you're hungry."

"Okay. I'm pretty hungry."

"Oh, yeah? What did you eat this morning?"

"Nothing. I went for a run and forgot all about breakfast." Nicole glanced away as warmth spread long fingers of pink across her cheeks. Just being close to Marcus did silly things to her insides, making her feel nervous and excited, sensual and frustrated all at once.

His strong hand touched her chin, his thumb turning her face back to his. He caressed her lower lip, his breathing husky, deepened with passion.

His slow decent to her lips was halted by the ringing of his phone.

It rang three sharp chirps before he tore himself away. A rush of disappointment hit Nicole in the gut as he turned, answering his cell and reaching for an open file. He jotted down notes as he spoke to the caller. *I've always hated cells. I'm getting rid of mine.*

His tone changed from bedroom to boardroom in a single beat of her heart. She heard his voice but didn't really hear his words or care about making sense of his side of the conversation. She watched his profile. His brows creased; then a grin widened his lush lips.

Lips that'd been about to kiss her moments ago.

Crossing her legs, Nicole tried to dull the ache between her thighs, knowing it would take more than that to sate her desires. She bit her bottom lip hard enough to feel a sting of pain, but even that didn't lesson the sharp edge of lust.

A few moments later Marcus folded his phone shut and slipped it onto the glass table with a slight click. "All's good." He rose, flipped the chair forward in one smooth motion, and slid it beneath the clear-top table. "Let me get dressed and we'll head out and find something to fill you."

Nicole gasped, catching the double meaning in his words.

He sauntered several feet down the hall toward his bedroom before he paused, tossing her a glance over his shoulder. Nicole met his gaze, tempted to rise and follow him. Determined to prove to herself she had a tiny shred of control, she held her breath as the moment was suspended between them.

The sizzle of awareness snapped when he turned away and disappeared behind his bedroom door. This was why she'd come; to be with Marcus. She should walk down the hall and catch him naked. Perhaps he was even waiting for her to join him.

A pulse of longing leaped to life as Nicole fought to catch her breath, which seemed to linger and burn deep in her lungs.

Marcus emerged minutes later wearing gray sweat shorts and a white T-shirt with a small Raiders logo above his heart. She knew he still loved the Raiders and wondered if he missed playing for them. Surely after three years of belonging to a team he must have been disappointed when an injury to his knee caused him to retire early. He should've had a longer career.

He'd used his business degree well, and opened an agency using both his name and his contacts within the organization to establish himself in the field. He'd done pretty well, despite being tucked away in a relatively small town like Sacramento, where professional sports graced the city with only the River Cats, the Monarchs, and the Kings. Well enough, in fact, that he'd garnered the attention of a large agency in Atlanta. *The job offer was too good to pass up,* she thought, understanding why he'd accepted it.

Nicole was proud of his accomplishments. She'd seen his struggle and knew what drive it'd taken to reach his dreams. Still, there was a small part inside of her that didn't want him to leave. But as his friend, she'd never ask him to stay. He had a right to pursue his aspirations. She wanted it for him, too.

"Everything all right? You still want to go eat?" he asked, giving her a quizzical look.

"I'm fine. Just daydreaming. Let's go."

"I'll drive," he said, snatching his keys from the counter.

"Sure." It was better he drove anyway, since she doubted she'd be able to concentrate on the road with him seated beside her and the need to touch him as strong as it was.

She followed him out the door, then waited while he locked up. He pressed a button on the key chain, unlocking the doors to his truck. He walked to her side, smiling as he opened her door. Nicole's heart flipped over in her chest. She knew she was in trouble. Deep trouble.

She pretended her heart didn't rev and slid into the seat. He went around the truck and slipped in beside her.

The music came on as soon as the engine purred to life, Mary J.—and Nicole's excuse to visit him. She smiled as Mary J. cried out a sensual song of making it in life without love, all on her own, but Nicole could feel the hint of loneliness in the singer's voice, which hit oh-so-close to home.

Marcus maneuvered the truck onto the street, then weaved his way through the traffic with expert skill.

"So what do you feel like eating for lunch?" he asked, tossing her a quick glance.

Nicole looked at him, one strong hand wrapped around the steering wheel, his finger tapping the leather binding in time with the smooth beat. The smile on his pronounced profile exuded charm.

"You choose," she replied. She knew what she wanted in her mouth, and it had nothing at all to do with food. "Drive slow."

Nicole pulled her shoulder belt and tucked it behind her, shifting in the seat so she could get closer to Marcus. She touched his thigh right where the hem of his shorts reached. Running her finger along the edge, she toyed with the material.

His fingers stopped tapping in rhythm with the beat, and instead held the wheel with a tight-knuckled grip. The bulge at his groin grew beneath the thick gray cloth, and she heard the faint shift in his breathing, a rasp of air leaving his lungs.

"You know, Marcus, you could take a long route," Nicole said, sliding her fingers up the material, feeling the bunching of his muscular thighs as she slowly skimmed up his leg toward the elastic waistband of his sweat shorts.

"What are you up to, Nic?" His breath was jagged.

"Going to lunch with a friend," she teased. She slid her hand under his loose T-shirt, running her fingernails lightly over his skin, feeling with the pads of her fingers the line of hair descending into his shorts. His stomach tightened, leaving a narrow gap at the top of his shorts.

She took advantage of the opening and slid her hand down, fingering the edge of his boxers beneath his shorts and the hard length of his cock that rose to meet her exploring hand. Knowing how aroused he was heightened Nicole's own desire. The need to touch him, to feel him, to taste him, became overpowering.

With the back of her hand she lowered the band of elastic keeping him bound, revealing the smooth, satiny head of his cock. She brushed her thumb over the small slit at the top, drawing out a pearl of moisture and a husky growl from Marcus. She used the tiny drop to dampen his skin. Biting her bottom lip, she wondered how it would taste upon her tongue.

"Damn, Nic. You sure know how to convince me to drive slow."
She saw him ease off the gas pedal and felt the decrease of mo-
mentum in the truck.

She shoved the shorts lower, allowing the full length of him to
be free, then curled her fingers around his shaft and stroked down
to the base and up again, drawing another bead of precum from his
erection. Again she swirled her thumb in it, using it as lubricant as
she stroked him, turning her hand as she cupped his balls.

"How's your concentration these days?"

He tossed her a quick glance. "Pretty good. Why?"

Nicole bent forward.

"Oh," Marcus groaned when her lips brushed against his flesh.

The skin on his head felt like satin on her lips. She lightly
brushed over him. Wanting to taste him, she opened her mouth and
closed around him. He smelled like soap and cologne and tasted
salty, heady, and masculine. She swirled her tongue over the ridge,
feeling his pulse throb against her lips.

Opening her mouth, she took him deeper—so deep he brushed
against the back of her throat, filling her with the heat of his solid
cock. She sucked as her tongue lapped against him, caressing the
curve of his width as she lifted her head, then lowered again, taking
him in, feeling the satin of his penis caress the roof of her mouth.

Insatiable, Nicole massaged his tightly drawn sac in the palm of
one hand. She used the other to stroke against his shaft, where his
length prohibited her from taking him in all the way. Up, then
down. She lifted until the shiny tip of his dick slipped from her wet
lips, her tongue running across his bathed flesh, her teeth nibbling
and nipping at him.

Moisture seeped from her sex onto her panties. She was hot, and
damned wet. But she wanted to please Marcus more than she
wanted to appease her own hungry flesh. Besides, she was getting
off just from the taste of him, the fullness of his hard flesh pressing
into her mouth, and the broken grunts and harsh pants escaping his
lungs. Her power heightened her arousal.

She rocked her body forward so her legs rubbed together, squeezing her thighs. The pressure of her tight muscles created a jolt of pleasure of her own, and she knew it wouldn't take much to push her over the edge to climax.

With an urgency kindled by her need to make him cum, Nicole leaned into him again. She felt his body tremble as he gave up control, while trying with desperation to keep focused on the road. He groaned from the center of his gut, a sound that nearly did Nicole in. She whimpered, allowing her lids to drift closed as she feasted upon his body. Her hardened nipples brushed the smooth leather of the seat.

Nicole wrapped her hand around the base of his erection, holding him still while she moved, using the undulations of the road to set her speed. She lifted her lips, catching the ridge where his sensation centered. A guttural sound escaped his lips. His uneven panting drove her wild. Tightening her lips, she amplified the pressure of her hand and increased the rhythm of her mouth.

"I'm going to drive us . . . into another car." Marcus paused to suck air between his teeth. "I can't drive . . . if you're making me . . . lose my mind," Marcus managed to say between jagged breaths.

Nicole felt the truck shift lanes. Lifting enough to whisper, Nicole teased him, "Stay away from big rigs; they'll be able to see right in."

"Yeah, and be jealous . . . as hell. I have to pull over . . . before I cause an accident."

She responded by taking him into her mouth again.

Marcus forgot about signaling as he shifted lanes, causing the car behind him to lay on the horn. He pulled into the empty parking lot of a business center deserted on Saturday.

Not caring how he angled, he stopped beneath a tree to shade them from the springtime sun, shifted into park, and dropped his hands from the wheel as he leaned his head back against his seat.

Glancing down at the back of Nicole's head moving in long, steady strokes up and down his cock, he wanted to touch her the way she touched him, to bury his erection within the welcoming folds of her tight, slick heat.

Her fingers caressing in time with her tongue, his muscles begged for release—release lingering like the ball of fire in the sky at sunset, just beyond reach.

He lifted his hand to her head and gently tucked a lock of hair behind her ear, then ran his thumb down the slope of her cheekbone to her damp, open lips encasing his dick. He had the urge to wrap his hands around his base and give a few quick jerks, ending his suffering, but the torment was pure heaven.

Dropping his hand away from her face, he moved to her shoulder, feeling the muscles in her neck work as she increased, then slowed her pace. He skimmed down her back, the thin material of her cotton dress the only thing keeping him from feeling the smoothness of her caramel skin. He lowered his hand and released his seat belt, then hers. She fell forward, her slight weight causing his thoughts to scatter.

His fingers found the bottom of her skirt and pulled it up, revealing a slip of pink lace panties. Not bothering to pull them down, he slid the narrow strip of cloth to the side and dipped his finger into a pot of melted milk chocolate, as tempting and as sweet as the purest candy he'd ever tasted.

Damn, he was close. "Did you bring any condoms?"

Nic paused. "Yeah, but I left them in my car."

"From the cookie jar?"

"Uh-huh."

"I'm close, Nic. I don't have any either."

"That's okay, Marcus," she murmured against him. One hand continued to stroke down his shaft while her other deft fingers caressed and massaged his balls. She pressed an openmouthed kiss to the head of his cock.

"We don't need a condom. I want to taste you. I want to feel the pulse of your climax throb against my palm." She stroked down his dick, slick and lubricated from the wetness of her mouth. "I want to taste your explosion, feel the heat on the back of my throat. I want to make you cum in my mouth." As if to put proof behind her words, she closed around him, drawing him deep and tightening the fingers around his shaft.

The climax ripped through his body, causing a roar of pleasure, pure and unabated, to pour from his chest. Hot, thick liquid jetted from his dick. "Ahh." His body was milked while the muscles in her throat caressed him as she swallowed. One hand became a fist; the other stilled with fingers halfway plunged into her vagina in search of the pearl of her clit.

Shaking from the power of his release, Marcus waited as the tilt of the world righted itself, until his mind recovered, until the pleasure surging through his veins abated enough for him to think.

"You're amazing, Nic," he said, his breathing uneven.

She lifted her head, her lush pink lips slightly swollen and shimmering with the remnants of how her mouth had made love to him. She smiled, the tip of her pink tongue running across her lower lip as she sat back, her face a strange combination of both satisfaction and strain.

"You liked that, huh?" she asked, her voice heavy with humor, husky with desire.

"Hell, yeah, I liked that. Come here." He placed his hand behind her head and dragged her forward, slanting his head as he claimed her lips. He tasted what remained of his sex, heard her slight whimper tinged with need. Her small hands gripped the front of his shirt as she rocked gently in his direction, a pace reminiscent of the one she'd used on his cock. He knew she needed fulfillment.

He released her lips and pulled away. A hungry plea escaped her. "Come here," Marcus said, placing his hands on her narrow waist, turning her so her back rested against his chest. He circled her body with his arms, one large palm coming to rest on her left breast. His thumb stroked across her pert nipple, drawing a shudder from her supple body.

"Does that feel good?"

"Yes." Her head to lolled to the side.

Marcus chuckled at her open invitation to nibble her slender neck, its tone a warm caramel. Not one to resist a beautiful woman begging to be touched, he lowered his head and pressed his lips to the pulse point on her skin, then kissed a light path to the hollow of her throat.

With one hand massaging her breast and tweaking her nipple, he dropped the second hand lower, back to the pool of moisture between her legs.

"You're wet, Nic. And hot." His fingers slid past the well-trimmed patch of hair to the damp folds protecting the treasure of her clit.

Parting her lips, Marcus slipped one finger inside the well of her body's liquid heat, then two, stroking and teasing. "I want you wetter," he said. The timbre of his voice had dropped, and although he was sated, blood rushed to his flesh again, leaving him half-erect with the new stirrings of arousal.

"Wetter?" she panted.

"Wetter. I want to feel your liquid fire on the palm of my hand. I want to make you cum." He turned his hand, keeping his fingers buried deep inside, his thumb finding the pearly bead of her clit and brushing against it. She trembled in his arms.

"Marcus," she whispered, her head rolling from side to side.

He rubbed against her again, pushing in a slow, steady rhythm. His fingers slipped from her, dragging wetness to the patch of hair, across her lips, then teasing the opening of her vagina before plunging back in.

"Marcus!" she cried out. Her voice was tight. Her body shook in his arms.

He knew her release was near. Knowing how close she was to climax, he gathered her tightly in his arms so that when she leaped off the crest of pleasure she'd know she wouldn't fall. With her body pressed close to his, he lowered his lips to her throat once more.

Spreading a dusting of kisses along the line of her jaw, Marcus circled his thumb around her clit two quick times. She exploded. Her body convulsed, each of the tiny tremors of her flesh gripping his buried fingers.

"Marcus?" Her voice was low and filled with wonder.

"I got you, love," he replied, enjoying the beauty of her release. From her profile, he could see the shadow of her long black lashes resting against her soft cheek, and her parted lips slightly trembling from the rush of orgasm.

Awed, Marcus had no idea he could take so much pleasure in getting a woman off; yet with Nicole he couldn't even imagine taking his own release and not offering her the same. It had never mattered to him before. But this was *his* Nicole. *My Nicole for now; she'll move on once I'm gone.* Was it jealousy that twisted in his gut?

Long minutes ticked by. The CD paused at the end before it started over again, reminding Marcus just how long they had been at play. When her breathing slowed to normal, she slanted her head and looked back at him, a shy smile flashing across her face.

It was the shyness that undid him. His Nicole, audacious and confident, successful and bold, felt shy about the intensity of her climax. Her wary glance tugged at his heart. Wanting to reassure her, he repeated his earlier appraisal: "You're amazing, Nic."

Her eyes sparkled. Tossing a glance back at him, she laughed, her brashness back. "You promised lunch, and I'm starving."

"So am I." Marcus realized just how hungry he was now that one appetite had been sated. Leaning forward, he placed a quick kiss on her lips before he turned away to right his clothing.

Nicole giggled as she shimmied her cotton summer dress down her hips. With her soft laugh the newness of lovers eased away, replaced by a time-tested friendship.

After they'd clicked their seat belts back in place, Marcus lowered the volume on the CD player. With one hand casually draped on top of the steering wheel, he asked, "So what type of food do you want?"

"Something close. I didn't realize just how hungry I was until now. Whatever, but make it soon."

"No problem." Marcus shifted the truck into gear and rolled away from the shade offered by the canopy of leaves into the brilliance of the springtime sun. He pulled into light traffic and cruised down the road, making a left at the following light.

A few blocks later he pulled into a small parking lot filled with cars before a small café. Round white tables were scattered upon the sidewalk, each with a large green-and-white umbrella offering protection from the sun. Guiding Nicole to the last empty table, he held out a chair for her to sit down.

"You know, I need to use the bathroom first. Order me a soda, okay?" Nicole smiled, waiting for him to nod; then she turned away.

Marcus sat down and watched her retreating backside, a perfect swell atop shapely, long legs. Her hips swayed as she walked, a come-hither siren's call. *Damn.* And he was lured to her like a bee to honey. *Bad analogy,* he thought, shaking his head. *A bear to honey, maybe? Nah, a bear to chocolate.* He grinned.

Easing back in his seat, he glanced around the café, noticing at once that he wasn't the only man who appreciated Nicole's beauty or her sexual appeal. Several men had their eyes glued to her rear end, and openly appraised her with lust written clearly on their faces.

A surge of anger filtered through his blood. Shaking his head, Marcus tried to cleanse his mind of the fierce possessiveness he felt toward Nicole. They were friends and had no strings attached. Despite the fact that they'd been making love every Saturday night for the last month, he had no claim on Nicole.

A few moments later Nicole returned and sat beside him. When the waiter arrived they ordered Cokes and cheeseburgers, with a big basket of fries. Chatting between bites, Nicole told him with animated eagerness about how her promotion to junior partner would change her duties at her law firm and give her a new office with a big window.

And then her face changed with her tone. A spark of passion

flared in her eyes as she told him of several women at the shelter she was representing.

With them both busy with their careers, Marcus had really missed just hanging out for the afternoon with her as they'd done so many times over the years. He'd yearn for this once he moved. Though the thought of asking her to move with him had played through his mind, he knew he shouldn't. He wouldn't ask her to leave her job. Her work was important.

Marcus stared at her profile, committing it to memory as she talked. He had to wonder what would happen once they were living three thousand miles apart.

"Marcus? Marcus?" she repeated.

His attention snapped to her face. "What?"

She flashed him a kick-ass sexy smile that rushed blood to his cock, leaving him fully erect again. *Can I not get enough of this woman?*

"I asked if you wanted to go for a walk."

"A walk sounds good."

They finished their meal, and Marcus paid the waiter, leaving a generous tip on the table.

Side by side, they walked down the narrow cobbled sidewalk, past the large glass windows of various shops, each displaying their wares. A cool breeze rustled the flowers planted in large wooden barrels at each section of the sidewalk, lifting the freshness of their blossoms into the air.

Still able to catch the hint of sex upon Nicole's skin when she walked close or brushed against him, Marcus had the desire to see her upon a bed of flowers, naked and waiting for him.

"Marcus," Nicole said.

He was so caught up in his fantasy of her, he hadn't even realized she'd stopped walking and stood gaping at a display of dresses in a shop window. He walked to her side, placing his hand on the small of her back, and looked at the simple pastel-colored gowns.

"They're pretty, aren't they? I really like the pale yellow."

He looked at the pale yellow slip of silk. Tiny white roses had been woven into the material around the short hem, short enough to show the glory of her legs. "Do you want to go in and try it on?"

For a moment he thought he saw a glimpse of whimsy in her rich dark eyes, but she shook her head no. "Actually, if you don't mind, I have a few things to do before you come over later. Could we head back?"

"Sure."

After walking back to his truck, they drove to his condo in silence, though on several occasions he caught her yawning.

Back in his parking lot, he walked her to her car, then folded her into his arms for their usual good-bye embrace. While he held her pliant, lush body to his, he flipped the back of her dress and took a peek at the tag. He couldn't help grinning when he saw it was a size six, remembering how hard she'd worked to get down from a size fourteen.

"I'll see you in a few hours," he said, helping Nicole into her car. He stood there watching as she drove away.

There was something he wanted to do. He'd skip watching the end of the draft and get an update on ESPN later. Once Nicole was out of sight, he turned back to his truck.

Chapter Five

HE COULDN'T STOP THINKING about her. Marcus stared at the steaming black fluid in his coffee mug, but didn't see coffee. Rather, the dark, rich brew reminded him of the color of Nicole's expressive eyes and the shimmering moisture in her gaze when she climaxed. A surge of blood hit him in the groin. He was in trouble, and smart enough to know what a fool he'd been to allow this to happen.

"What's her name, man?"

Glancing up, Marcus saw Jay approaching, a wide grin spread across his lips, like he knew just what Marcus had been thinking about. "Huh?" he asked, pretending he hadn't heard.

"The girl." Jay grabbed a towel from his bag and swiped the sweat from his face, then draped the terry cloth over his wide shoulders.

"Who's what girl?"

"You can't fool me. I've seen that look before. Don't forget I have brothers, all of them married. So are you going to tell me who she is?"

Marcus felt a lump form in his throat. Was he so obvious that this kid, fresh out of graduation, could see how he felt about Nicole? Did he have it smeared across his face like the remnants of a powdered doughnut? And just how did he feel about her?

Shrugging, he released a deep breath and pasted an easy, carefree smile on his face. Whatever he felt for her, he wasn't willing to share it with Jay. Or with anyone, for that matter. Hell, he didn't want to think about it at all. She wanted no strings, and that was exactly what he planned on giving her.

No strings, but a whole lot of sex.

"You got it wrong, man. I was thinking about looking for an apartment in Atlanta. I've been on the Internet searching, but it's hard to tell without going there." Marcus cleared his throat, then lifted his gaze to Jay's. "When I've started my new—"

"I'm signing with you," Jay cut him off. "I like you, man. I trust you can get me the contracts I want. I just need to know you have the power of a company like Dynamic behind you." He stuck out his hand to shake.

Marcus took hold and gave a quick pump. "You're a smart kid."

Jay laughed. "Yeah, a kid with the 49ers making offers. Hurry up and move, will you?"

Marcus nodded. His thoughts skittered back to Nicole and the upcoming end of their physical relationship. To ease the tension, he rolled his shoulders. "Don't sign anything they offer. I want to make sure we have a good attorney look at everything first."

Jay shrugged. "Do you have one in mind?"

"Yeah, Nicole Davis. Contracts aren't her usual thing, but she knows her stuff."

"Nicole? Why's that name ring a bell?"

"You met her. She went to dinner with us a few months back. She's a friend," Marcus replied.

"Right, the babe with tits made for licking and a body meant for sticking." Jay laughed as he stuck out his tongue and motioned as if he were licking an ice-cream cone.

Something tightened deep in Marcus's gut—something fierce and raw and angry. He curled his fingers into tight fists to keep from slugging his soon-to-be client.

"Hey, man, she's a lady, classy in every way. A little respect." Marcus hoped his demeanor didn't betray to Jay that he was full of shit, and it'd been Nicole he'd been thinking about earlier. Irrational as it was, he was angry.

He shouldn't be. The kid was playing around, the kind of talk often heard in locker rooms before and after games. The guys could joke about girlfriends, but no one made fun of wives. To him, Nicole was neither wife nor girlfriend, and he shouldn't have cared. He did. Precisely the problem.

"No disrespect intended," Jay said, putting up his hands, his wry grin reaching his eyes.

Feeling the sting of fury and having no one to blame for his anger but himself, Marcus nodded.

"Yeah, she'll do. Set it up." Jay chuckled. "By the way, if you're going to be setting something up, do you think you could hook me up with her?" He swooped to retrieve the bag, then fell into step beside Marcus as they walked away from the practice field, toward the parking lot.

"You don't need the hookup. Looks like you got some fans already," Marcus replied, tilting his head to where a group of college-age girls had gathered to watch Jay run a few plays. Relief washed over him.

Jay smiled. "Hey, let me know once you've moved. Then you can set up the meeting with the attorney. I'll catch you later," he said as he turned in the direction of his new admirers.

What the hell was wrong with him, feeling relief when Jay left and hadn't pursued the issue of being set up with Nicole? Grinding his teeth, he went back to his truck and slipped inside, then allowed his forehead to rest on the steering wheel. He inhaled, catching the lingering scent of her floating in the cab. The sweet scent of roses and the moist, feminine fragrance of her sex assaulted his senses and made his semiaroused cock stand full-mast.

Oh, yeah, he was a fool all right, but as long as those condoms lasted and until he moved, he planned to keep playing right along with this silly act of indifference, even though he knew he was in way too deeply over his head.

Chapter Six

THE SHRILL CRY OF THE ALARM CLOCK blasted the silence of dawn. Nicole woke with a start, her head pounding. Reluctantly tossing back the covers, she stalked to the kitchen, not bothering to turn on any of the lights. She opened a cabinet, dumped two white tablets into her palm, and reached for a glass. Once she'd swallowed, she grabbed the phone and dialed. It rang twice before the service answered.

"Law Offices."

"Lydia, it's Nicole Davis."

"What can I do for you, Miss Davis?"

"I need my appointments for today rescheduled. While you're at it, do the same for tomorrow. I won't be in."

"Should I forward your calls?" asked the night receptionist, who worked graveyards to field emergency calls from clients facing dangerous situations.

"No. Let voice mail pick up. I'm not feeling very well and not up to talking to clients," Nicole replied, resting her forehead against the cabinet, the cool wood a welcome relief.

"Would you like me to make you a doctor's appointment?"

"That's all right. I think I just need some sleep and a couple of Tylenol. I'll be back Monday."

"I'll inform the partners."

"Thanks."

"My pleasure. Is there anything else I can do for you?"

"That should cover it," Nicole answered, allowing her lids to drift closed. She was so tired; sleep beckoned.

"Okay, then, take care of yourself and get some rest."

"Thanks," Nicole repeated, then clicked off the phone. Dragging in a deep breath, she wearily retraced her steps back to her room. In the faded light of morning, the room appeared gray, the half-closed blinds filtering the brightening light of the sun emerging from the eastern horizon. She spun the blinds all the way closed, turned off the ringer on the phone, and fell back into bed.

When Nicole awoke again, the room was alight with sunshine despite the protest of the miniblinds and sheer window coverings. She glanced at the clock: 11:43. *At least the headache's gone.*

It felt decadent to be sleeping when she should've been at work. She laughed into her pillow as she rolled onto her side and snuggled into the warmth of her bed. But sleep didn't come again. The pleasure of oversleeping vanished at the memory of her and Marcus's parting after having worked out the previous night.

So powerfully different from their other farewells, Marcus's impassioned good-night kiss still loitered on her palate. Their mouths had met, searing, yet tender. He'd lingered, his tongue touching her lips, but not bold enough to enter. It'd been a mere caress, a devotion-filled brushing of lips. A melding of souls.

It left Nicole shaken. Soon it'd be a kiss good-bye.

What was I thinking? I set up the rules, and I've broken every one.

In Marcus's wrinkled button-down workshirt, she stood and stretched her arms above her head. The rumpled cotton was soft against her skin. She lifted the collar and inhaled, the masculine scent assailing her.

Like Marcus—spicy, slightly musky, Polo cologne, Ivory soap, and—*oh, God;* tears sprang to her eyes—so familiar it was like being home. Like strong arms and an even stronger presence. Like love.

I'm in love with him. Her knees weak, Nicole collapsed onto the bed behind her and buried her face in her palms. When had she begun to love him? *When have I not,* she chided herself. She'd always loved Marcus; for six years he'd been her closest friend. But it was not friendship tightening her heart. It wasn't the love of a friend that suspended her breathing.

Why did I let this happen?

Minutes ticked by. The air burned in her lungs, the ache returning behind her temples. The simple game of mutual pleasuring had turned serious. Lifting her head, she studied her reflection in the mirror. She was a woman, almost thirty, without a man to call her own. But she couldn't risk losing her best friend. Ever.

Despite the distance of miles that would separate them when he moved to Atlanta, they'd always remain friends. He must never know of her feelings, for he certainly didn't feel the same. Sex just for sex—friends always.

Secure in her resolve to neither tell Marcus how she felt nor change their present relationship, Nicole shoved Marcus's shirt beneath her pillow and headed for a shower. *Focus on the physical. Forget what's in your heart.*

Once she was dressed, Nicole checked the voice mail at her office. Two messages—both from Marcus. Punching her code, Nicole listened to Marcus's deep voice over the phone.

"Hey, Nic. I'm headed out of town for a couple of days. Seems the Atlanta Hawks are ready to talk business and offering Brian Brook the figure I requested. I'm staying an extra night, since I'd like to check out a couple of apartments. I'm taking a red-eye home Friday. Have breakfast with me Saturday morning? See you then. Bye."

Breakfast? *Definitely.* She smiled. *I'll make you breakfast in bed,* she thought as she waited for the second message. Nicole bit her lip. In bed? After all these weeks they'd never had sex in either of their beds. Being in bed with Marcus would've been too close to making love; perhaps they'd both subconsciously avoided it—choosing the floor, the sofa, and his truck instead. Bed would be far too risky to her emotional well-being.

Marcus's voice began again.

"Nic, check your front door when you get home."

Nicole grinned like a schoolgirl playing hooky. She wasn't supposed to be home. She felt naughty as she pressed number three to save both messages. Hanging up the phone, she made her way to the front door.

Nicole glanced down at her stoop, where a box neatly wrapped in white paper with swirls of pink tea roses and a big pink satin bow sat on her top step.

"Marcus," she said, bending to pick up the gift. She went inside to open it, setting the small card to the side before reading it. She opened the gift and pulled the lid off the box.

There, secure in a frothy bed of white tissue, was the pale yellow dress she'd admired in the shop window. Tiny stitches of rosebuds lined the hem and the bustline. "Oh, Marcus." With a sigh, she lifted the silken material from the box. Her heart flipped; the earth felt unsteady. She glanced at the tag, the price thoughtfully removed, and saw that it was just her size.

Several times she'd thought about going back to pick up the dress, but the days were too short and her schedule too full.

Thankful, she clutched the smooth material to her. She'd show him her gratitude Saturday morning.

Grabbing the envelope she'd set on the table, she tore the seal and pulled the card from the encasing, then read: *You're beautiful.*

That was all—no signature, but she didn't need one to know Marcus had left it for her, easily recognizing the scrawl of his writing in those two simple, yet profoundly meaningful words.

Unable to squelch the rising emotion in her chest, Nicole carried the card and the dress to her room. She slid the card beneath her pillow, joining his shirt for later enjoyment, then hung the dress on a hanger on the outside of the closet door so she could see it whenever she entered.

Feeling lighthearted, Nicole called her mom and set up a late lunch date. They met at their favorite Indian restaurant, and spent several hours catching up over the meal.

That evening, Nicole gobbled up a to-be-read book on her night-stand. With the alarm left off, she slept in for a second time. She spent the next day in the garden, finishing her book, and tidying her house.

But by Friday night Nicole was restless. She could hardly wait for Marcus to return. She missed his smile. His scent. His whis-pered words and subtle innuendos. She missed Marcus.

With Marcus gone, Nicole got a glimpse of how life would be once he moved. They had no future but what remained of the con-doms in her rose-shaped cookie jar.

In the kitchen she found a fluted glass and opened a bottle of wine. She needed something to help her sleep. After having a cou-ple sips, she grabbed the ceramic rosebud cookie jar and tipped the contents onto the counter, counting what remained of her intimate relationship.

Eleven. Damn, that was it? Just under half of what they had started with? For a moment Nicole pondered the idea of restocking her supply. She doubted Marcus had been keeping track. But she dismissed the idea. They'd made a deal, a verbal contract, and, being an attorney, she knew she shouldn't breach it no matter how tempting.

She gulped the rest of her wine and refilled her glass.

Flopping onto the couch, she turned on a late-night video show and cuddled under a throw. Hours passed before she was able to fall asleep.

A persistent tapping jarred her awake to the creeping gray light of dawn. She scurried to the door and yanked it open. Marcus stood on her stoop. A fine woven jacket hugged his broad shoulders, gray like the pale morning light, over a shirt a softer shade of the same color. The adorning necktie was printed with small Raiders em-blems—another of her gifts.

"Hi," he said, his voice husky.

"Hi, yourself. Come in here," she said, placing her hand on his forearm and drawing him into the house. In a stupor of wine and sexual frustration she'd forgotten about making him breakfast in bed. *Darn.*

As soon as he'd stepped inside the house he pulled her into his arms, wrapping her tightly to his chest. His mouth didn't find hers, but settled in the hollow of her throat, where he murmured softly against her skin. He held her there, secure in his embrace for several long moments. Slowly he released her and stepped away.

"Did the trip go well?" she asked, taking his hand and guiding him to the living room.

"Went off just as planned. We got the contract we wanted. The Hawks got the player. Everyone wins."

"You must be tired."

"Yeah, I'm beat. I also found a couple of nice neighborhoods I wouldn't mind living in."

Nicole nodded, ignoring the way fear made her pulse speed. "Have a seat and I'll make us some coffee."

"Sounds great, Nic." Marcus plopped down on the couch, kicked his feet up on the ottoman, and leaned his head against the plush pillows. "How was work?"

"I didn't go in the last couple of days," Nicole replied over her shoulder as she entered the kitchen. She started the coffee.

"Is everything all right?" His words were followed by a yawn.

"Yeah, I just needed a little R and R. It felt great. I even had lunch with my mom. My sister called yesterday. She'll be in town next weekend. We're going out Saturday night."

"Oh, yeah? Where?"

"Must Be Paradise. Her favorite club." Nicole found two mugs, then leaned against the counter while black liquid dripped into the glass carafe. "Hey, Marcus? Did you work out yesterday morning?" she asked loudly enough for him to hear her on the couch, feeling a bit guilty about missing their routine, especially after how long it'd taken her to get in shape.

"Not in the morning. Just before lunch a few of the guys and I went to the gym to shoot hoops. Those dogs are relentless, and throwing bows with them is a workout. Did you?" His husky mumbling faded.

"No. I slept in." She poured the coffee into two mugs, adding cream and sugar as she talked. "Actually, I felt funny about going to the gym without you. . . ."

Nicole lifted the mugs and walked into the living room, only to find Marcus fast asleep, the blanket she'd used draped over him. She put both mugs on the side table and sat down on the couch, careful to not disturb him. She slipped beneath the blanket, snuggling closer to his warmth and studied his profile, content to have him back in her arms no matter how brief their time would be.

Marcus glanced down upon Nicole's sleeping face, her body tucked into the crook of his arm. Her cheek rested against his chest, and one of her small hands was curled into a fist beneath her chin. With his arm adorning her shoulder, he couldn't resist the urge to tug her closer. She murmured softly but didn't awaken, before cuddling back against his side.

Though it wasn't the first time during their six-year friendship that they'd both fallen asleep on the couch, it was the first time it had felt so right. Hell, he wanted to wake every morning with her sleeping next to him, to awake every day gazing upon her beautiful face.

Despite the ever-present lust he felt for Nicole, he didn't want the day to be about sex. He wanted this day to be so special that even after he was gone, she wouldn't forget.

Slipping his hand into his pocket, he withdrew his cell phone and flipped it open, punching in the number to his friend.

"Chuck here," a gruff voice said when the ringing was answered.

"Hey, man, it's Marcus," he said, keeping his voice low. He was having one hell of a time forgetting about his throbbing hard-on with Nicole's leg draped over his thigh.

"How's it going?"

"Good. You know that thing we discussed last week?"

"Yup. You ready?"

"Yeah, can you get it set up now?"

Chuck laughed on his end of the phone. "Do you want pink or red roses?"

"Red. You have everything else, right?"

"I said I'd be ready, and I am." Chuck's laughter broke out again. "Do you want me to pop the cork, let it breathe?"

"Champagne doesn't need to breathe," Marcus replied, knowing his friend was giving him a hard time.

"I know that, man. I like harassing you. Don't worry, Marcus; you told me how you want it set up, and I'll have it ready."

"Good," Marcus said, then snapped the phone closed without saying good-bye.

Inhaling a deep breath, Marcus thought over his resolve to keep the day from getting sexual no matter how badly he wanted Nicole.

Nicole shifted, her hand drifting lower onto his lap. He bit back a groan, his arousal pressing sharply against the fly of his gray slacks as the woman he desired wiggled, all soft and feminine against him.

He caressed her cheek. His fingers followed the shell curve of her ear, traced the line of her lips, hovered over her long, dark lashes resting peacefully upon her perfect brown skin. Marcus tightened his hand on her shoulder and nudged.

"Nic, time to get up, love. Come on, sleepyhead." When Nicole didn't rouse at first, he was tempted to let her sleep. But he was eager to get on with it. He'd been planning this for weeks, just waiting for the perfect moment. No time like the present.

"Nicole Davis, this is your get-up-and-get-'em call. I've got plans for us."

"What kind of plans?" she whispered, burrowing into his side and refusing to open her eyes.

"To get something to eat and go for a ride."

Nicole sat up, blinking her eyes. "A ride?" she asked, her voice dropping to a seductive purr.

"Yes, a ride." Marcus shoved off the couch before smoldering turned to fire. Standing, he stretched his arms over his head, easing the tension in his shoulders and neck. It'd been a long couple of days and an even longer plane ride to get home.

"Let's get out of here; I'm starving," he said, brushing the wrinkles from his jacket. "I just need to get my bag from my truck and change into a pair of jeans. You going to get dressed?"

Nicole rose slowly, arching her back like a cat, then strode toward her bedroom. Twenty minutes later she emerged wearing the pale yellow silk dress he'd left for her on the way to the airport. The lines of the dress perfectly complemented the swell of her breasts and the narrowness of her waist. The fine material clung to each of her lush curves, shimmying down her body to fall midthigh, with a hem intertwined with the brocade dusting of roses.

With her hair pulled into a loose bun, black ringlets fell around her face and tumbled down her back. Her legs were freshly covered with a rose-scented lotion that made her brown skin shine as if it had been sprinkled with glitter.

"You're beautiful." His voice was husky with awe. She certainly did the dress justice.

"Thank you," she replied, her gaze dropping to the floor and a becoming blush covering her cheeks.

He cleared his throat, and she looked up, her eyes reflecting a fathomless amount of emotion. "Do you like it?"

"Do you need to ask?" She closed the distance between them. "I love it. Thank you." She lifted on tiptoe and pressed a kiss to the corner of his mouth, but stepped back just as he reached for her.

"My pleasure. I knew it'd look great on *you*. We should get going. I'll drive." Marcus walked to the front door, holding it open as she went past. *I can't wait to see her face when she sees what I've planned.*

Once they were out the door, he placed his hand on the small of her back and walked her toward his truck. "Let's go for a drive."

"All right," she said. "But I thought you were hungry."

"I am, and we'll stop for something to eat in a little while."

Marcus started the truck, keeping the music low so they could talk, but neither said anything as he got on Interstate 80 and headed east.

With his gaze shifting from the freeway to her bare legs to the perfect profile of her delicate face, Marcus had the overwhelming sense of belonging.

He exited on Douglas Boulevard and headed toward Folsom Lake.

"Where are we going?" Nicole asked, turning away from the window.

"To Folsom Lake."

Nicole laughed. "We're hardly dressed for swimming."

"We could go naked."

"Marcus, it's May, and way too chilly for what you have in mind. If your offer were a hot tub, we'd have a deal."

"I'm just playing," he replied with a laugh, settling his hand on her thigh just below the hem of the silk. Her skin was warm and soft beneath his fingertips. Nicole scooted in his direction.

Douglas Boulevard narrowed as they drove through Granite Bay. On each side of them were narrow streets where the houses were large and the neighborhoods established. Giant maple trees hugged the paved roads, their sweeping canopies acting as an umbrella from the brightness of the sun, and sending a dappling of light onto the shaded ground.

Vast yards, lushly green and carefully manicured, dressed with white picket fences, spread out on all sides of them. Birches and cottonwoods lined each snaking black driveway, and set off in the shade, emblazoned with beds of flowers, were homes, all well kept and expensive.

Nicole had always loved this neighborhood. With longing, she stared at the wonderful homes, watching as a gray squirrel scampered up a tree and a blue jay took flight. But something else caught her eye, a scattering of FOR SALE signs that graced a yard here and there.

Glancing down at her purse, she thought about the slightly crumpled brochures of homes on the market that she kept tucked away in case she was ever in the area to check them out.

Sliding her gaze back to Marcus, she asked, "Do you ever plan on getting married, Marcus?" *I hope I sounded natural.*

He startled, as if the question had taken him off guard, but he kept his eyes fastened to the road and shrugged. Silence filled the small cab, a moment of tension, a hint of sexual awareness, then was replaced with the comfort of longtime friends.

"I guess I do. What about you?" he finally answered.

"Yeah, I do. I guess you could say I want it all, Marcus." She tried to laugh, but it ended up sounding like a sigh. Either that or a sob. She wanted these things with Marcus, but knew it would never be. She thrust her palm out, making a sweeping gesture to the houses outside. "You know, a husband, two-point-five kids, white picket fences . . ." With an ache in her heart, she went back to gazing out the window. "A dog, maybe. A cat."

"Yeah, that'd be nice."

Nicole held her breath for a moment, worrying her bottom lip between her teeth. "Marcus, I need a favor."

"Anything," he replied immediately.

"I'm selling my house." She'd meant to talk to him about this before, but the timing had never felt right. "I'm not content living downtown anymore. I want something bigger. A place where I can have an office, someday room for kids. I'm ready for something more permanent, long-lasting—secure."

"I know what you mean. So what can I do to help?"

Don't go! she wanted to scream. *Stay here! Be with me!* Gulping, Nicole turned her head away, refusing to let him see the arrival of tears. He had to pursue his dreams, just as she had to. She had an established law practice, but she could easily relocate, if only he'd ask. There were women all across the country who could use her help. Sacramento or Atlanta didn't matter to her.

Drawing a breath to steady her tone, she looked back at him. Her voice quavered slightly before she corrected it. "I have a list of homes for sale in this area. Maybe you could come with me to look at a few today?"

He flashed her that sexy-as-hell half grin of his, the one that made his dimple prominent, then finished it up with a wink. "I'd love to. But do you think we could eat first? I'm starved."

When Nicole nodded, Marcus turned the truck onto the road leading to Folsom Lake. Within a few moments they neared a private beach. In a patch of sunshine stood a picnic table, covered in white linen cloth.

Giggling, Nicole leaped from the truck as soon as it rolled to a stop, and skipped toward the table. "Oh, Marcus, what have you done?"

"I wanted you to know I missed you," he replied with a sheepish grin.

Nicole banded her arms around his neck, pressing a kiss to his full lips. "You couldn't have planned all of this, this morning." Her gaze dropped to the table, where fluted glasses lingered alongside strawberry baskets and fresh red roses.

Marcus chuckled. "Nope, not this morning. I always miss you when you're not around."

Marcus heard the hitch in her breathing. Stepping from her embrace, he moved them toward the table. Once she was seated, he served her the ham-and-cheese omelets from the white carry-out boxes, still warm from when Chuck left them. He mixed the champagne with orange juice, then settled beside Nicole.

They laughed and talked as they ate, feeding each other, kissing between bites. The sun was overhead by the time they finished eating breakfast, and Marcus was completely enlightened. He was head over heels in love with this woman. *I'm supposed to move and leave her behind? She's going on without me, fool,* he berated himself, thinking of the bigger house she wanted to buy and the husband who wouldn't be him.

He cleared his throat as he repacked the box of supplies, cleverly hidden under the table. "So how about looking at some houses? You have the list handy?"

"Yeah, sure," she answered, fishing in her purse for the papers.

"Choose one and we'll call the agent and see if we can get a look inside."

"Do you think we can?" she asked, her milk-chocolate eyes warming.

"Probably. Which one do you want to see?" He waited until she'd touched her fingernail to the paper, then pulled the cell from his pocket and punched in the agent's number. The real estate agent readily agreed to meet them at the address.

It took them only a few minutes to drive from the lake to the house. The agent, a middle-aged man, arrived about twenty minutes later and opened the lockbox on the front door.

The entry was covered in Italian porcelain tiles, flanked with dark hardwood floors that ran throughout the rest of the first level. The ceilings vaulted to the second floor, and a gently curved staircase swept upward. The room was bright, floor-to-ceiling windows allowing in the brilliance of the clear spring sky.

As they walked through the house, the agent pointed out features: marble countertops, a walk-in pantry, chef's stove, paneled refrigerator doors that made the appliance blend in with the mahogany cabinets. There was an office—complete with DSL and cable-wired—a guest suite including full bathroom, a library, a den and family room, as well as a formal dining room.

In all, there were 5,500 square feet, which included six bedrooms total. The click of Nicole's sandals against the tiled floor in the master bathroom drew Marcus's attention.

When he reached her side she stood motionless, not looking at the bathroom but staring past the mirrored wall above the sinks to a walk-in closet damn near the size of his condo. The walls were lined with mesh organizational baskets and several tiers of hanging rods.

"Marcus, I love this house. I can afford it." She gulped, but her gaze didn't waver from the closet. "But I'm alone. This place is big," she whispered, her hand instinctually gripping his without so much as a glance down.

He almost laughed, and would have if she didn't sound so down. After all her oohs and aahs over this house, the closet was what had sealed the deal in her mind. So typically womanly. So feminine. So Nicole.

He grumbled a comment, hating to see her not have everything she wanted. No matter how sexist it sounded, to him a home reflected the woman. He liked this house, too. It suited Nicole well. But then images flashed in his mind of her raising children and playing wife to another man. Pain seized his heart. *And where will I be? Moved on with my life,* he realized sadly.

"You want to keep looking? I'm sure there's something smaller on your list."

She shook her head no, her gaze still intent on the huge closet. "I'm alone," she repeated. "I think I was wrong. I don't need a bigger house. Not now anyway. I've changed my mind."

Shrugging, Marcus huffed. *What just happened here?* Why did Nicole suddenly look so sad despite the fact she'd damn near glowed while looking at the rest of the house? He searched the gigantic, bare closet for an answer, but found only an empty space. Placing his hand on the small of her back, he said, "Come on; we should get going."

Nicole reluctantly turned away, then fell into step beside him as they retraced their way out of the house. They met the agent outside.

They shook hands. "We'll be in touch," Marcus said, opening

the door for Nicole to get in. A few minutes later he was seated beside her, and they were driving away from the house she'd obviously adored.

Marcus headed back toward downtown Sacramento, the freeway starting to fill with late-afternoon traffic.

"Do you want to stop by and pick up a few movies before we get back to my house?" Nicole asked softly when they got off the freeway.

"I know it's Saturday night, Nic, but I haven't been home since Thursday and have a few things I need to take care of. I'd come see you tomorrow, but I'm playing golf with the fellas."

"Oh, okay." The disappointment in her tone tore at his heart.

"Nic, I'll make it up to you, I promise." He gave her a quick kiss, then was gone.

Chapter Seven

NICOLE KNEW she had to put some distance between Marcus and herself, especially after the crazed incident where she'd just about had a panic attack staring at an empty closet. It was the emptiness that had gotten to her. She loved everything about the house, except that it came without the most important thing: Marcus.

He'd be long gone by the time she went to her closing. Better to suffer his loss in her old home, where they had good memories. She didn't want the big house to remind her what she'd forfeited when Marcus moved to Atlanta.

She needed a distraction from the melancholy thoughts of her best friend and short-term lover. Taking a sip of her peach margarita, Nicole was relieved by the muddled fog of tequila and grateful to be out with Natalie.

Spinning the barstool, she scanned the crowd for her sister. She found Natalie on the dance floor, shaking her hips, bumping and grinding with a decent-looking guy in his midtwenties. *What am I doing here?* Nicole asked herself. *This place is a meat market. I'm too old for this shit.*

The heated wash of alcohol seeped into her blood, warming her bare legs and tamping down the miserable self-pity. The sensual, soulful rhythm of the music vibrated off the walls and bounced back at her. The throb of the crowd created a dizzying effect that had them swaying and pulsing in time with the bass blaring from the five-foot speakers.

Nicole slid from her barstool, then made her way through the throngs of gyrating couples, past the bumping and grinding, to where her sister grooved on the dance floor.

"Nat, I'm going out to get some air."

Natalie paused in her dancing, putting her hand on her partner's shoulder to slow his slick moves that a slightly younger crowd considered dancing. "You all right?" she asked.

"Yeah, I'm fine. Go back to your dancing." Nicole turned, intent on finding the closest exit, but a firm hand on her upper arm halted her progress.

"Don't leave, gorgeous. Dance with me." Nicole was yanked into the arms of a stranger. Good-looking though he might be, he was no Marcus. *Damn.*

Placing her palms against his chest, she eased away, putting a good distance between them. "Not right now; I need some air," she shouted back, to be heard over the volume of the sensual song pounding through the room. She bit her lip, realizing that was the wrong thing to say to a brother who'd zeroed in on hitting on her.

"Some air? You shouldn't go outside alone. Don't you know it's not safe?" He smirked. "I'll go with you." His hand was back on her upper arm. His fingers caressed her skin through the thin material of her silk blouse.

Nicole fought the urge to roll her eyes. It was so typical of a man to want to follow her out into the dark and hope to have his way with her. It wasn't going to happen, not tonight—not with her.

"Let's dance," she returned, starting to sway her hips in beat with the bass and the soft hum of male voices harmonizing. She'd give him the rest of the song, then make her escape—alone. She glanced at her sister getting a bit freaky with the guy she'd been dancing with. Natalie didn't look like she'd be ready to go for a while.

For the rest of the song, Nicole avoided the man by dodging his groping hands like they were lobster claws. His not-so-subtle winks and thrusts of his hips gave her the creeps.

It was hard to imagine how fun this had been a few years back. Now, despite the soothing affects of two shots of tequila and two peach margaritas, she wanted nothing but the quiet of home, the warmth of a bubble bath, and the passion she felt in Marcus's arms.

"Thanks for the dance," she said, easing away and slipping between two bodies before he could stop her. She made her way to the perimeter of the room, deciding that outside might not be the safest place, particularly if she might run into more fools with over-practiced pickup lines.

Feeling the light-headed effects of her drinks, she closed her eyes, tilting her head to the side. The sensual, passionate call of the music guided her in a gentle movement that tilted her hips and rocked them back and forth. She could see the words, a picture behind closed lids, a fantasy of lovemaking. Silken white-sand beaches, cool ocean breezes, the sun melting her in the arms of a lover.

She felt the body behind her too late. Strong arms folded around her shoulders. Nicole started, engulfed by a powerfully possessive grasp, and was pulled up against a chest as firm as the wall had been. But the quickening of her heart, the strangled breath of fear, quickly changed to excitement, for her body recognized the masculine frame wrapped around her. Heat churned in her belly, her nipples hardening to peaks.

Marcus.

"You're beautiful," he whispered against the slope of her neck.

Heat sped down her arms to the tips of her toes and rushed to her core, making her wet with desire. The liquor hummed in her system, the light buzz magnifying her emotions. Leaning back in his embrace she could feel his long shaft, hard against her bottom. A giggle burst from her lips.

"Marcus, what are you doing here?" she asked, leaning her head back onto his shoulder so she could see the profile of his handsome face.

He took advantage of her exposed neck and nibbled on her skin, spread a dusting of kisses that felt like the flutter of hummingbird wings against the base of her throat. His tongue brushed against her pulse point before he answered.

"You mentioned where you and Natalie were going last weekend. I had to decide between a pickup game at the gym or coming here. Luckily, I chose right." His long fingers fanned out over her lower belly and dragged her even closer against him. She went willingly deeper into the security of his embrace.

"Luckily?" she asked.

"Mm-hmm . . ." he mumbled, kissing a path from the hollow of her throat, his tongue gliding over her skin until he reached her ear. Drawing the soft, fleshy part of her earlobe into his mouth, he bit down, then swirled his tongue against her sensitive flesh.

The rumbling of his voice when he spoke against her sent a quiver down her spine to join the rising desire that dampened her panties and made her knees weak.

"Luckily, because I missed our movie night. Two whole weeks without . . . Damn, girl, I needed to see you."

Needed? Needed was not the word she would have liked him to use. How about *wanted*? Yeah, *wanted* to see her would have been nice, but flush against his rock-solid body, his arousal pressing into the small of her back, and his strong arms wrapped around her, she'd take whatever she could get, weak though that might be.

Marvin Gaye's "Let's Get It On" began to play.

"Come on. Let's dance," Marcus said, stepping away from her, then grabbing her hand and leading her through the crowd of couples to the center of the dance floor. He spun her, bringing her firmly against his chest, his large, possessive hands settling on her hips.

With his strong pecs rubbing against her breasts, the lace of her bra felt wickedly erotic upon her skin. *I'd like to have his tongue there instead.* His erection pressed to the apex of her thighs and brushed against the patch of hair protecting her clit. Shafts of pleasure tore through her body, causing Nicole to melt into his embrace.

"Let's get it on," Marcus whispered into her ear, as he swayed their bodies like blades of grass in the wind.

She balled her fist and jabbed him in the side. "We're in the club."

"So." He claimed her mouth, his kiss thorough, hot, and demanding, laden with repressed need. They stopped dancing, yet stood locked within each other's tender embrace, feasting upon passion.

She could taste the beer on his breath—Corona with lime—and smell the subtle hint of his cologne. She couldn't stop kissing him. She didn't want to, yet she knew damn well that the effects of the alcohol she'd consumed loosened her inhibitions. She shouldn't be kissing him so wildly standing in the middle of a bar. It wasn't like her.

But just as she was about to protest, he slowed the kiss. His lush lips moved away from her mouth to kiss the skin below her ear. She giggled when he starting humming along with the words of the song.

"Marcus, stop." Damn, she knew her tone hardly sounded convincing. She wasn't convinced. Her body screamed for him to go on.

"Why?" he asked, pressing kisses to her skin between the words of the melody.

"We're supposed to be on the down-low," she responded, rolling her head to the side to allow him better access to her neck. *Yeah, that's convincing.* She trembled when one of his hands slid between their bodies and cupped her breast. His thumb stroked across her hardened nipple.

"Down-low, huh?" He licked her skin. "I don't remember that being part of the arrangement."

"My sister's here." Nicole hated the breathy way her voice sounded, but couldn't deny how he was making her feel. As though she'd had more than just the two shots of tequila—like sipping fine wine.

"Natalie looks busy to me," he replied, slanting his head in the direction of Nicole's sister, slow-dancing with the same guy as before.

"She's drunk. I should get her home before she does something she'll regret," Nicole said, turning her head so her cheek rested above his heart. She took comfort in the steadiness of his pulse.

"Yeah, we should get her home. I'll drive you two."

"I brought my car."

"Then we'll pick it up in the morning."

"I guess you're right. I drank more and faster than I'd planned."

Marcus smoothed a palm down her back, then slowly retraced his path to her shoulders. "Let's get out of here."

Nicole nodded, leaning away from Marcus as she reached through the crowd to tap her sister's back, hollering to be heard above the din. "Nat, it's time to go."

Natalie stepped away from her partner. "Hey, Marcus, I didn't know you were here."

"I just arrived. How've you been, Natalie?"

Heat spread over her cheeks as Nicole met her sister's questioning gaze. Natalie's eyes swept over Marcus's arms, possessively wrapped around Nicole's waist.

Natalie grinned knowingly, then turned back to Marcus. "I'm good. How about you?"

"Can't complain. You ready?"

"Just let me say good-bye. Oh, Byron, this is my sister, Nicole, and Marcus."

Byron grinned while shaking Marcus's hand. "Hey, you're Marcus Patton. You used to play for the Raiders, right?"

"Yeah, that's me. Come on, ladies; let's go."

Marcus nodded at Byron. With his hand on her back, he guided Nicole toward the exit door. Natalie quickly jotted her number for Byron, then followed them out.

The night air was crisp compared to the sultry club. A sprinkling of stars twinkled against the velvet backdrop of night above the city lights. Never having released her hand, Marcus still held her fingers intertwined with his as they made their way through the parking lot to his truck. Nicole could feel her sister's stare sizzling on her back, but his warmth was soothing despite the fact that she'd play Twenty Questions next time her sister got her alone.

Marcus unlocked the passenger-side door and held it open while Nicole slipped in and scooted to the middle. Natalie got in beside her before he shut the door and rounded the truck, getting into the driver's seat. He got on the freeway and headed east up 50 to Cameron Park, where their parents lived, and where Natalie was staying for the weekend.

Trying to sit up straight to avoid leaning into Marcus while he drove, Nicole listened to them chat about school classes and majors. Though tamed by her sister's presence, desire hummed in her system, intensified with every rub of her leg against his hard thigh, with every jostling of the truck that brought her into contact with him.

Maybe her intense need sprang from the fact that it had been two weeks since they'd made love. Or perhaps it was the knowledge that their time remaining was so limited. Awareness of Marcus beside her was like a potent drug to an addict. She needed him; she wanted him more.

Nicole was relieved when the truck pulled up in front of her parents' home and they all got out to say their good-byes. Marcus gave Natalie a quick hug, commenting on how nice it was to see her again, then got back in the truck to wait while Nicole walked her sister to the door.

"What's going on with you two?" Natalie asked.

"We're friends."

"You've been friends for years, but I've never seen him hold you like that before."

"We were dancing."

Natalie laughed. "Oh, dancing's what it's called now, huh? Holding hands in parking lots?"

"We're friends, Nat," Nicole stated, trying to keep the quaver from her voice.

"You know what they say: Friends make the best lovers."

Nicole forced a laugh of her own. *If you only knew.* "I'll keep that in mind." She kissed her sister's cheek, then skipped off the porch, heading back to the truck, where Marcus—her friend and *lover*—waited for her. "Tell Mama I'll come for brunch after church tomorrow," she tossed over her shoulder.

"Good night," Natalie said with a wink just before she stepped inside the door and disappeared into the shadowed interior of the house.

Nicole hurried into the truck, smiling at Marcus as she shut the door. The alcohol buzz had faded, replaced by the purr of sexual awareness.

Marcus could tell by the shimmer in Nicole's eyes what she intended as he pulled onto the road and retraced their tracks back to the freeway. Blood surged to his cock, making him pulse with want. Gripping the steering wheel, he glanced at her, her dark eyes glowing with hunger. Being in his truck was a cruel reminder of when she'd taken him into her mouth and nearly caused an accident.

When she shifted on the seat toward him, he put up his hand to stall her, though his dick bucked in protest beneath his denims.

"God, I want you," he said.

She flashed him a smile and licked her lush lips, so he added, "Not while I'm driving, Nic. If I drive like I did last time, I'm sure to get pulled over, and I've had a beer. Facing a cop with a hard-on and liquor on my breath probably wouldn't be such a great idea."

"You're right," she whispered. In the pale light of the full moon and the warm glow of the overhead streetlights they passed beneath, he could see a slight stain of blush cross her brown skin. Her gaze dropped to his lap and lingered.

"But you'll come in, won't you? You won't walk me to the door and then leave me wanting? Not like last week."

"No, Nic. Not like last week, I'll come in tonight." If she only knew what he had in store for her—but it was a surprise. He tried to lighten the stifling mood loitering in the truck's cab. He slid a glance in her direction, caught her gaze, then winked before he slanted his eyes back to the dotted yellow lines on the road. "Did I leave you wanting last week?" he teased.

"Um, yeah." She turned away, staring out the window, mumbling, "You're a cruel, cruel man."

"I promised I'd make it up to you. I don't break promises."

She shrugged but didn't say anything. After a while she broke the silence. "Natalie was asking questions."

"What kind of questions?" he asked, fighting back a smile.

"She kept hinting that there is something going on with us."

"There is."

"Yeah, but I know she'll think we're *involved*."

"And what would be wrong with that?"

Again, the cab was swathed in silence. The stereo had been turned down so low he could just hear the soft hum of music but not make out the lyrics. There was the sound of his tires moving over the pavement, and the muted sound of wind as they cut like a streak of metal through the spring night.

Nicole took a deep breath, then sighed. "But we're not involved. Not the way she thinks."

"What did you tell her?" he asked.

"I told her we were friends. But she didn't believe me. She thinks there's more to it."

"Nic, I don't care what she thinks. I don't care what anyone thinks. This is about us. You and me. About what *we* want. What's right for us." He looked at her again, hoping to see the brilliance in her eyes alight with the same joy he felt. It was like gazing into a mirror.

They drove without talking the rest of the way down Highway 50 and as he maneuvered the quiet streets of Nicole's quaint neighborhood downtown. When he pulled into her narrow driveway, he shifted to park and shut off the ignition. Bounding out of the cab, he rounded the truck and opened her door. Marcus took Nicole's hand in his, stroking his thumb across the smooth skin on her palm while he helped her out. Once her feet were on the ground he pulled her into his embrace.

He whispered into her ear, "This feels right to me, Nic." And he felt her body quiver in reply.

She snuggled closer into his embrace; he could feel her head nod beneath his chin as she mumbled, "Me too," her warm breath caressing his skin.

"Let's go inside," he said, releasing her and stepping away. He clasped her hand in his and led her to her front door. He withdrew his key ring and unlocked it.

"I forgot you still have my key," she commented, tightening her fingers in his.

"Yep, ever since you were out of town last year and I watered your plants. Do you want it back?" he asked, dangling the key ring between them.

She smiled in an interesting combination of innocent sweetness with a dash of sexy she-devil. "Go ahead and keep it." A becoming blush crept over her cheeks.

Suppressing his grin, he held the door open for her to enter.

When she went to flick on a light, he placed his hand over hers. "No, Nic. Come here." He took her hand, bringing her soft palm to his face and placing a brief, yet surprisingly intimate kiss to her skin. "I want to show you something."

Marcus led her down the dimly lit hallway, where the sweet floral scent of roses wafted in the air. From the corner of his eye he could see how her gaze widened in surprise. He felt her ever-so-slight hesitation as he guided her toward her bedroom.

He understood the significance, for they had yet to have sex in a bed—a gesture that closely symbolized lovemaking, and a commitment they'd agreed they weren't going to make. He wondered if she was apprehensive about taking such a step.

They reached the bedroom door. Silvery shards of moonlight

filtered through the half-closed miniblinds and cast the room into a pale, milky darkness. Marcus left her side, withdrawing a lighter from his pocket.

Nicole watched as Marcus strode from candle to candle, setting each tiny wick aglow with flame until her entire room was bathed in gold. The vanilla scent lifted in the air, mixing with the strong fragrance of spring roses. Though she wondered where the floral scent came from, she couldn't keep her gaze from tracking Marcus's every move. His wide shoulders moved like rock beneath river current, as the smooth material of his shirt shifted over his vast, muscular back.

Nicole withheld the questions dancing in her mind. She didn't wish to do anything that might spoil the sensual mood settling over the room with the warmth of sun-colored fire. The pale, cool light of the moon was replaced by yellow and gold flickering shadows.

The ivory of her bedsheets and comforter was dotted with red. Narrowing her eyes, Nicole took a tentative step closer. Rose petals littered her bed—soft pinks, vibrant reds, tones the color of rich burgundy. Each silken petal had been delicately removed from its bud and scattered about, creating a soft bed of roses.

A surprised smile widened her lips. Her heart constricted. "What did you do, Marcus?" she asked, not suppressing the wonder in her voice.

Marcus grinned like a cat that had found cream. "Candles and roses, Nic. You deserve candles and roses." His voice was deep, husky. He lit the last candle. Though he stood on the opposite side of her queen-size bed, his heated gaze was like a caress to her skin. The dark depths of his eyes bored into her soul. Her heart felt exposed to him. She trembled. Moisture seeped onto her panties, released from the ache between her legs that heightened from her knowing what Marcus had planned.

"When did you . . ." Her voice trailed off. She released his gaze and allowed her eyes to settle on the bed.

"When you were at the club," he said softly. "I promised I'd make leaving you . . . *wanting* up to you. And I mean to keep that promise. Here. Tonight."

Nicole's gaze snapped back to his. A mischievous smile played around the curve of his lips. In long, smooth strides he rounded the bed, never tearing his gaze from hers, and came to stand before her.

He framed her face in the palms of his hands, his strong fingers fanning out into the curls about her temples. His thumbs brushed along the underside of her jawbone. He slanted his head, her lips yearning for a taste of him, for the overwhelming feel of him crushing against her.

It took a lifetime—forever—for him to close the distance. When he kissed her, it was nothing more than a light stroke of lip upon lip as he feathered his attention across her skin. Her knees buckled and she collapsed into him, her hands coming to rest on his chest. The steady cadence of his pulse throbbed beneath her palm.

There was such tenderness in his kiss. The affection was her undoing. Tears sprang to her eyes, yet she forced them away, willing only to savor the moment and forget about regret—regret that with each used condom, their future dwindled.

Marcus's lips hovered above her, his tongue smoothing a path across her mouth, whetting her palate, increasing her appetite for him. Moaning, she gave way to the sensations stirring within her blood, to the building lust hinting of thunderstorms, to the tidal wave of desire.

When she neared begging, he deepened the kiss, slipping his tongue into the depths of her mouth, thrusting, seeking, exploring—staking claim. She met his tongue with hers, the tips touching, then retreating, swirling and dancing as if in an ancient mating ritual.

Marcus slid a hand down from her cheek, coddling her shoulders, lower to her breast, where her pert nipple stood astute beneath her thin shirt and pink lace bra. His thumb found the peak and rubbed over it, tweaking it between his fingers, before his hand fell to the waistband of her suede skirt. Deft fingers unfastened the top button and, with a flick, released the small zipper.

Marcus slowed the kiss, pressing his lips to the corner of her mouth, lightly caressing a trail of dampness to the sensitive skin beneath her ear, down her throat, to the hollow of her neck. Nicole's head lolled to the side, her knees weak, her inner thighs trembling.

Before she knew it, her shirt was pulled over her head, his hands urging her skirt off of her rounded hips, leaving her standing in nothing but a skimpy lace bra and tiny matching pink panties. Nicole moved her hands to Marcus's shirt, wanting to divest him of his clothing, wanting him naked against her. His warm palm settled over hers.

"Tonight is about you, Nic," he murmured between laps from his tongue to her skin.

"I want you," she whispered, her breathing, sharp and eager. She inhaled his masculine scent, a perfect contrast to the feminine scent of vanilla candles and the lushness of roses. He was musky with the subtle hint of sweat and soap.

Marcus chuckled against her flesh, an action that sent his vibrations pulsing through her body and centering deep in her gut. "I'm glad." He kissed her thoroughly. "Mmmm, but in due time."

Marcus stood back, releasing his hold. She wobbled before she found her balance without him. He removed his shirt, unbuckled his belt, released the fly on his jeans until only his boxers kept his straining erection from freedom. He made no move to allow the glory of his hardened cock liberation from its cotton prison.

The muscles of his pecs bunched beneath the perfect shade of rich chocolate skin, the golden rays of candlelight flickering and glistening on his naked chest. Nicole's gaze drifted over the wonder of his body, to the path of curly dark hair gathering at his naval and descending. His body reacted to her open appraisal, bucking behind the cloth.

Bringing her gaze back to his, Nicole gasped and stepped away, shocked by the supreme intensity of his stare. "Marcus?" she whispered, not knowing what to make of the depth of his eyes, feeling it sweep through her body, find her soul, and capture it.

He stalked her like a wild beast did prey, stepping toward her, closing the slight distance she'd created by stepping away. It was not fear that made her retreat, yet she trembled. After tonight, she knew deep down she'd never be the same. Letting Marcus go was going to break her heart.

The backs of her legs hit her bed, and she stumbled onto her mattress, crushing rose petals under her weight. Marcus kept coming, a slight smile waltzing across his face, his dimples deepening. The mattress dipped as he knelt on the edge, but Nicole scooted to the center, dizzy with want, awash with the heady scent of spring.

His strong hands wrapped around her ankles, his fingers stroking the skin on the pads of her feet, working the muscles on her calves. Lifting one foot, he brought it to his lips, pressing a kiss to her arch.

"Marcus, what are you doing?" she asked through a mouthful of giggles. She leaned back on her elbows, her hands brushing against dozens of silken flower blossoms. Their scent—stronger now as their thin skins broke and seeped onto the bed—permeated the air.

He licked up her ankle, then on the inside of her calf. "Tasting you. Mmm, sweet. You're like honey."

There was no room for melancholy in the rise of pleasure his touch evoked. She gave herself over to it, forgetting everything but him pleasing her.

His mouth traveled up her leg, passed her opened knees to the quivering flesh between her thighs, nipping at her skin. Marcus's hands explored, caressed, and stroked. The glide of his tongue moved up her inner thigh; then he openmouthed kissed the crotch of her panties over her damp and eager vagina.

Feeling at ease even with Marcus poised between her legs, she allowed her eyelids to slide closed as her arms buckled, sending her shoulders to the bed upon a pillow of roses. A slow breath escaped her parted lips. "Marcus."

Marcus smiled with triumph. "I'm here, Nic," he responded, slipping his fingers into the top of her lacy panties. He worked the material down her hips and past the triangular patch of pubic hair that glistened, damp, proof of her arousal. His cock thickened into a painful erection. As he slid the underwear past her vagina, his thumb brushed against her clit, eliciting a whimper and a tremble from Nicole.

He loved the way her body responded to his touch. To him. With her panties out of the way, Marcus knelt between her open legs. He lowered his mouth to her, kissing the wetness, two fingers sinking into her welcoming, hot flesh, spreading her labia so that his tongue could find her clit. The aroma of her sex mingled with the scent of roses and the vanilla from the tapers he'd arranged around the room.

"M-M-Marcus." A cross between a moan and his name.

Lapping at her, he swirled his tongue against her skin, devoured her essence, thrusting into her as he would if it were his dick. A sheen of sweat broke out on his shoulders from holding himself in check. *I don't think I've ever wanted a woman more.* He'd never guessed that pleasuring her could bring about satisfaction of his own. His own climax threatened and he'd yet to enter her.

"I want you, Marcus," she said. Her voice sounded as if it were about to snap.

Lifting his eyes, he glanced up her body, her caramel skin shimmering in the shadows and diffused light of the twinkling candles. Her body was damp, her breasts firm and full in her bra. Delicate rose petals stuck to her skin. She was beautiful and bewitching, her alluring body ripe and humming on the edge of orgasm.

Marcus slid his fingers into her, curling them forward, finding her G-spot. His tongue found the nub of her clit and he circled it, then nibbled.

"Marcus!" she screamed, her body shaking violently as her muscles clamped down, convulsing on his fingers in tiny spasms, each shudder of her climax driving him closer to the brink of sanity.

While Nicole lay relaxed, her eyes closed, her body still quivering from the aftereffects of crescendo, Marcus rid himself of his boxers, tossing them to the floor to join the rest of their discarded clothing. He moved up her body, kissing the slight mound of flesh beneath her belly button, her tight abs, and her ribs until he came to the lace of her bra.

Slipping one hand beneath her, he twisted the hook, releasing her breasts for him to feast upon. Cupping a round globe of flesh in his hand, he planted a kiss to her puckered brown nipple, then opened his mouth and drew it in. Her hands landed upon his shoulders, holding him to her. Her back arched to greet him. He couldn't help smiling at Nicole's tender urgings.

He left her nipple and trailed kisses to her face. Finding her mouth, he seized it. Supported on his elbows, he bracketed her head. Marcus could think of nothing but being one with his friend—his lover. Nicole's knees bent, drawing him into the cradle of her thighs. Then she wrapped her supple legs around his lower back, holding him to her. His cock brushed against her wet core. In mindless need, he plunged inside of her, grinding pubic hair to pubic hair.

Being inside of her was calming to his soul, quiet, peaceful, like when a winter rainstorm turned to snow.

Marcus drank in her cries of pleasure, answering with a gruff moan that echoed through his chest. Slowly he withdrew and entered again, finding a rhythm too staid to bring about a quick end.

She rocked her hips upward, taking him deeper, thrusting into him, stirring lust like fire consumed wood in a hearth. Yet the tenderness of her touch completed the ultimate feeling of rightness.

Nicole kissed him back as she ran the soles of her feet down the backs of his legs, then found his butt and pushed with the heel of her foot, lifting her hips to welcome him. A second wave of pleasure exploded, her body trembling beneath him. She moaned her release into his mouth, her body convulsing around him, each spasm a warm, wet glove that sucked him deeper.

"Grr . . ." he grumbled, trying to hold back the rush of orgasm but unable to succeed. "Damn, Nic. I'm cumming." His back arched, every muscle in his body going rigid as his climax ripped through him. He spiraled away from the bed, his whole existence revolving around the pleasure of Nicole. When the shaking subsided, he lowered his body to hover just above her, resting his face in the curve of her throat, his semihard cock buried deep inside of her.

Between light kisses and nibbles on her earlobe, he asked, "Are you all right, Nic?"

He could hear the smile in her voice, feel it in her touch as she smoothed her palm down his spine. "I'm good."

Marcus rolled to the side, gathering Nicole into his embrace. Reaching behind him, he grabbed the edge of the comforter and tossed it over them, encasing them in warmth and silk rose petals. Against his chest Nicole's breathing slowed.

The light dwindled as the candles burned themselves out. Marcus shot a quick look at the clock. Three thirty. He smiled and tightened his hold on the woman sleeping in his arms. He was in her bed. He was spending the night.

Chapter Eight

Nicole came awake slowly, securely enveloped in the warm cocoon of Marcus's embrace. With their naked limbs twisted and entwined, she was reluctant to move for fear of disturbing him. He slept peacefully behind her, his chest pressed against her back and the long, thick shaft of his morning erection tucked against the cheeks of her butt. Inhaling deeply the faded scent of vanilla candles, crushed rose blossoms, and the pungent odor of sex, she warmed with the joy of waking with a man in her bed, along with a pang of heartache.

All this would come to an end within two weeks. Two weeks in which to enjoy the tender loving and passionate embrace of the man she now knew, without a doubt, she loved. Not the kind of love she'd felt for him as a friend, but the deep-down, head-over-heels love a woman felt about a man she wanted to spend the rest of her life with.

Nicole exhaled and squeezed her lids together. She'd made an arrangement with Marcus, one that involved the body but definitely not the heart. And certainly not a lifetime. She'd promised no regrets, and that was exactly what she'd deliver on the day Marcus packed up and drove out of her life to begin his job in Atlanta.

Easing open her lids, Nicole took in her bedroom, bright sunshine streaming in through the narrow slats of her window coverings. The streaks of light shimmered as if dusted with glitter.

Glancing at the clock, she realized they'd miss the Sunday service, but she had a few hours before she was expected at her mama's for brunch.

Without warning, Marcus rolled her onto her back and came up on one elbow on his side. His midnight gaze was assessing as he studied her face. Nicole almost felt like blushing. This was the first morning they'd shared together this way. The first time they'd made love in either of their beds.

Did he wonder, as she did, what it meant? Was it just another place to have sex, or did he sense, too, that something had changed? Something was different?

The poignant moment passed, and he smiled a charmingly boyish grin and bent forward to nuzzle into the hollow of her neck. Between light kisses, he said, "I'm starving." He softly nipped her collarbone.

"My mama's serving brunch at eleven o'clock. Do you want to come?" she asked, not caring what Natalie would think when she arrived with Marcus, after their talk the night before. Her mama wouldn't mind. She adored Marcus and had even warned Nicole several times that good-looking men and women couldn't simply be friends. Nicole had argued back then, but now realized dear old Mama was right.

"So do you want to come?" she asked again when Marcus hadn't answered.

"There'll be enough food?"

"Have you ever known my mama to not cook enough food?"

Marcus chuckled. "Nope, I guess not." He rolled away and in a smooth motion stood from the bed. "I'm going to grab a shower." He rubbed his palm over his stomach. "I'd ask you to join me, but we'd never make it to your mama's, and I'm starving." He winked as he turned away and headed toward the bathroom.

Nicole lay still, watching his perfect physique retreat.

When he reached the bathroom door, he paused. Leaning one elbow onto the frame, he glanced over his shoulder at her. "By the way, when we're done at your parents', you're all mine," he stated matter-of-factly.

"Oh, yeah? What've you got in mind?"

"Shopping." He slanted his head toward the wad of comforter on the floor. "You need new bedding. I think we've ruined yours." He entered the bathroom, not closing the door.

Chapter Nine

MARCUS LISTENED to the tweeting of birds in the vicinity, heard the rustling of leaves as a warm summer breeze scurried across the backyard of Nicole's parents' home. Tucked beneath a pair of curving old apple trees, the hammock swayed lazily, lulling him in the drifting place between consciousness and sleep.

As he cracked his lids slightly, it took him a moment to orient himself. The June sun had crested the sky and lingered middescent in the west. The overhanging apple branches were void of their springtime blossoms and covered in the tiny buds of what would be apples come fall. Stretched out on his back, he had his legs crossed at the ankles, one arm bent and tucked beneath his head, the other protectively wrapped around Nicole, who lay cuddled up all warm and cozy next to him.

Was it any wonder we fell asleep? he mused, thinking of the lovemaking the night before. With his stomach stuffed from Mrs. Davis's cooking and his body sated, he and Nicole had strolled the backyard looking at her mama's flower garden, before lounging on the hammock. Marcus had kicked back and pulled Nicole with him. That was last thing he remembered before he'd fallen asleep.

The murmuring of nearby voices registered in his foggy brain. His lids drifted closed so no one would know he was awake. He was far too comfortable to move, let alone disturb Nicole. She needed her rest for what he'd planned for them later. Holding back a grin, he focused on Nicole's soft body, half on the hammock, half draped across him. She smelled sweet, like roses, and fresh, like soap. He could imagine how her skin would taste later, but it was more than just sex between them; it had to be.

Drowsily, he half listened to the conversation of Nicole's family, only to realize they were talking about him.

"Mama, not so loud. You're going to wake them up." It was Natalie who'd spoken.

Marcus damn near groaned. She'd been giving him the *I know what you've been up to* look since he'd arrived with Nicole. And she was right.

"Oh, hush now. You're the one who's going to bother them," responded Mrs. Davis. "Nat, what do you think is going on with those two?"

"Are you asking me if I think they're involved?"

"Yes, I guess I am. Do you know something I don't?"

"I don't know *anything* for sure, and Nic denied it when I asked her," Natalie replied.

Mr. Davis's deep voice cut in. "Girl, I don't believe that for a second. Do you see the way that boy looks at her? Nat, do you want some iced tea?"

Marcus gave himself a mental scolding. He'd better check himself. He heard the rattling of another chair and clink of ice in glasses. "Thanks, Daddy," Natalie said. "So you think they're *in love?*"

"I don't know about Nic, but I know what that young man is feeling. I used to be one, remember, honey? He loves her all right. Now it's just a matter of making sure he does the right thing," he said protectively.

"He's leaving in a less than two weeks, as I understand it," Natalie said.

"He's such a nice boy." There was a pause and the movement of the ice-filled glasses. Mrs. Davis sighed, then added. "He won't go if he loves her."

Marcus wanted to leap from the hammock and pound on his chest like a respectable caveman. He wanted to shout, *Hell, no, I'm not going.* He wanted the entire world to know it *was* love, all right!

More than that, he wanted Mr. and Mrs. Davis to know he'd marry Nicole if she'd have him. That they'd have a bunch of mini Nicoles to call them grandparents. There'd be nothing more he'd like to do than to admit his love for their daughter. To admit he'd actually fallen six long years ago when they'd met in college. Despite the growing need to shout from atop every roof and at the top of his lungs, he didn't. He kept his mouth shut and pretended to be asleep.

Nicole hadn't asked him to stay. As far as he knew, she was happy with the arrangement. She had a house, a job, friends.

Keeping still, Marcus tasted the bitterness of regret. Not over what they'd started, but because he was afraid to confess what he felt for her. And why? he asked himself. Because he'd give up the physical part of their relationship if it meant not losing her as a friend. He couldn't risk the loss of their friendship any more than he could risk the sting of her rejection. Regret because he was a coward.

Nicole stirred at his side.

Arching her back against him, she removed the single leg she'd tossed over his thighs as they'd slept. But her soft palm on his chest remained in place, and drew small circles as she spoke.

"Mama, why'd you let me sleep so long? I was supposed to help with the dishes." Nicole sat up halfway, leaning her weight into Marcus, keeping the shifting hammock from tipping.

"Don't worry about the dishes. Nat helped, and you needed the rest. You had a nice nap?" her mother asked.

"Yeah, Nic, were you warm enough?" Natalie teased, her words clearly hinting at the fact that she lay cuddled up with Marcus.

Nicole nodded, but went tense beside him, sucking a sharp breath between her teeth. Playing off the gasp of air, she glanced at her watch. She sat up fully, swung her feet to the ground, and halted the slow swing of the hammock. Marcus grumbled at the chill caused by the absence of her body heat. She turned toward him, her dark, liquid-filled eyes fixed on his.

He felt her nervous gaze down to his gut, the silent plea to get out of there—quickly—and he wondered if she'd heard every word he had. With a wink to reassure her, Marcus rolled from the hammock to his feet. Extending his hand, he pulled her up beside him.

"Mama, Daddy, thanks for brunch—and the use of the hammock—but I've got to go. I have a dinner appointment with a client," Nicole said in a sleepy voice.

Again, her eyes fixed on his, the look imploring him to play along. He placed his hand on the small of her back.

"Marcus needs to drop me off at home so I can shower and dress."

"On a Sunday night, Nic?" her mother questioned.

Nicole shrugged and gave her mom a quick hug. "You know, Mama, some women are beaten on weekends, too." Retrieving her purse, she asked Marcus, "Are you ready?"

"Yeah." He smiled at her, though he couldn't help wonder what shifted her mood. "Mr. Davis." He shook her father's hand and kissed her mother on the cheek. "Thanks for the meal. As usual, it was terrific."

"It was nice to see you again, Marcus." Her mother spoke to him, although her dark gaze remained fixed on Nicole's face.

"That's right, boy, don't be a stranger," her father added, also giving Nicole a pointed stare.

"I won't. Thank you again. Nat, good luck in school if I don't see you again before you head back."

Marcus didn't object when Nicole grabbed his hand and dragged him out the front door. As he thumbed his key chain and unlocked her truck, he could tell she was on edge. She bit her bottom lip as she slipped silently into the passenger seat with a quick wave good-bye. He started the engine and put it into drive. Within a few minutes her parents' house slid from sight, but sitting tensely beside him, Nicole didn't relax a bit.

Chapter Ten

WERE HER FEELINGS FOR MARCUS so transparent? Nicole withheld the threatening whimper, but settled for burying her face in her hands.

"You okay, Nic?" Marcus asked.

The concern in his voice tore at her heart. She blinked hard to rid herself of the hot stinging in the back of her eyes. Tears were ridiculous, she knew. This was all her own doing.

Pasting a grin on her lips, she turned toward Marcus. The forced smile instantly became genuine the moment her gaze settled on his beautiful face. "I'm fine. Just a little embarrassed. My dad caught me sleeping in your arms. Did you notice that look he was giving me?"

Marcus made a gruff noise at the back of his throat, sounding a lot like a groan. "Nah, he's just acting like your father. We were on the hammock, not in bed."

Nicole didn't miss the slight way he rolled his eyes when he glanced back at the road. He'd noticed her father's look all right, she was sure. She didn't mention the conversation she'd overheard, and she thanked God that Marcus had been asleep.

Nicole exhaled a relieved sigh. "You're right. I'm grown. I don't need my daddy's approval for an afternoon nap."

"Nope, you're one hundred percent woman. Over eighteen, right?" Marcus paused before he went on. "But your parents care about you and want what's best. That's all."

"I know." After a quiet moment, Nicole leaned forward and turned up the stereo. Gazing out the window, she stared at the broken white lines speeding by in what seemed like perfect beat to the fast-paced music.

As they made their way down Highway 50 from the foothills of the Sierras and back toward the valley floor, a sign they passed caught her attention.

Nicole leaned forward and lowered the music. "Hey, didn't you promise me shopping? Something about a ruined comforter?"

"I sure did. You want to go home first?" Marcus asked, sliding her an amused smile.

"Just find me a place where I can get a good iced latte and I'll be ready to shop."

Marcus laughed out loud. "Leave it to shopping to cheer you up."

"It's the thought of the iced latte," Nicole said, punching him on the arm softly.

Marcus cocked an eyebrow at her and gave her a menacing look. "Watch it, young lady, or instead of shopping I'll be liable to spank you." The dimple deepened on his cheek. His lips twitched into a charming smile.

"Oh, yeah? Maybe I'd like that. You want to give it a try?" she taunted. Though she meant it as a joke, her nipples puckered beneath her cotton blouse. She could imagine Marcus's fingers there instead, his other hand giving her a solid whack to the butt.

Marcus flashed his teeth, his dimple carving into his cheek. "You want me to pull over?"

Biting back the moan his suggestion elicited, Nicole responded, "No, I want to go shopping. I need a new comforter." Her gaze dropped to his lap and the growing bulge that got bigger as she examined it. Under her breath she added, "One we can ruin later."

Marcus burst into laughter. The sound of his mirth warmed Nicole's heart and brought about her own giggles.

"You're funny. That's why I lo . . . like . . . you." *Stupid! Stupid!*

Stupid! Nicole rolled her eyes at her own near slip. To hide the creeping red staining her cheeks and slithering down her neck, she turned her attention out the window.

A few quiet moments passed before Marcus took her hand in his and give her a little squeeze. "I like you, too, Nicole Davis." He stroked his thumb across her palm, sending a scattering of goose-flesh across her skin.

Marcus drove to the closest coffee shop. Twenty minutes later Nicole sipped a frozen vanilla latte as they rode the escalator to the second floor of the department store. Still holding hands, they began their search for linens, weaving their way through the house-hold goods, toaster ovens and waffle irons.

Nicole chitchatted between sips about an annoying deliveryman who'd been hitting on her secretary.

He caught most of what she said, something about needing to call the security guard to see this guy out, but the details seemed like mumbo jumbo. Nodding his head as she spoke, Marcus let his mind wander to the memory of Nicole's face when they'd gone to look at the home she'd been interested in and the conversation they'd had previously. She'd been straightforward: *They* were just for fun, and when he moved it would be another guy she'd marry.

Oh, and the luminous look in her milk-chocolate-colored eyes when she'd seen the master closet, all wistful and dreamy. Had it been how many shoes she'd be able to fit into that closet, or could it possibly have been visions of her future as a wife that'd caused the shimmer in her eyes?

Letting a rush of air escape through his teeth, Marcus shut his eyes to the sharp pain aching in his chest and leaving a cold, empty space in his gut. He didn't want to imagine Nicole with another man.

With his new job in mind and the opportunity it presented, he couldn't see any way around leaving town.

Sliding her a glance, he saw her lips pucker around the straw, her cheeks hollowing as she sucked. Damn sexy lips of hers, and the little slurping sounds she made jolted him from contemplation right into a full-blown erection.

Marcus thought about the supply of condoms he'd picked up from the drugstore. Now that brown bag full of a good two dozen condoms was stuffed beneath his seat until he had a chance to sneak them into the cookie jar to be mixed with the chocolate Kisses.

He'd done the math. If they used two a day for the next two weeks, they'd need more than what remained of Nicole's original supply. So what if he cheated? He wasn't ready to give up their sexual relationship just yet.

The condoms would be replenished tonight. He meant to take full advantage of every chance he got to bury his cock deep in Nicole before he had to leave for Atlanta. He grinned from ear to ear.

"What?" Nicole asked, pausing in speech and movement.

"Nothing." He tugged her hand. "I think comforters are over here."

"Nothing?"

"I was just thinking, is all. Are you done with this?" he asked, to change the subject. He took her empty latte cup and tossed it in a waste can.

A few displays later they came to the bedding section. Miniature beds were set up to show off each design, and behind them were stacks of folded comforters, pillows, sheets, and matching blankets.

Nicole flashed him a smile; turning away, she began looking at the different patterns offered.

Marcus licked his lips as he watched her retreating backside, the perfection of her build apparent in her summer dress and mid-heeled sandals. Beneath the hem of the thin printed cotton, her toned coffee-with-milk-and-sugar legs stretched for what seemed like a mile to where her ankles were strapped into her sexy-as-hell, come-and-get-me shoes.

"Come here. Look at these," Nicole tossed over her shoulder, looking at a large display of cream-colored raw-silk comforters.

Glancing around to make sure no one was watching, Marcus stalked forward, hearing only the "come here" and taking it as an invitation. Back in the corner of the store, she was well hidden by the height of the bedding piled floor to ceiling. Marcus realized there was only one way into the alcove. It was completely private. Anyone approaching would be heard before they were seen.

He reached for the display on either side of Nicole's head, effectively pinning her to the wall of silk and cotton. His fingers dug into the five-hundred-thread-count Egyptian-cotton sheets. Leaning his weight into Nicole's back, he pressed her forward until her forehead rested against the smooth material.

His cock begged for contact, so he tilted his hips, brushing his rock-hard erection to the small of her back.

"What are you—" Nicole began in a hushed voice.

"Shh. Don't move." Marcus nudged aside a loose curl at her temple with his chin. Bending, he nestled his face into the curve of her neck from behind. "Close your eyes." He waited a brief moment. "Are they closed?"

Nicole nodded.

Using one knee to press between her legs, he edged them apart enough so that she rode high on his thigh. "I'm going to fuck you." He went on, undeterred by her slight gasp: "My hand is slipping beneath your dress to find your breasts. Yeah, they're so full and heavy. You want me to touch you, don't you? To take you in my hand, to kneed your flesh in my palm. To find your pert nipple." Marcus sucked in a winded breath and rotated his hips into her ass. His hard shaft rubbed against the small of her back.

"My mouth's there, sucking your nipple into the hot depths and swirling the extended tip with my tongue. Your nerve endings are on fire. Can you feel me, Nic?"

Again she nodded, only a sigh escaping her lips.

"Imagine me lifting your skirt, Nic, my fingers brushing up the hem, working over the smooth skin on your inner thighs. I'm going higher, Nic, to touch you. Are you wet for me, baby? Can you feel my fingers find the edge of your panties and ease them to the side? Ahh, you're slick. Do you want me inside you?"

His descriptions continued. "My mouth is there now, kissing a trail to your pussy. Can you feel my tongue suck on your clit? You taste like honey. You're so sweet, Nic. I can't stop kissing you. You don't want me to, do you?" Marcus asked taking a moment to scatter light kisses on the sensitive skin below her ear, on the wild pulse racing on her neck. He could feel her body gasping for breath as he leaned against her.

Nicole gulped down the raw emotion building. Her chest burned from holding her breath, the words and images Marcus provoked so real.

"No, I don't want you to stop," she whispered, her mind no longer in the department store but on a bed of silk, with her naked in Marcus's arms.

She could feel his words like stroking fingertips, like a gentle caress, like a fevered wind on a hot summer afternoon.

"I don't want to stop touching you. I want to fuck you, Nic, not with my tongue, but with my dick." His open mouth nibbled against her skin as she sucked in a breath.

Marcus shifted his bent leg so it brushed against her sensitive vagina, already on fire, wet, and ready for him.

"I want to be inside you, baby. I want to feel your pussy close around me. To tighten on my cock with each of your wild shudders of orgasm."

He rocked his leg again. Shivers began, centered on her clit. A slow, low moan bubbled from her lips. "Mmm . . . Marcus," she said, her words breathy and panting. With her eyes still closed, Nicole allowed her head to loll back and rest on Marcus's chest.

"Do you want me to slip my hand on your breasts? Do you want me to pluck your beaded nipple with my teeth, to roll it in my mouth with my tongue?"

Another guttural moan eased from her lips, only louder than the last. Marcus's moved his hand from the bedding and slid his fingers over her mouth, softly yet effectively covering her lips.

"Shh, baby, this is just for me," he whispered in her ear.

Nicole could hardly think to keep her voice down. Not with his muscular thigh rocking against her flesh. Not with the image of his hand groping her breast and his tongue working at her hungry nipple. With his hand lightly resting over her mouth to muffle her cries of passion, Nicole focused on breathing through her nose and the incredible rhythm of his hard thigh mimicking lovemaking against the apex of her legs.

Then the spasms started—small at first, but the tremors built like an avalanche consuming the mountain, the first thrusting her over the ledge, then soaring into pleasure.

Nicole kept her eyes closed, listening to the rich timbre of Marcus's voice, feeling the orgasm grip her and wrench free her cries.

"Are you cuming for me, Nic?" he asked, his aroused husky voice vibrating against her skin.

Some far-off place in her mind, where reality still dwelled, reminded her where she was. To keep her passionate yells from summoning every assistant in the store, Nicole leaned forward and buried her face into the wall of silken bedding, inhaling the subtle scent of their newness. Her climax cascaded around her.

In time, her labored breathing slowed to normal. She became aware of Marcus's strong fingers stroking up and down her arm, reassuring her that he was right behind her.

"Marcus?" she mumbled, her face still sunk into the bedding.

"Yeah, Nic?" She registered the concern in his tone.

"I'll take this."

There was a moment of silence. She composed herself.

"Nic, this what?" he asked.

Letting out a cleansing sigh, she eased from the shelter of his arms and turned to face him. She smiled when she saw the confusion on his face. "This bedding. Remember? That's why we're here."

His glance swung to the folded comforters behind her. "Oh, the bedding. You want this one? It's similar to the stuff you have."

"I like the stuff I have." She leaned forward and placed a quick peck to his lips. "Until it got ruined. Besides, Marcus, this stuff is supersoft against my skin."

Seeing the spark of interest in his deep-chocolate eyes, Nicole pursed her lips into a pout.

Marcus grabbed a set of bedding. She fell into step behind him as he wound his way out of the alcove and through the aisles. Her knees wobbled at first, taking a moment for her postclimax legs to function properly.

He winked at her as he neared the cash register. "We'll test these out later."

Marcus was pulling out his wallet by the time Nicole thought of a fitting response, but the presence of the saleswoman kept her quiet. She was getting a quizzical look that made her think of her junior high school teacher who'd caught her passing notes.

The purchase complete, they headed out of the store. Stepping onto the escalator one stair behind Marcus, Nicole leaned onto his back and whispered in his ear, "Thank you, Marcus."

Tipping his head to the side, Marcus looked back and captured her mouth with an unexpected kiss. "You're welcome. Anytime."

Chapter Eleven

"IT'S NICE, don't you think?"

Marcus tossed a look over his shoulder to see Dani Clark walking up behind him. Her long legs dripped to the floor from her way-too-short miniskirt, entirely inappropriate for business attire.

"It's all right," he replied with a shrug. She certainly wasn't what he'd been expecting when the secretary at the Dynamic Agency had said they'd be sending Danny to meet him at the hotel and show him around town.

Danny had turned out to be Dani, a tall, gorgeous woman with voluptuous breasts. Glancing back at the oversize kitchen in the fourth condo they'd looked at, Marcus realized he didn't like it at all. There was something missing.

"So do you want to call it a day and look more tomorrow? You must be hungry. What do you say I take you out to dinner?" Dani asked, placing her hand on his arm.

Marcus glanced down at her manicured nails slightly gripping his skin. A sizzle of apprehension skidded down his spine. Was she hitting on him? Maybe he was just imagining things. It'd been a long day, and he hadn't gotten a hell of a lot of sleep the night before. Knowing he was getting on a plane just after dawn, he'd made love to Nicole with a frenzied passion several times during the too-fast stretch of night.

Dropping his arm so Dani's hand fell away, he turned from the kitchen and headed toward the front door. "Nah, I think I'll get something back at the hotel. Thanks for the offer."

"Are you sure?" she asked, following behind him.

Marcus closed his eyes. The pounding headache was getting worse. It'd been throbbing behind his temples since he'd kissed Nicole good-bye that morning, knowing that moments later she'd drive away in his truck. No sense paying parking costs, he'd told her.

He planned on lining up his new condo so he could have his things shipped directly there, without having to put them into storage. Then he'd drive across the country to his new life . . . and away from Nicole.

Was it the forlorn look in her eyes as she bade him a safe trip that had started the ache in his gut and the lonely pain in his chest? Or was it the fact that she'd still never once hinted that she wanted him to stay?

Feeling Dani's hand settle on his shoulder in a light caress jolted Marcus from his memories of the morning.

"Are you sure?" she repeated, a seductive purr in her tone.

"No, thanks. It's been a long day."

He yanked open the door with more force than necessary and stepped into the strange false brightness of streetlights, and the faded glory of the sun. He started walking toward the parking lot.

Dani came up behind him, the quick tapping of her high-heeled shoes telling him she'd had to walk pretty fast. She grabbed hold of his elbow, stalling his retreat to the car. When he turned to face her, she licked her bottom lip, her pink tongue darting out to wet it.

Her hand slipped from his elbow down to his wrist, and she pulled it behind her and stepped into his chest, leaning her tits against him. With the noxious odor of her perfume burning his nostrils, she wiggled as she made the contact complete.

"Marcus, come back to my place," she whispered. Her hand reached for the back of his neck. Her other hand reached between them, firmly grabbing hold of his dick, which was limp despite her coercing.

Withholding an irritated groan, Marcus shut his eyes. A year ago he would have accepted the blatant invitation to her bed. She was a beautiful woman.

Opening his eyes, Marcus reached back and took hold of her wrist, then stepped from her grasp. He was a man now, and a real man didn't dally in the bed or arms of a woman when another held his heart. Though he'd made no promise to Nicole, he was committed to her just the same.

Knowing women like her didn't take subtle hints very well, he was blunt. "You know, Miss Clark. I'm not interested in the type of dinner you're suggesting." Marcus took another step back from her and released her wrist.

A flash of disappointment flickered in her eyes. "But I was told I should welcome you to Atlanta. I was told that you'd be open to the idea."

"Who told you that?" he asked, gritting his teeth as anger surged through him. "No, don't bother answering." He knew it was the bosses at the Dynamic Agency who had sent her to welcome him. What type man did they think he was? *One with no dignity or self-respect, apparently.*

To hell with Jay. If Jay wanted him as his agent—and he was a damned good agent—then the kid would have to accept him on his terms, on his *home* turf.

Marcus walked away through the half-filled parking lot.

"Wait. At least let me give you a ride back to the hotel," she called after him.

Jamming his hand into his pocket, Marcus retrieved his cell phone. "I'll call a cab." He kept walking.

Fighting off the stinging in her nose and the hot burning behind her eyes, Nicole was determined not to cry. Leaning back against the seat, she dropped her hands from the steering wheel. Grabbing several shredded tissues, she swiped them beneath her nose.

It'd been a long day that was preceded by a night of passionate lovemaking. The alarm had sounded at five thirty, but she'd already been awake, watching Marcus sleep.

She'd tried to memorize the handsome lines of his face, the carved dimple that deepened when he smiled, the small pucker between his nose and lush lips. Gazing at the rise and fall of his chest, she imagined the way his heartbeat would feel against her cheek. Needing to burn this memory of him into her brain forever, she couldn't waste their final minutes with sleep.

When he'd risen she'd rubbed her hand across her new sheets, the fine texture smooth beneath her fingertips, feeling what remained of his lingering heat.

The sheets would be cold now.

Exhaling, she knew she couldn't hide in his truck all night, despite feeling the need to remain in the cab where gentle reminders of their lovemaking remained. Ever since she'd dropped him off at the airport that morning, she clung to the knowledge that she'd see him at least once more, when he came back to get his truck. With a sigh, Nicole opened the door and slid her feet to the ground. She entered the dark house, silenced the alarm, and kicked off her shoes.

Nicole left the lights off, not wanting to see how empty the house was.

After watching Marcus walk through the security gate at Sacramento International Airport, she'd rushed outside to watch his plane take off. It lifted into the morning air and into the rising sun, making an appearance on the eastern horizon. She'd watched long after the plane was out of sight, feeling alone and empty.

Then, after buying a latte at a local café, she'd worked all day. Accustomed to being with Marcus at night, she stayed late so she wouldn't have to return to an empty house.

Now she was home. Alone. Her house was dark. The sheets were cold, and the cookie jar would be empty except for the chocolate Kisses. Stifling a sob with the back of her hand, Nicole went to the kitchen and opened the fridge, hoping to find a bottle of chilled white wine. Pale fridge light spilled across the tiled floor, giving the dim room a little illumination. She poured a glass of wine, then took a sip as she leaned against the counter—where she and Marcus had first become lovers. Where it had all begun.

Lifting the goblet to her lips, Nicole drained the wine in one deep swallow, immediately feeling the rush of dizziness to her head. One glass and she got an instant buzz, undoubtedly since she hadn't eaten a bite all day.

She grabbed the phone and speed-dialed number seven.

"Extraordinary Pizza. Dine-in or delivery?" a young woman asked.

"Delivery," Nicole responded.

"What can I get you?"

"Small, thick crust, double cheese, double pepperoni, and black olives." Liquid filled Nicole's eyes. This was her first dinner alone in weeks.

"Anything else?" the girl asked.

"One of those small chocolate Bundt cakes you had on special as dessert."

"I'm sorry, but we're all out of those. Did you want to try the lemon?"

"No, thanks. I need chocolate," Nicole responded, closing her eyes against the wave of melancholy.

"Okay. Thirteen dollars and forty-three cents. It'll be there in about thirty minutes," the girl said, then hung up.

Disconnecting, she placed the phone on the counter and reached for the ceramic rose-shaped cookie jar. Setting aside the lid, she dumped the contents onto the tiles. Silver-wrapped chocolate Kisses spilled everywhere, along with something else that caught her off guard. "Condoms?" she whispered. A bunch of condoms.

Picking one up Nicole marched over and flicked on the lights. The foil package was similar to the brand she bought, but not quite the same. It didn't take a genius to realize that meant Marcus had replenished the supply. There were seven left of the new type.

Closing her eyes, she attempted to count how many times they'd made love. She shook her head. After the first few nights, she couldn't recall. Tossing the foil-wrapped condom on the counter, she wondered how long ago—and how many times—Marcus had replaced them.

She gasped as realization hit her full force. He'd gone against their initial agreement. They were supposed to have ended their sexual relationship when the condoms were gone.

Why had he purchased new condoms? Did he not want the sex to end? It was damn good sex. Or was there something deeper? Was there some other reason why he wouldn't want things to end between them? Nicole placed the chocolates and condoms back into the container, then poured a second glass of wine, sipping it this time. She mulled the same questions over until the doorbell rang.

After paying, she stood holding the warm cardboard box, the pungent scent of the pizza filling the air. She couldn't eat, not with her stomach flipping and her mind on Marcus.

Leaving the pizza untouched in the kitchen beside her empty wineglass, she made her way to her bedroom, dropping clothing as she walked, not caring where it landed.

Standing naked in her bedroom, Nicole glanced at the bed, neatly made with the two-week-old bedding. A pale sliver of yellow seeped in through the blinds, casting an insipid gold light on the off-white cloth. She was temped to delve into the bed for warmth, but looking at the smooth Egyptian cotton and raw silk, she thought it appeared plain and lonesome without Marcus in it.

Again, the sting of tears threatened behind her eyes. Holding off the flow of sorrow, Nicole thought about the feel of Marcus's touch, the softness of his kiss, and the passion in his embrace. Needing to feel closer to him, she turned from her empty bed toward the closet.

Nicole retrieved the folded off-white comforter that was stained with splotches of pink rose petals, and scented with vanilla candles and the heady fragrance of their sex. Refusing to throw it out when it'd been replaced, she was glad to have it now. She shook out the folds and tossed it around her naked shoulders, snuggling into the familiar feel.

Back in the living room, Nicole settled onto the couch, securely encased in the comforter. She closed her eyes, instantly conjuring up images of Marcus.

She couldn't pretend, despite how she tried, that he was with her. A strangled cry spilled from her tight throat. Given freedom, one sob turned into many and she wept out the sorrow she'd contained for so long.

"Why'd you have to go?" she asked, knowing in her heart the answer.

How could she possibly begrudge him the life he deserved? She'd seen his struggle to make it in the NFL, only to be forced into retirement by a devastating knee injury. She'd seen him work his way up as a sports agent, building a reputation and clientele he could be proud of.

She'd longed to ask him to stay. To give up the job offer that could potentially make him millions. She'd been prepared to beg, if need be, for him to remain in Sacramento and by her side. But she'd swallowed down the plea because she knew in her heart of hearts she would never hold him back from his dreams. If she tried, one day he'd grow to resent her. She'd never back him into a corner. "I'd have gone with you," she whispered.

Her sobs turned to muffled cries, then faded to whimpers. The long night and painful day finally took their toll. Her lids flush against her cheeks, the last sob escaping, she cried herself to sleep.

Marcus paced his room until he'd worn a trail in the carpet. So he walked the halls of the hotel heading to the pool and weight room. He even considered working out to burn the rapid growth of his agitation and anger. But workouts were meant to be shared with Nicole. He kept walking.

Under the half-moon sky, no stars were visible, all drowned out by the city lights. But he knew they were up there. Just as he knew he didn't belong in Atlanta at all.

"Fuck!" He swiped a palm over his face, scrubbing away the mask of indifference to be replaced with what he was truly feeling—love.

Love for Nicole laced with a whole hell of a lot of irritation about his situation. Where he should have been was three thousand miles away, in the arms of *his* woman, not pacing the deserted hotel lobby trying to figure out what to do.

"What am I doing here?" he asked through gritted teeth.

Is this the step I want to take to further my career? Hell no! The answer came roaring back at him. He had a lucrative, well-respected agency of his own that he was damn proud of. So what if the position with the Dynamic Agency would offer him bigger-name clients and more prestige. It wouldn't offer him self-respect. It sure as hell didn't offer him Nicole.

He didn't want to own a condo, but a large home designed for a wife and kids. For the family he so longed to embrace when the right woman came along. Only she had. She'd always been there, and he wasn't willing to risk losing her—if it wasn't already too late. "I belong in Sacramento. I belong with Nicole."

Turning on his heel, he rode the elevator to his room. Once there, he gathered up his wallet, briefcase, some loose change, and his household keys, along with his cell phone.

He flipped the phone and punched the preprogrammed number to the airline. "Yeah, I need the first flight out of Atlanta flying to Sacramento International Airport."

Chapter Twelve

Tapping his knuckles against the door for a third time, Marcus sucked in a deep breath of the balmy air, unusually humid for the Sacramento Valley, and wondered what could be taking Nicole so long.

Clearly she was home, judging by her open garage door and the fact that her car was inside and his truck was parked in her driveway. Stepping from the shaded stoop, Marcus squinted against the bright ball of fire lifting into the fathomless, pale blue sky, and scanned the empty street for any sign of her.

He spotted a splotch of color in the back of his truck out of the corner of his eye. Marcus glanced into the bed, which was filled with several bags of topsoil, potting mix, and compost. On the floor closer to the cab were about half a dozen flats of vibrant flowering plants. Lifting the bouquet of roses he held in his hand, he laughed.

Gardening, he decided, rounding the paved and cobblestone path toward the back of the house. He reached the chest-high wooden fence and scanned the backyard.

His gaze fell upon Nicole a heartbeat later, kneeling in the grass with her back to him and her hands enfolded in the rich brown soil. Her hair was pulled into a ponytail, though several stray ringlets clung to the damp skin on her neck. A pair of headphones circled her head.

Nicole's hips swayed to the beat drumming through the tiny

speakers, her shapely round ass slightly rotating. Her voice drifted across the ten-yard space of grass.

The sensual sound of her hum resonated in Marcus's gut. The sweet echo grew louder as she mixed in a scattering of words. "Don't need him," she sang out. Pausing, she scooped up something beside her and lifted it to her lips. A medium-size plastic bottle of water, the condensation glistening in the sun. Draining the bottle, she tossed it aside, humming again.

Watching her slender body move to the music only she could hear, Marcus thought about this moment. Hell, he could think about little else.

He'd caught a couple hours of sleep, here and there, on the long red-eye flight back across the country. He had a cup of coffee during the short layover in Dallas, and despite not sleeping more than five hours combined over the last two nights, he felt exhilarated.

After running his cell phone until the battery pack had given out, he finally had everything all arranged. Chuck had picked him up at the airport and driven him to the real estate office, where he'd signed the needed papers to make sure his plan went smoothly.

Everything went as planned. He could only hope the rest of the day was as successful as this morning. There were just two final things that needed to be done.

Marcus walked away without Nicole noticing. He let himself into the house, making his way to the kitchen.

Grabbing the ceramic cookie jar, he slid it in front of him, setting his bouquet aside. When he removed the lid the scent of chocolate wafted into the air, giving him a nostalgic glimpse of love.

He knew how he felt, but what if for Nicole nothing had changed? He shook off a moment of doubt, concern over her reaction tightening in his gut. There was no time for that now. Counting all the remaining condoms, he removed them from the cookie jar and slipped them into the garbage under the kitchen sink. He then dropped the surprise he'd gotten for Nicole inside with the Kisses, swirling them together before he replaced the ceramic lid. Pushing it back to its original location, Marcus grabbed the flowers and exited the kitchen.

Finding his truck keys on a side table, he dropped them into his pocket. His gaze swept over her furnishings, a welling of emotion rising in his chest. He left her house and made his way back to the fence.

Her hips had slowed. She no longer sang out but mumbled low and husky, the sweet sound like a siren's song.

Marcus plucked off a rosebud from the bouquet. Taking the blossom, he tossed it in her direction. It landed by her side.

She didn't notice.

Tugging off another blossom, he tossed it, too. Still she didn't detect his presence. He thrust another at her but got the same response—nothing.

Growling in frustration, Marcus grabbed a handful of flower petals and tossed them over the fence, but they landed around her in a rainshower of color everywhere but where Nicole knelt on the ground. With her head tipped back, he could see that her eyes were closed against the intensity of the sun, her caramel skin shimmering golden and bright. Her lush lips were parted and glistening, and moved to some song playing from the earphones.

Frustration a brewing beast in his gut, he grabbed a handful of rosebuds from the bouquet, tearing them from their stems, and tossed them at Nicole's feet. A single bloom went astray and hit her on the back of her head.

"Ahh!" She let out a startled scream, ripped the headphones from her head, and twisted around to see who'd hit her. "Oh, Marcus, you scared me to death." Her faced changed from angry surprise to something more akin to joy as she struggled to her feet and wiped the dirt from her hands against the sweat material of her shorts.

"Sorry, Nic. I didn't mean to scare you," he said, opening the wooden gate and walking through. "Or hit you. You okay?"

Nicole lifted her soiled fingers to her head and rubbed the spot where the flower had struck her. "I'm fine. But . . . what are you doing here? I thought you were in Atlanta."

"I was."

"Yeah, so what happened?"

Marcus strolled across the yard, pausing a mere step from her, mulling over what his response should be. "I came back."

Nicole could scarcely breathe past the lump tightening her throat and the crazed surge of her heartbeat. Her heightened state of alarm when the flower had hit her was nothing compared to the awareness of having Marcus—in the flesh—standing before her.

"Why?" she squeaked, not intending for it to come out like the croak of a toad, but it did anyway. She cleared her throat, to little avail, and tried again. "Why'd you come back?" she inquired just above a whisper.

"Something was missing in Atlanta," he replied in an even tone, his warm breath swooshing across her skin and causing a shiver to run down her spine.

"What was missing?" she asked, then smoothed her tongue across her bottom lip to moisten it. With his rich, dark eyes locked on her face, her mouth felt as dry as sandpaper.

Marcus leaned toward her. His hand cupped her cheek. His fingers fanned out into the fine, twisting hair by her temples, and he dragged her closer to him.

"This." His mouth brushed over hers in a light kiss. In the space of a heartbeat he settled fully upon her mouth and nibbled her bottom lip between his teeth.

Nicole's bones turned to butter, and she melted into his embrace. Her arms instinctively encircled his neck. The tips of her breasts brushed against his hard chest, causing a jolt of fire to flame at her core. Moisture—hot and immediate—pooled between her thighs. When her knees buckled, she allowed all of her weight to be supported by Marcus's superior strength.

The kiss changed from soft and tender to wild, needy, and thorough. His tongue thrust into her mouth, searching, exploring, conquering. He traced her teeth, found the darkest corners of her mouth, and bathed them in his heat, all while his thumb made small circles upon her cheek.

Sliding her tongue forward to greet his, she felt the sizzle of his wet caress all the way to the tips of her toes.

Marcus's tongue retreated, yet when she attempted to follow, he did the unthinkable and slowed the kiss, before breaking it off completely.

"Marcus," she whimpered, trying to follow. Her body ached for his returned touch. His hand slid from her face, down her arm, to settle at her bicep. He gripped her there, holding her away from him for a moment. His midnight gaze locked on her lips, and an odd look came over his face.

Unsure whether he was going to thrust her away or offer her the pleasure of a second kiss, Nicole stared back into his face, only to notice how the dimple in his cheek seemed to dance with life and the corners of his yielding lips twitched as if wanting to grin.

Instead of kissing her again, Marcus tugged her to him and banded his arms around her shoulders, hugging her tightly. A sigh escaped her lips as she took comfort in the ease of his embrace and the familiar feel of being pressed against him. His pulse throbbed against her cheek.

Pressing a kiss to his exposed collarbone, Nicole asked, "Missing my kisses brought you back three thousand miles? Maybe I should bottle them," she teased.

He chuckled. "Yeah, potent kisses like that could make you a fortune." He released her and stepped away, taking her hand in his. "Until the condoms are gone, they belong to me."

They'll never be gone if you keep replacing them. She smiled. She'd be his forever and reserve every passionate kiss under his name if only he'd ask her to. "Yeah, until they're gone, or you are. What are you really doing back here?"

Marcus started walking toward her back patio, tugging her by the hand behind him. He settled onto a porch swing and brought

Nicole down on his lap, then kicked the slider into motion. "Let's just say Atlanta wasn't what I'd been expecting. And not what I was looking for."

Nicole chewed her bottom lip. "Did you look at condos? You don't want to miss your Monday meeting with the Dynamic Agency," she said, enjoying the closeness of him.

"I'm not going back. I'm no longer interested in the job."

"What!" Nicole gasped. She attempted to get up but he held her to him. "I thought this was a chance-in-a-lifetime opportunity. What's changed?"

"I have. I've grown up."

For a moment Nicole remained quiet, thinking over the meaning of Marcus's statement, and wondering what had happened in Atlanta that had made him change his mind.

"I don't—"

"Shh," he said, putting one finger to her lips to silence her. "Stop talking and kiss me again."

With a demand like that, was there any way she could refuse? *Hell, no.* Nicole turned on his lap. "Kiss you, huh?" she teased, leaning forward so her breasts were level with his face. "You kiss me."

He made no response, but nuzzled his lips into her cleavage visible in her V-neck T-shirt. Tilting his head, he found her nipple with his tongue, beaded and begging through her shirt and bra, and sucked her into his mouth.

He suckled her deeper, pulling the taut flesh fully into his mouth until her back arched so he could get more complete contact. A low moan passed her lips. "I missed you," Nicole admitted with a sigh.

"I missed you too, baby," he mumbled against her flesh, causing a vibration to rumble through her limbs. His nimble fingers found the bottom of her T-shirt and shoved it upward, pulling the cup of her bra as he went and leaving one breast exposed to the warm sun and his hot gaze.

His mouth was on her again. His hands on her backside kneaded her flesh, pulling her into him. He rotated his hips in a slow but sensual rhythm, until deep down in her core, Nicole knew she was close to orgasm.

With Mother Earth still clinging onto her hands, Nicole held Marcus's wide shoulders and rocked with him, feeling the cooling zephyr created by the movement of the porch swing on her mouth-dampened skin.

"Make love to me, Marcus."

"In a minute, Nic. I want to savor you," he replied against her skin.

She tilted her hips against his erection, driving onward in her quest for climax, spurred on by the throaty groans rumbling against her tit. But the feel of his hard cock encased behind his pants and rubbing her clit wasn't enough. It did nothing to soothe the need for him that throbbed deep in her core.

"Make love to me, Marcus," she repeated with more urgency. She settled her hand at the top of his button fly. Her fingers divested the first and second button in record time.

"Yeah, baby. Go get a condom," he responded, lifting his talented mouth from his fondling.

With an excited yelp, Nicole leaped from his lap and skipped toward the sliding glass door. She slipped inside. Once her eyes adjusted, she trotted into the kitchen, straight to the rose-shaped cookie jar.

Nicole dropped the ceramic lid to the counter with a clank, and stuck her hand inside to retrieve a condom. She twirled her fingers in the Kisses but found only the candy.

"I know they're in here." She grabbed hold of the cookie jar and dumped it upside down, spilling the contents onto the counter.

Silver foil–wrapped chocolate adorned the white tiles. She fumbled her fingers in them, spreading them out so she could see clearly. In contrast to the silver wrappers of the chocolates, a shimmer of gold caught her eye. Her fingers closed around the metal and lifted it.

It was a golden key ring holding a single key and a heart-shaped key chain, engraved with what appeared to be a street address. With her hand trembling, she flipped the heart over and saw her first name had also been engraved, but there was a blank spot where her last name should be.

Marcus! He must have taken the condoms and replaced them with the key chain. Her heart quickened, while she fingered the cool golden metal in her hand. Not willing to speculate on the meaning of the key ring, she turned and walked with as much calmness as she could muster toward her yard.

His truck roared to life. Confused, Nicole gripped the key as she jogged around the front just in time to see the tail end of Marcus's truck disappear around the corner at the end of her block.

With her cheeks burning, she ran into the house, grabbed the phone, and dialed his cell number. She was greeted by the computerized voice mail. She hung up.

Uncurling her fingers, Nicole stared at the heart-shaped golden metal and the address engraved there. There was something vaguely familiar about the numbers and the street address in Granite Bay. Some feeling that churned in her belly and beckoned her to understand what it meant.

An address?

Quickly cleaning up, Nicole decided the only way to figure it out was to go there. Fetching her keys and purse, she left her house.

A little over a half hour later, Nicole pulled her car up in front of the house she'd looked at with Marcus a month and a half before. Strange that once she started driving, she had no problems remembering how to find the place, even though she'd been there only once. Marcus's black truck was parked in the driveway.

With hesitant steps, she walked past the white picket fence and followed the stone path that cut through the perfectly tended yard to the front door. Biting her bottom lip, she pushed her finger to the bell, then waited. She rang twice more, but nothing happened.

Nicole flipped the key over in her hand several times and felt the hot sting of tears in her eyes. The world shimmered for a moment before she was able to get the tears under control.

Holding her breath, she slipped the single key into the hole and twisted. It unlocked easily, and the solid wooden door swung open.

Shocked, Nicole took a step back. Scattered all over the tile entryway was a trail of rose petals, silken and so fresh they still smelled of morning dew. "Marcus," she shouted, taking a step into the foyer. Her voice echoed off the high-vaulted ceilings and came back with no reply.

Stepping inside, Nicole followed the trail of hushed pinks, vibrant reds, and sunny yellow flowers. It led her to the kitchen, where a large glass vase stood proudly on the center island, filled with the yellow roses and tiny white heads of baby's breath. A white piece of paper was folded in half and propped at the base. Her name was scrawled in red ink on the outside.

She lifted it and read the words written in Marcus's hand.

The heart of a home is the kitchen.
The heart of a man is his family.
Leave now, or follow the path where your heart leads you.

Nicole scoffed. She could no sooner leave than she could stop breathing.

Glancing around the kitchen, Nicole noticed the rose-petal trail continued on, only the yellow rose blossoms absent. Swallowing down the rise of nervousness, Nicole followed the path of pink and red rose petals up the vast curving stairs to the end of the hall, where a pair of double doors led to the master bedroom suite. The door was slightly ajar and the roses continued inside.

The thick carpet silenced her entry. Standing proudly in the center of the bedroom was a king-size bed, dressed in the identical cream-colored raw silk and Egyptian cotton bedding she and Marcus had picked out together. The trail led straight to the bed, and the entire thing was covered with soft pink and lush red roses.

In the center was a folded white piece of paper. The room blurred with her tears. She took three calming breaths and exhaled slowly, then walked to the bed and lifted the paper.

The bedroom is where passions flare and hearts become one.
Where lives are created.
Where the past was seconds ago and there's only the future.
If there's no doubt, follow the path of your heart.

Nicole stood staring at the note shaking in her trembling hand. The trail of red roses continued on the other side of the bed and led toward the master bathroom. Only red roses; the pinks had stopped on the bed, she noticed, just the way the yellows had stopped in the kitchen.

As she stepped around the vast bed, her breathing became tenuous. Her shallow panting left her feeling light-headed as her mind tried to keep pace with the raw emotion of what she was feeling.

She followed the trail of red, careful not to step upon the blossoms for fear of staining the light carpet under her weight the way she and Marcus had on her bed. Her shoes clicked as she left the bedroom and entered the large marble bathroom. There were red roses everywhere. The tub was filled with blossoms—and something else that caught her by surprise: foil-wrapped chocolate Kisses.

The candies joined the trail that wove its way through the tiled bathroom and stopped short at the entry to the giant closet, where the doors had been opened wide and a pile of chocolates towered.

Nicole stepped forward, her gaze fixed on the trail. As she glanced higher, her eyes collided with Marcus, kneeling upon the floor, surrounded by the red flower petals and the sparkling foil-wrapped Kisses.

"Marcus!" she gasped, unable to withhold the sob. Swiping a tear from her cheek, she studied his face. His dark eyes were glowing and deadly serious, the dimple unusually shallow. Her gaze dipped lower, to find the pulse of his heart beating heavily on his neck beneath the perfect shade of milk-chocolate skin.

Her eyes traveled lower, over his muscular shoulders to his carved chest hidden beneath the thin material of his shirt, to where his arm was extended. She was so stunned it took her a moment to think straight, for her brain to realize what she was seeing.

In his hand he held a small velvet black box, with the lid propped open. Secure in the folds lay a gold ring, topped with a one-carat princess-cut diamond. Its meaning dawned clear.

In awareness her gaze snapped from the little box back to Marcus's face.

He wasn't smiling, but his dark eyes twinkled with a hidden delight. "Hello, Nicole," he said in a smooth, melting tone.

She shook her head, trembling and on the verge of tears. "What are we doing here? Whose house is this?"

"Yours."

She shook her head again and tried to steady her suddenly rubbery legs. "Mine? I decided not to buy. It's too big to live in alone."

"You won't be alone. I'm not moving, Nic. Everything I've ever wanted is right here. I'm staying here, and if you'll have me, we'll share the house," he said, lifting the velvet box slightly in her direction.

"Wh-what are you doing?" she managed before a sob broke free.

"Shh, don't cry, Nic," he soothed. "I'm doing what I should have done a long time ago." In a single fluid motion, he stood and crossed the space to stand before her.

With his free hand, Marcus took hold of her hand gripping the key and the notes, and turned it so it was palm up. His touch was comforting. He removed the items she held and slid them into his pocket, his thumb stroking the palm. Still holding her fingers in his, he dropped to one knee before her. "I'm asking you to be my wife."

Nicole closed her eyes, the events since their first consummation flashing behind her lowered lids. She must be imagining this.

Too much wine the night before to commemorate his departure from her life. This was a silly trick being played upon her from her dreams. But when she opened her eyes, Marcus was still there, and his hand felt warm, solid, and real against her skin.

"To marry you?" she whispered.

"I love you, Nicole Davis, and I want you to be my wife. I want you to mother my children. I want you to rock by my side on hot summer afternoons out by the pool and watch our grandchildren play. I want to spend my entire life with you." He kissed her palm. "I want you to be my partner. You've been in my heart from the moment I met you more than six years ago. And most important, Nic, the condoms are gone and I want to know I'll never lose you from my bed or my life."

He released her hand and lifted the ring from the box, holding the gold band at the tip of her ring finger. "Will you marry me, Nicole?" His timbre dropped an octave or two.

"You love me?" she asked, emotion welling so high in her chest she could barely swallow.

"With all my heart."

"You're not moving? You're not leaving me?"

"I have a business here. I'll do whatever it takes to make it successful. I'm staying. This is everything to me. You're everything."

"Yes. I'll marry you." Nicole dropped to her knees amid the rose petals and chocolate Kisses. Holding her breath, she waited as he slipped the diamond onto her finger—a perfect fit. She tossed her arms around his shoulders and buried her face in the curve of his neck. "I love you, Marcus." She snuggled closer, dusting tender kisses on his throat. "I didn't know where this was leading when I proposed becoming lovers. But I'm so glad I did."

"So am I," he said, scooping Nicole up in his arms, getting to his feet and carrying her to the king-size bed. Laying her back upon the roses, he didn't give a damn if he needed to replace the comforter again. Stretching out beside her, he covered her in chocolate kisses.

♥ ♥ ♥

Renee Luke believes in mixing the bitter with the sweet, as long as it's all dipped in chocolate. She dreams up her stories amidst the beauty of the Sacramento Valley with her hero husband and four children, sharing the candied kisses, sweet hugs, and salty tears that add flavor to life. It's Renee's belief that there's nothing better than good books, great friends, and that real strength is the ability to break a candy bar into four pieces and only eat one. For more sugary treats and sensual romance, visit her on the Web at www.reneeluke.com.

8022